ARKANSAS

JOHN BRANDON

McSWEENEY'S BOOKS

SAN FRANCISCO

www.mcsweeneys.net

ISBN: 978-1-932416-90-9

For Oscar Owen Brandon (1924–2002)

PART ONE

BOREDOM IS BEAUTIFUL

Swin Ruiz was born in Tampa. He spent his childhood flipping through the reference books of a neighbor lady, a former teacher with no family. He didn't like the lady, and liked to be left alone with the books. He spent time wishing he had a brother, wondering what the point of T-ball was, managing crushes on sitcom actresses, and observing the adults in his neighborhood, whom he pitied. Most adults, he noticed, had little range to their personalities. There was a guy across the street who tried to be funny all the time, and if people didn't laugh at him he got peeved. There was a widow who was always in a panic, and when people acted composed around her she fumed. Swin's mother was resigned. Swin's father, cranky.

When Swin was twelve, his father drowned himself in the bay. Though a weepy note was left behind, no body was found. Swin's mother thought her husband had staged his death in order to escape child support. Swin had a lot of sisters, each more striking than the last, all with toned torsos and straight hair, each a lovely burden for Swin, who was outnumbered and couldn't look after them all.

When Swin was thirteen, his mother married a Dutch man who moved the family to Kentucky. Swin was against the move and against the Dutch man, and hid himself in schoolbooks. His grades in high school were impeccable. He had an ability to visualize microscopic goings-on that allowed him to excel at science. He went to Vanderbilt on a scholarship which stipulated he keep a 3.7 GPA. The fall semester of his sophomore year he took humanities and turned in a paper he'd written in high school. He didn't realize that in support of his college application, his high school history teacher Mrs. Donaldson, who had always given Swin preferential treatment because he was Hispanic, had sent his paper on French colonialism to the Dean of Admissions, who sent it to the Chair of Humanities, who put it in a file the department kept for examples of fine freshman-level writing. How the paper went from that file to the attention of his professor, Swin did not know. He got a D in the class and lost his scholarship. He didn't tell his mother or stepdad, and took out loans in order to continue school in the spring. He stewed over all the rich kids with their parents' bottomless credit cards and their roving, spotless trucks. He missed his stunning sisters and hated the idea that they were now loyal to their stepdad, with his rules and yellow, feathery hair. Swin was no longer around to remind them that this guy had dislodged them from their neighborhood and ignored their culture and dragged them to Kentucky, land of Baptist, horse-crazy hill folk. Swin wasn't there to suggest that his mother had been seeing this man before their father's death.

Swin did not go home for the holidays. He ate tuna from the can and carrot sticks. He sat motionless in front of his window. He tossed pencils against the brick walls of his dorm, trying to break the points. He stared himself down in the mirror. Disconnected his phone. The last hours of December, icy and frank, made him feel hardened. He could be cold-blooded, could read the slightest evil in people.

January was the most boring month of Swin's life. He attended Organic Chemistry, Exceptional People, Thermodynamics, and History of Architecture. He watched the professors fiercely, knowing he would never write a word for them. When bags were unattended or cars left open or display cases unlatched, when laps were swum and basketball played, when watches and bracelets were left in shallow boxes behind counters, waiting to be repaired, he stole. At parties he would slip into bedrooms. In the library, when a lone girl went to the bathroom, Swin would get in her purse. He pawned the women's jewelry and wore the men's. The chance that one of his victims would recognize his necklace or ring thrilled Swin. It was not the fashion, at a private college in Tennessee, for men to wear prodigious jewelry. People gave him looks. One of Swin's professors, a black man, held him after class and asked what the hell the joke was. This was tough love— guidance. Swin told the professor not to hate, but instead, congratulate. Swin walked out and never returned to the class. He quit wearing his spoils, hoarding them in a rubber container under his bed. He lifted weights. He wondered how much a tattoo would hurt. He began to worry about the fact that he owed the Department of Education thousands of dollars.

Swin founded an organization for students of part-Latino, part-Scandinavian descent. He assured the members that trips abroad separated organizations from mere clubs. He suggested stops in Spain, England, Norway, and Iceland. The student government's secretary of overseas studies, Lindsay, was Jamaican and Icelandic. Her hair had puffs and slick patches. This girl, Swin knew, would help organize and sell the trip because she wanted to date him. Swin gave her the idea he'd had a rough life. He took up for underdogs and solemnly shook his head at backwardness. Down with racial disharmony. Up with... pluralism. He got disgusted without calling people names. While flirting with Lindsay, he acted awkward. She was plump but not flabby. She had round eyes, tiny teeth, and prim hands and feet.

For the cost of copies, slides, SSLO T-shirts, and letterhead bearing the logo of the invented travel company UGO4CHEAP, he collected dues—$60 from each of the twenty-four members. Dues made their inclusion in a group of like peers official. He made ID cards. He claimed to have experience with UGO4CHEAP. The company offered nice hotels that were not in nice neighborhoods, so you could experience the real country. In the slide show, Swin included filthy areas where food was sold and doors were ornate. To keep the members busy, he chose a gross injustice. They set up a booth and dispersed literature. The writer types drafted letters to congressmen. They held car washes. There was a rock group sympathetic to the cause and Swin mentioned getting them to play a benefit. At the next meeting, he stormed in proclaiming that rock bands were all talk. Using a whiny voice, he said, "We're taking a break from performing. We're tired and stressed out." He asked if injustice took a break. When enthusiasm for the cause ran low, he questioned whether the organization was fighting on the correct side of the issue. He kept lauding the trip, painting a picture of dignified partying and rough edification.

Toward semester's end, in order to cement Lindsay as an ally, Swin accepted her invitation and went to her place one late afternoon for homemade soup. He checked his watch and said, "You know, I'd like that."

Lindsay's apartment was cramped with overlapping rugs and tapestries. There were countless houseplants. Incense was burning. Lindsay had a poster of Tom Cruise. She explained that she didn't like his movies, but admired him because of this emotional 911 call he'd made when his daughter was ill.

"Turned out okay," she said. "They thought she drank a bottle of lotion, but she'd rubbed it all over the dog."

"The dog was shaved?"

"Then she went into a deep sleep."

"The daughter?"

"Tom Cruise panicked, and that shows a parent is always a parent no matter who they are. How many kids do you want? Not that it matters."

"One," Swin said. "At the most."

Lindsay went over to her stereo and held down a button. Her speakers were overrun with vines. The voice that came from the stereo was shrill with energy, the words unintelligible. The music didn't have enough notes to achieve a melody, just toots and cymbal crashes.

"Come along." Lindsay led Swin to the kitchen, where he sat at a bar. Her waist was small. Despite her chub, she had an hourglass figure and muscles in her arms. Her body seemed to change from minute to minute.

"I know it's not your kind of thing," she said. "But I wish you'd go to Paducah with me. It looks great on your résumé."

She was referring to a leadership conference where, from what Swin could tell, serious young people dressed up and congratulated each other on having bright futures.

"My sister's birthday is that weekend," Swin said. "I'm no leader. I can boss people around, but—"

"I disagree. I'd follow you."

Lindsay tasted and seasoned the pot of soup, uncorked wine, and set the bar. She was graceful and sure in her kitchen, which made it easy for Swin to sink into the bemusement he'd been fighting since entering the apartment. There were so many scents and colors and leaves. Textures and steam. It occurred to Swin, as Lindsay peered into her pot, that she could be a witch. What *were* witches? Maybe leadership conferences were coven meetings. Lindsay rested a bowl in front of Swin and touched his head. He focused on the soup, which contained lentils, sausage, tomatoes, corn, and celery. All of it tasted like table pepper.

"Aren't *you* hungry?" he asked.

"I want to know about your sisters."

"Why?"

"Your life is unique."

"If you knew me more, you wouldn't think so."

She grabbed his bicep with two hands and pulled near him, sliding along the low, wide windowsill, her ample ass sweeping the wood. "You'd never believe the kind of stuff you make me think about," she said. When Swin didn't answer, her neck and ears turned red. He kissed her and her mouth felt generous but not loose. She made a squeak. He held her under the chin and, not knowing what to do with his other hand, put it in his pocket. Her fingers pushed on his stomach and he backed away. He realized he'd never considered having sex with her.

"I'm only Dutch by marriage," he said. "I lied."

"I know that."

"How?"

"And Holland isn't Scandinavia."

"It's not?"

"I know you're doing something shady with the trip. I hope that's not true, but I wouldn't tell if it was."

Swin thanked Lindsay and squeezed her hand. He escaped into the parking lot, where a tree was dropping pink flowers into a dumpster. He never spoke with her again. Swin didn't bother to tell anyone he was leaving Nashville. He took his books and CDs and a couple other things, made his bed and left his school bag sitting on it, left his posters on the walls. He took the dues and trip money he'd collected from the SSLO kids to Little Rock and bought a huge pickup at a military auction. He didn't know how to go about getting a new identity, so instead he got a crew cut and put down false information when applying for a video-rental card. He came to a dead halt at stop signs, did not litter. He frequented a dive called Hondo's. He would organize himself at the bar during the dead part of the day, the only patron for hours, and skim Aristotle, thinking not about the tenets of logic but about what it must've been like to walk around in a robe amongst white pillars, munching on grapes and washing your feet and contemplating the universe. Hondo got a kick out of how many pages there were in the Aristotle book. He got a kick out of the fact that Swin drank wine coolers. Swin told Hondo he'd been kicked out of a university and Hondo got a kick out of that, too.

"I've concluded something," said Hondo. "You're cut out for breaking the laws of the land."

Swin squinted up from his book.

"You know," Hondo said. "Professionally."

Swin's brain churned at this, but he looked levelly at Hondo.

"You got the laziness," Hondo reasoned. "You're kind of a weird guy."

"Taking enjoyment from reading doesn't make one lazy or weird."

"You weren't really reading, though," Hondo said. "You were gazing at the words."

Swin ordered another Bartles & Jaymes. Hondo explained that there was a man named Frog, and that Hondo knew the guy who ran Frog's business in Memphis, a fellow named Colin. If Swin wanted, Hondo could put in a word.

"Doing?"

"Making runs."

"Memphis, huh?"

"You wouldn't have to move. You wouldn't have to leave all this."

"It entails what, just a bunch of driving?"

"That's right. I wouldn't even call it a bunch."

Until Swin got used to what he was doing, he thought of himself as a delivery driver, dropping off pizzas or paperwork. The exchanges were not tense. The cops never pulled him over. The job was easy—a lot of downtime. Swin quit going to Hondo's. In his bare apartment, he watched documentaries while lifting weights. He found that a person with cash in Little Rock lived worse than a poor person at Vanderbilt University. He knew that, as a criminal, his intellectual talent would wither. He missed the world of ideas. He missed the vague promise of secretaries, luncheons, investments, golf. Occasionally he put on all his stolen jewelry. Occasionally he remembered the bare affection of Lindsay's kiss.

After Kyle's mother died, he lived with a friend of hers for a week and a half before jamming his stuff in a green bag and taking a bus to Athens, Georgia. Athens was a young, hilly place. Kyle took long walks and eyed tan girls with pretty toes. These girls owned big dogs, wore backless tops, and pretended to be impressed with nothing. In the afternoons Kyle did push-ups and ate and hid in his apartment from his neighbors, who liked to pull the sun down with chatter.

He drank 7-Up and bourbon. He would walk up the road to a nicer complex with a pool and sit next to the water with his bottle and glass and 7-Up, pine needles falling on his head, feeling that his mind was clear, that with bourbon he could have useful thoughts, that before long he would be able to forge a tidy philosophy of life.

One night, down the street at the pool, Kyle watched a guy on in-line skates coast by with a girl. They were having a giggly argument about music videos. They clunked over the grass to their poolside apartment and skated inside. Kyle kept swallowing whiskey for another hour, thinking of little else but the fact that a guy who wore earrings and skintight jeans and went in-line skating had been rewarded with one of Athens's well-formed peaches.

Kyle went to the guy's patio, hoisted a lounge chair over his head, and slammed it to the ground, making it collapse into itself with a low crunch. There was another chair. Kyle bashed it until it was a scatter of painted shards. He looked at his hands, looked around the courtyard. He'd been wanting to destroy something for a long time. He didn't know about the table; it was made of steel pipe. He tested its weight. He heard the door slide open beside him and stumbled off the patio. The guy was in his boxer shorts, squeezing a bat so that his muscles flexed. His girlfriend was hanging on his arm, leaning back like she was trying to open a heavy door. She was angry that the boyfriend thought proving his manliness was more important than preserving their wonderful future. She dug her nails into his stomach, not even glancing at Kyle. The boyfriend was yelling about his friend who was a cop. He inched toward Kyle, who couldn't find any words. The guy was so scared and the girl was so pissed. They were a bracing wave of feeling, and Kyle allowed himself to wash away from their patio and out of the courtyard. He envied the way the guy had gotten caught up in the moment, envied the guy's fear. Kyle couldn't remember ever in his life being as scared as the guy or as angry as the girl.

Other things happened. A wobbly black woman tried to steal Kyle's clothes at the laundry; when he caught her and twisted the bag from her hand, she went on standing there like nothing had happened, like Kyle had been rude to point out her attempted theft and she was choosing to ignore this rudeness. A waiter recognized Kyle and had him kicked out of a restaurant. It was a place Kyle went once every couple weeks. He would order water and scarf a basket of bread, then pretend to remember something urgent and rush out. Kyle sulked through a poster sale on the college campus, dazed by how many famous things there were—paintings, movies, bands, cartoons, slogans, mountains, causes—dazed by how many famous things these college students required, by their frantic need to proclaim what their favorite famous things were. This was how they chiseled out a philosophy of life: posters.

Kyle didn't live in a good or bad part of town, where stealing might've been difficult. He lived where stores didn't sell anything too valuable, where shoppers weren't desperate or emboldened. He molded his diet toward what was easy to take—macaroni and cheese, bacon, packs of trail mix. He stole cigarettes from the convenience store and sold them to his neighbors. At the liquor store, he'd buy a six-pack—they didn't ID him; no one ever did—and brush out the door with a fifth hidden under his stretched-out T-shirt. He sold the fifths. He sold bottled water. One lucky day a clerk went to take a leak and left a case of metal lighters on the counter. At the level Kyle did it, stealing was no trick. He stole what was available and he stood up straight and spoke to people every chance he got, because shoplifters, everyone knew, were hunched and solitary. Shoplifting for a living released Kyle from any thought of being a stand-up citizen. He didn't enjoy it. Shoplifting made him feel petty and dependent.

Kyle saw a HELP WANTED sign in a window and carried it inside. It was a bicycle-repair shop. A fat guy made a serious face and said, "Kyle, do you really want to work?" The whole thing took maybe four minutes. Kyle was amused to have a job. He had to show up the next morning at a certain time. Each Friday, he'd get a check. He walked home feeling brisk. He went outside after dinner and gabbed with his neighbors. He found himself telling them about his new job, found himself feeling proud. Maybe he could be like them: kept happy because of low-stress work that occupied their minds, tired out their bodies, and gave them something to complain about. Their evening beers were all they needed.

The fat guy, Matthew, wore sandals and had a lot of energy. He didn't know how to fix bicycles that well, but he didn't mind taking them apart and putting them back together until he got it right. Instead of attempting to teach Kyle anything, he invented tasks that involved cleaning and lifting. The two of them were alone in the shop most of the day, but the radio kept them from having to talk. Often, unprompted, Matthew would show Kyle a new bag of fireworks he'd added to his arsenal under the counter.

Matthew's sister stopped by several times. She was zealously nice to Kyle, always bursting into the room and halting there with an expectant look, making Kyle feel he was supposed to say, "What a great fucking day!" She would rearrange things Kyle had already rearranged. She would run her finger over flat surfaces. She'd ask Matthew a bunch of questions, and then they'd go in the next room and spit whispers at each other. This woman was older than Matthew. She was a professor at a college in Alabama—a pigeon-toed woman who, naked, Kyle imagined, would've resembled a raw turkey. She wore a fanny pack that held a paperback book and rolls of Life Savers. She offered to treat for sandwiches one day and when Kyle said he wanted double meat on his she acted burdened, like Kyle was wily—white trash that would never miss an opportunity to get a lot of whatever was free. After every talk Matthew had with his sister, he headed straight out back to the sun-drenched parking lot and let off a flurry of his loudest fireworks.

Friday, Kyle came in to find Matthew sitting in the middle of the floor, gazing at a wrench.

"Did you fall?" Kyle asked.

Matthew set the wrench down softly. "I'm closing."

"*Closing* closing?"

"Afraid that's the case. I've been asleep at the wheel of the American dream."

Kyle had never seen Matthew gloomy before. He didn't like seeing a fat guy who was gloomy.

"Sorry," Matthew said.

"What?"

"About your job."

Kyle had been startled to get hired and was now startled to get fired.

"But don't you think it'll pick up when the weather gets warmer? Or cools off? What's biking weather?"

Matthew frowned good-naturedly. "This is my sister's place. I owe her up the wazoo for it."

"Ah," said Kyle.

"Look outside that door, why don't you."

Kyle pushed the back door open and saw breeze-blown piles of damp confetti. Matthew's fireworks had been ruined.

"She did *that?*"

Matthew explained that his sister was a bona fide cunt. She hadn't given him a birthday or Christmas present in two years, instead deducting the cost of a gift from his debt. She'd told Matthew he needed to cultivate a hippie look, that the sandals were a good start but he needed hemp jewelry and a pot T-shirt.

"I thought hippies liked Volkswagens," Kyle said. "Not bikes."

Matthew gripped the wrench, looking like he might laugh. "I hit her in the shin with this thing."

Kyle stared at him.

"Didn't break a bone or anything. Got rid of her, though."

Kyle smelled the grease and the dust. A clock ticked behind him. He had attempted working in the straight world and doubted he'd ever attempt it again. He couldn't believe people crammed their lives into belittling routines just for steady money. What was the big deal about getting money steadily? Was that so enticing, getting a tiny check made tinier by taxes every two weeks for the rest of your life, continually voicing the same stale complaints that working stiffs have been voicing for centuries, that the people in Kyle's apartment complex voiced each evening? Alarm clocks, layoffs, cigarette breaks, backaches, carpal tunnel syndrome, company parties, and always the steady little checks.

Kyle sometimes drank in a bar—in the afternoon, when bars were empty, when there wasn't some wailing band in Converse sneakers. He sat in the shadowy corners and tried not to talk to anyone. People in irreverent T-shirts would trickle in, making faces and using long words while discussing the local music scene. They could spend forty-five minutes comparing one noisome quartet to another. What made one of these bands better than another, aside from their outfits or how high they jumped, Kyle had no idea.

One day a tall guy drinking Gibsons started giving Kyle a hard time. He was an anthropology PhD. He was pissed off about something remote, about the way of the world. Kyle tried to ignore him but the bar was quiet and the guy was looking right at him, saying he wanted to radiocarbon-date Kyle's hairstyle.

"Ask me if I'm a lumberjack," he said.

"Are you?" Kyle asked.

"No, say the whole question."

"Are you a lumberjack?"

"Nope," the anthropologist said. He exploded in laughter.

Kyle raised his eyes at the bartender. "Check."

She wrote on a pad and punched the keys of a calculator. Kyle looked at what was left of his whiskey, threw a little back, and concentrated on the taste of it.

"Don't you say 'please'?" The anthropologist raised a finger in the air. "The expression is 'Check, *please.*'"

Kyle took his time getting over there, but still the guy froze as if a tiger had sprung down from the rafters. His face bunched up as Kyle cocked his arm. The anthropologist didn't even get his hands all the way up. Kyle meant to hit him in the chin but got him in the throat. The guy toppled off the stool in hacking spasms. Kyle had never hauled off and decked someone before. He didn't know what to do next. Drop down and keep swinging? Ask the guy if he'd learned a lesson? Say something dashing to the bartender? There was no telling what the guy would do when he got up, so Kyle got his balance together and booted him in the ribs. The gasp came not from the anthropologist but from the bartender.

"It's done, baby," she said. "If I was you I'd leave. I wouldn't even pay."

Kyle met a woman named Ester and within a month gave up his apartment and moved in with her. He didn't understand this decision of his, but he wasn't troubled by it. Ester lived in a neighborhood of tall, restored houses that all seemed to have dozens of people in them. These people shared cars and bikes and clothes and gave each other massages. Ester was crazy about dogs, but they had to be mutts. She had a gray tooth and wonderful hips. Nothing felt permanent around her. Time was malleable. Ester and her friends hung around in suffocating, screened rooms, listlessly figuring out the world. Ester wore bulky rings on her toes. She organized small parades. When a parade occurred that she hadn't organized, she deemed it amateur and listed its faults.

Ester had a boyfriend in Nebraska that Kyle never met, a guy she'd been with for eight years who was studying to be a surgeon. She said this thing with Kyle was a fling and had nothing to do with her long-term plans. Kyle was someone to hold her at night, someone from the real world who she could learn from. She was scared of becoming insulated from the real world. She was wary of corporations. She was terrified of pregnancy and wouldn't have regular sex with Kyle. Whenever they made out she waited about three minutes and then fell upon him with her mouth.

Someone from Kyle's old apartment complex introduced him to a man named Ron, a man with salt-and-pepper sideburns who would buy almost anything you had to sell. The guy could unload coffee beans, cases of pants, air fresheners. Ron owned a crappy gym with a big basement. He ate protein bars and listened to speed metal.

Kyle took to trolling parking lots, looking for booklets of CDs, radar detectors, cell phones, sporting goods. The gold mine was golf clubs. Kyle would put on a pastel shirt and go into a Nevada Bob's, take some practice swings, mention the names of a couple courses, buy a three-pack of balls, slip a driver down his pant leg and breeze out. Kyle paid no rent and soon saved enough to get a car. He didn't get one, though. He didn't want to share it with all of Ester's friends.

Suddenly Kyle had been living with Ester for a year and a half. Many of her neighbors had moved on and been replaced, but the new ones talked about the same things in the same screened rooms. The conversations seemed to belong to the rooms and not to the people—conversations whose very appeal was that they never yielded answers. There were fewer and fewer dogs. Ester got angry with Kyle, something she never used to do. She got angry about Kyle's hair, about what he did with his time, about his ignorance of certain music and certain books. She demoted him from blow jobs to hand jobs.

One morning she announced she was going to visit her boyfriend and Kyle asked if he should water the plants while she was gone.

"Water the plants." She seemed exhausted. "Water the plants?"

She threw her version of a fit, a grave lecture with a lot of pauses. She put her thumbs to her temples and whispered the word "fuck." She wanted Kyle to be jealous. She wanted him to say enough's enough with the hand jobs, throw her down and screw her brains out. She wanted him to hate people and get sad about things, to tell her how he felt about her, to make her feel safe and feminine.

Kyle said, "What happened to the whole *fling* deal?" and Ester hurled her keys at him.

After this, even the hand jobs stopped. Ester wouldn't kick him out, though. She quit talking to him. She brought guys around. Kyle figured out that the guy in Nebraska didn't exist and wondered where she'd gone all those weekends. He knew it was up to him to leave, to dig out his green bag, fill it, hump it downtown, and sign a lease.

He could get a car now.

Ron asked Kyle if he was busy on Thursday. He knew a guy that needed a guy on Thursday.

"Who's the guy?"

"Colin."

"Don't know him."

"Guy from Memphis. He's under a few other people in a pretty good outfit."

"Oh, yeah?" Kyle said.

"Meet him at the kebab place at four."

"Did you have to vouch for me?"

Ron peeled open a protein bar and held it up to his eye. "No, no." He sniffed the bar, pinched it and rubbed his fingers together. "No, it's all between you and him."

Colin was cutting grilled vegetables into dainty bites when Kyle sat down across from him. Colin was pale and wore a tie. When he crossed his legs, Kyle saw his ankle socks. He said he'd been to Athens twice, once to do something with Ron and once when he was seventeen, when he'd dropped acid and spent a whole night staring at shop windows. He laughed, his head held still while his shoulders quaked. He explained what Kyle was supposed to do and it seemed simple enough. Kyle's only question was why Colin didn't just do it himself, but Kyle didn't ask. That seemed like a question you didn't ask.

That Thursday, as he'd been told to, Kyle walked into the Marriott hotel, stepped calmly into the EMPLOYEES ONLY area beside the check-in desk, took a long hall and some steps down to the laundry, opened the second dryer, and pulled out a small suitcase. He took it across to the kebab house, waited in line with it, ordered a big combo plate, and settled into a booth. He ate slowly, savoring the marinated meat hunks, watching for a wop with a yellow shirt. Kyle had been told that the wop would show up for the suitcase before Kyle could finish eating. Kyle paused between kebabs. He went and got one of every condiment packet the place offered, tore open each and squeezed it dry. He took the suitcase with him to piss, then sat back down. He ate all the vegetables, even the squash. He got a refill on his soda, sat and slurped it and let out a string of soft belches. No wop. He kept looking at the clock on the wall. Five, ten, fifteen more minutes passed. The guys behind the counter were starting to wonder about Kyle. It felt like the place was getting smaller. For a while he was the only customer and he couldn't get a full breath in his lungs. Kyle put his hands in his pockets and made fists. The zipper of the suitcase was secured with a tiny padlock that was meant to look inconspicuous. Kyle thought about busting it off with a hammer. He thought about going back to Ron's. He thought about taking the suitcase to the hotel and putting it back in the dryer. The wop was almost three hours late. Kyle slipped out of his booth, pins and needles in his legs, and carried the suitcase to his apartment. He put it out of sight and watched an awards show on TV until he dozed off.

Before dawn, there was a knock. Kyle looked out the peephole and his stomach dropped. It wasn't the wop. It wasn't Colin. It wasn't Ron. It was some guy with thinning blond hair and a toothpick in his mouth. Kyle kept quiet. The guy knocked a couple more times, then stepped back from the door and pulled something from his belt—something to pick the lock with. Kyle stepped into his shoes and leaned against the wall. The guy jabbed the knob unlocked and started working the deadbolt over. In a matter of seconds he'd be in Kyle's living room. He'd have a knife open and his eyes peeled. Maybe he had a gun. Kyle crouched, coiling his strength. The deadbolt wiggled and then flipped. The knob turned. When the door was open a foot, Kyle yanked it the rest of the way, tugging the guy off balance, and toppled him over the arm of the couch. Kyle used his knees and his weight. The guy made whining noises, spitting on the carpet. Kyle groped but could not find a knife or a gun. He dug in his elbow and demanded the guy's weapon.

"I don't got one," the guy said.

"What *do* you got?"

"Nothing I could hurt anybody with."

"Someone that fights like you should have a weapon."

"Trespassing is a lot different than armed robbery, smart guy."

Kyle made the guy take his pants off. He tied him up and put him in the closet and not fifteen minutes later Colin was outside the door, soaked in sweat, a gun in his waistband. There was nothing Kyle could do but open up and see what happened. He went over the events in his mind and knew he had nothing to hide. He swung the door open. Colin, seeming too tired to take a step inside, said, "Tell me you still got it."

Kyle nodded.

Colin came in and sat on the couch while Kyle got the suitcase. Kyle didn't know if he should tell Colin about the man he'd tied up, but what was *Kyle* going to do with him? If Kyle didn't tell Colin, then he was stuck with the guy. Colin asked for a glass of water and turned on the news. A freckled guy was announcing birthdays.

"You might want to go out for a while," Colin said. "Get some pancakes or something."

"Why's that?"

Colin held out his water glass and Kyle went and refilled it.

"A gentleman might stop by," Colin said. "If so, I have to shoot him."

"I got a guy in my closet." Kyle was relieved. "I don't know if it's the same one you're thinking of."

"Unarmed? Blond hair?"

"That's the one."

"Alive?"

"So far."

Colin ogled Kyle. He slid his water glass around on the coffee table, leaving a wet trail, then rested a paw on the suitcase.

"Got a car?" he asked.

"Just got it."

"Pack. Get out of here and meet me at Ron's in two hours."

"I have a job, don't I?"

"Yup. You're going to Arkansas."

Months later, many runs under his belt, Kyle found himself driving a Firebird to New Smyrna Beach, Florida, from his adopted home, Little Rock. He located a wet T-shirt contest. The contestants, most of whom looked better before the water was poured, whispered to each other instead of playing to the sparse crowd. The best-looking one had wide-set breasts and tanned feet. After the contest, Kyle told her she should've won and mentioned renting a Jacuzzi suite at the Sheraton. The woman declined with a twang. A half hour later, out of fascination with this woman who was acquainted with everyone in the bar but friendly to none, he gave her another try. She was sitting at a table singing along with "Wind Beneath My Wings." When she finished Kyle clapped, trying to appear as though her singing had touched him. She glanced at him, embarrassed, and left.

Kyle suspected that, as with many desirable things in life, he didn't want women as much as he should. He was just as pleased to get drunk, or to drink a bunch and not get drunk. He plopped down at the back of the bar and alternated between Bud and rum runners. He thought of his past, and none of the events seemed more distant than any of the others. All of them could have happened yesterday or a hundred years ago. Kyle tried to find some design in it all, in the things that he'd chosen and that had chosen him. This was impossible. His mind wasn't up to it. He wondered how long he'd live in Little Rock. He thought of Frog, Colin's boss, the dealer they all worked for. This guy, Kyle had heard, had a lake house so big that parts of it were closed up during certain seasons. He grilled steaks by his lily-pad–shaped pool, had money creeping all through the stock market. Kyle didn't feel jealous of him, and knew he should. Maybe Kyle didn't need a philosophy of life. Maybe it was only people who wanted things, who felt guilty about getting things and frustrated about not getting things, who needed a philosophy.

In the morning, Kyle bumbled around a gift shop and picked out a shark's jaw, a gift for his new girlfriend back home. He drove a Toyota Tundra to Tallahassee, stayed the night in a motel with a dry pool, then took a Ford Probe to Little Rock. He parked the Probe in the loading alley of a strip mall and knocked on Gregor's door. Kyle got buzzed in and found Gregor chewing pita and tomatoes, daubing mayo with a long fingernail. Gregor's hair looked shellacked. He pointed at a dolly, then flipped a page of the classifieds and put his face close enough to smell the ink. The room was full of brass parts that looked like prehistoric insects. Kyle left the dolly. He went to the Probe and retrieved eleven slim boxes covered with packing tape and labeled SHEET MUSIC.

"What kind of town is this? All I want is a periscope." Gregor rattled the classifieds, then dropped a wad of spit on them. His face lit up. "I read a book. Did I tell you?"

"You might have."

"It was about farmers. four hundred thirty-six pages long. You start on page thirteen, though. They count the table of contents and the part where the other writers say, 'This man, by damn, is a writer. If he was here, I'd give him a nut scrub.'" Gregor was grinning, full of himself. "Here's the trick." He pulled a paper shredder from under his table. "Every page I read, I tear it out and shred it."

Kyle told Gregor he was a unique individual, then he stood there and waited for his three thousand bucks, looking forward to feeling the tight lump of it in his pocket as he sat on the bus.

Kyle's new girlfriend, Nora, watched movies made in war-torn countries and was fond of the word "eclectic." Her jewelry was dangly and her tan lines out of whack. She often looked at Kyle with mild confusion, as if he were the wrong month of a calendar. She implored him to get a normal job and he replied that people held normal jobs because they'd been brainwashed to believe they wanted things. He wished he were brainwashed, he said, but for some reason brainwashing didn't work on him. He knew that no amount of possessions or height of position would make his life worthwhile.

The first time they'd met, to satisfy Nora's desire for sharing, Kyle lied and said his mother had molested him as a child. Nora bought this story and pampered Kyle for days, yet she thought he was lying when he claimed he'd lost a necklace he'd bought her. This amused Kyle. The truth was, his mother had raised him in an even-tempered, resigned way before being electrocuted when Kyle was a teenager. Kyle didn't feel that Nora deserved to know anything true about him. In time they would break up and then Kyle would never see her again. She would be no different from the people he'd known in Athens—Ron, Ester, Matthew—or the kids he'd gone to school with back in Lofton. They all came and went.

After graduation, you, Ken Hovan, stock groceries and build prefabricated sheds in the yards of rich guys out in Germantown. You work part time at a gas station and put vinyl siding on new brick houses. You snag a weekend doorman gig at a Memphis State bar and, during the week, mow lawns in the remote suburb of Collierville. Winter comes and the call for lawn service dries up. The bar where you work, whose owner can't contrive a drink special that's both profitable for him and enticing to college kids, goes under.

That February, the city of Memphis announces it's too broke to continue contracting repairs to its housing projects and will assemble its own low-paid troupe. You apply to be a roofer. You've never done roofing work but you know which tools are involved and that roofing, like stock brokerage or scooter repair or coffee-shop management or exotic dancing, can be learned in about three days. You work this job for over six years, applying for every bouncer spot that opens and getting turned down each time. As a roofer you acquire bulbous forearms and calves, and also the nickname Froggy, for the ease with which you spring from one project roof to another. You've always been the type of fellow people dare to eat the noxious and say the inappropriate, and you are now daily egged to leap ten-foot alleys and fling hammers into distant dumpsters.

In the spring of 1982, riding the goodwill of disco, a man from Mobile opens what he hopes will be the first multiracial dance club in Memphis. This man has bought a former coat factory on the west edge of Midtown and has sunk a million dollars into it. He hires twelve black bartenders and twelve white bartenders, white and black managers, a group of deejays that includes a Mexican and a Frenchman, and a total of thirty bouncers, one of which is you, Ken "Froggy" Hovan.

You have a stout, agile build that enables you to avoid ever being hit flush by a punch or body block. Like all small men who can fight, you are thought of as crazy. You allow the black bouncers to call you honky and cracker. In two months the club's patrons are all black. The white employees, other than you, quit, a development the owner doesn't mind because his black staff doesn't realize they're expected to steal. You attain a certain fame as the only white guy at the club. Everyone knows Froggy and asks how you're living, to which you answer, "Fat like Thanksgiving." You go to bed with black women and they do not act strangely in the morning. They roll over, stare at the clock a moment, curse, and matter-of-factly tell you they love you on their way out the door. They will not cook or even pour their own drinks. They demand that you sing to them and they striptease without being asked. You envy black dudes their women but not their business sense. When the club goes under, as all clubs do, the black bouncers will be the owners of Coupe de Villes for which they can't afford gas. They will march to the pawnshop and get ripped off by 60 percent on their chains.

It's March 1984 when the club dies. You find that your credit with the black bouncers and their women, as well as the feeling of being a vital cog in a scene, does not endure without the club. A new feeling you can't identify may be the grip of adulthood. You know you will not return to working in Germantown, slaving in the yards of Baptists who wear pastel shirts and live off investments. You doubt, in fact, that you will again have a boss or do anything you are dared to do. A space in a crumbling strip mall comes open and you think of leasing it. Over the next few days no better idea occurs to you and you want to have saved money for a reason so you pull the trigger, rent the space, paint FROGGY'S PAD on the front window, brush out the cobwebs, mop the floor. You buy a cash register and drink coffee behind it. You assume you need some sort of license, but you will not look into this unless you're forced to. You think of yourself one minute as a man who at twenty-seven owns his own business, then the next minute as a man who got so bored in his apartment, avoiding work, that he bought himself a place to be.

You put up a sign that reads BUY & SELL ANYWHERE and soon realize you know the market value of very few things. Your shelves fill with all manner of dolls, wreaths, teacups, ashtrays, pocketknives, and hand tools. You lose money for seven weeks until the beat-up guys start shuffling in. They're unshowered, bandaged.

You sense degrees of desperation in their twitches and coughs and hollow smiles. They sell you car stereos and cigarettes. A black guy with freckles who calls himself Testament comes in day after day, like it's a coffee shop. This worries you because he is not a junkie. He sells you collectible items one at a time—Elvis plates and German steins. Could be a cop. Could be casing the place. One day you dump your coffee out a window and tell him you know where a fellow could get ahold of some boxes. "Then you can bring all your crap up at once." You enjoy calling your inventory crap.

"I can get something you can move," he says. His lips are brown and stiff, like cardboard, his eyebrows unruly, one of his ears scabbed over.

He tells you he got the name Testament as a child. His parents liked to smoke a ton of opium and read Bible passages. He shakes your hand and tells you he is not a cop and wouldn't bother with you if he was. He will soon come into 140 cases of bootleg tapes and will split the profits with you for the use of your back-room shelves. You are happy for the prospect of customers. You were expecting this fellow to talk guns or pot, so the thought of trafficking unreleased pop music does not spook you.

When Kyle arrived at the lot, he saw a flatbed truck. He'd never operated anything bigger than a van, and had to hide his nervousness over this fact when a beige guy appeared and said his name was Swin. The guy tried to make small talk, but Kyle kept quiet until they were on the interstate. Something was up. The day before, Colin had told Kyle he'd have a partner for this run, something he'd never had before. Colin had told Kyle that a gun would be provided in the vehicle's center console, something which had never been provided before, and now the vehicle turns out to be a flatbed truck. Kyle didn't like the idea of having guns around when a deal was being made. He didn't know if Swin knew about the gun and didn't want to check the console with him watching. Kyle took a good look at the guy. He was a weights freak, with little muscles popping up where they shouldn't, on the back of his neck or his fingers. His T-shirt was a size too small.

"What kind of name is Swin?"

"A girl's," Swin said.

The load was faucets, more than a hundred cases, stuffed with bags of powder and plugged. This was another thing: Kyle knew what he was hauling. The way Frog ran his operation, his drivers simply drove a car to one place, got in another car, drove somewhere else. Sometimes the drivers handled money, sometimes not. Sometimes when Kyle returned to Little Rock he stopped off at Gregor's and unloaded something, sometimes not. Kyle preferred to be kept in the dark, but Colin had made a point to tell him about the faucets. Of course, he'd left out the amount. He hadn't let Kyle know he'd be captaining a highway barge.

Besides the faucets, Swin had also thrown on some miniature orange cones because, he explained, the randomness might throw off a cop. Their destination was South Padre, Texas. At a red light, rain started. Kyle knew the boxes wouldn't stay dry with Swin's shoddy cover job, so they pulled into a shopping center that included a hardware depot. The truck took two spaces. While Swin went for a tarp, Kyle bought rope and hurried back to the truck. He flipped open the console and there was the gun, reclined on sugar packets and ink pens and a tire gauge. Swin returned and they did their best with a roll of blue plastic that was meant to protect a small fishing boat. They got moving again and hit I-30. Swin took off his shirt and draped it on the seat to dry. A plus sign was tattooed on his right bicep, a minus sign on his left. Kyle asked if the left arm was weaker.

"It takes both for a charge. Step to me, you catch the voltage."

Kyle knew he could beat Swin up. "I've never wanted a tattoo," he said. "I've never seen one that didn't look stupid."

"You're not a sexy dude. If you're already sexy, a tattoo can enhance it."

"Don't tell me you're one of those witty people."

"I've been told that I am."

"You remind me of a game-show host."

"That's another way to say I'm brimming with charisma."

"No," Kyle said. "It's not."

"If you want to be the strong, silent type, you need to keep yourself from commenting on things."

Kyle tipped his chin back until his neck cracked. "It won't be right away, but at some point I'm going to knock you on your ass."

"You say that now, but soon we'll be friends. Everyone who meets me wants to be my friend."

Noonish they got a booth in a Southwestern restaurant with World Book place mats. Kyle's described belomancy, a process by which local Indians read the future by shooting arrows. Swin's was about Ford v. Wainwright, the ruling that made it unlawful to execute a crazy man. Kyle ordered a #7 combo. Swin was picky—didn't eat sour cream and didn't eat guacamole unless it was fresh. He and the waitress discussed what "fresh" meant. A woman with a baby sat down in a nearby booth and began nursing.

"That's good to see," Swin said.

"You're sad."

"A lot of women don't breast-feed anymore, which is a shame. Breast-fed kids get fewer syndromes. I was a formula baby. You, I'm guessing, had a mouthful of the real deal."

"No idea," Kyle said.

"Yup, I think you did."

"I lied about my mother once to get out of trouble with a girl. What do you think of that?"

"How much trouble?"

"Does it matter?"

"Is your mother in trouble now?"

"She's dead."

"Because you lied about her?"

"No. She's been dead."

Swin looked toward the ceiling, thinking. "A conversation this vague, really no point in having it."

"She was a great lady," said Kyle. "*Great* lady." He ate a chip.

"When people act sappy after someone's dead, that means they feel guilty."

"What do I feel guilty about?"

"How would I know?"

"I was always good to her."

"Not guilty about how they treated the person; guilty to have life and not know what to do with it."

When Kyle envisioned his mother, she was in a white bed, bandages on her left elbow and wrist where the shock had burnt off the skin, fingertips black, head shaved. Her face looked as though she'd been informed of a rude change of plans. Kyle would return from a walk to find her arms in a different position, and always it was just that a nurse had shifted her. Each Wednesday, he'd put her favorite program on, a game show about finding fake bombs. He began to settle into a routine, to get used to having his mother that way. It wasn't a bad way to be. She'd made an escape. For a time, Kyle hadn't wanted her to die or wake up, but to remain in peace, away from her life.

Swin opened a travel-size lotion and rubbed some on his elbows. "If one of my sisters died, I wouldn't care."

"What a stupid thing to say."

"I just don't care for women."

31

Kyle stared.

"I like them for *that*," said Swin.

"How about we both shut up."

They munched on chips for a time and slurped their drinks, the restaurant filling with nurses. Swin pointed without raising his hand off the table. "Caregivers."

They weren't far past Dallas before the tarp came loose again. They pulled into a truck stop and bought duct tape. The boxes were fraying. They did what they could with the tarp and got back on the highway, Kyle staying in the right lane and doing five over.

When Swin woke up, the sun was setting and the rain had stopped. He pulled the map out and did some measuring with his fingers. "If we go eighty-three the rest of the way, we won't be late."

"Getting pulled over with drugs makes you *really* late."

Swin looked over more maps from the glove box. There was one for each state, plastic booklets. "Here I go again," he said. "I'm learning again. You don't get this smart by accident."

The sky became a weak yellow, then abruptly it was night. They got off the interstate at a cluster of fast-food restaurants that all shared one lot, and parked in the far corner. They chose an all-you-can-eat restaurant where waitresses circled with bowls of pasta and salad and breadsticks. Kyle ate himself stunned. He planned to sleep away a good chunk of the remaining drive. The check came, with two peppermints, and he took care of it. Kyle and Swin were chewing the mints when they walked outside and saw a tall bald man snooping around the truck. He leaned over and peeked under the tarp. The man wasn't dressed as a cop, but he had a badge patched on his sleeve. Kyle told Swin to do the talking. When they got close, the guy stood up past straight, hand to his chin. Swin shook his hand and introduced himself as Mike. Kyle said, "Hey, now," then climbed in the cab.

"First-aid kit's in the seat console," Swin yelled.

He knew about the gun. Kyle kept still and listened. The guy's name was Pat Bright. He was some kind of ranger.

"Headed far?"

"Corpus Christi," Swin told him.

"I noticed your rig needs some help."

"Not sure I agree with that a hundred percent. Though all things give out eventually, don't they? If you're patient." Swin's voice was even.

Kyle opened the console and lifted out the loaded nine-millimeter with two fingers. "What's better for a headache?" he called. "Tylenol or—" he tucked the gun under his leg, "Aleve?"

"Got to get more rope," Pat Bright was telling Swin. "Go corner to corner."

"We were in a hurry this morning. Still are."

"What's the haul?"

"Faucets. Some computer tycoon's place. Used to be oil, now it's computers."

"There's no faucets in Corpus Christi?"

"He's got to have that adobe-marble core."

Kyle pushed the mirror out and saw Bright beaming with tolerance.

"Let me take a look how you've got them stacked," Bright said.

"How many styles of stacking are there? To me, stack always meant one on top of the other."

"I'm a safety expert in this state."

Kyle heard the tarp crinkling.

"See there," said Swin. "Now we really need to haul ass."

This wouldn't be a huge deal, Kyle thought; they would pull the body in the cab and be on their way, then dump Bright in some field. The only trouble was the shot. Kyle and Swin could act confused and run back into the restaurant, asking if anyone knew where that shot came from. Then again, this was Texas. The diners might just look around for a moment, then continue stabbing their battered vegetables. This wouldn't be a big deal. It wasn't that complicated, was it? The biggest worry was that this ranger already knew what they were moving and was stalling until his backup showed. Shit, Kyle thought. Shit, here goes. Kyle stepped down from the cab with the gun showing. "Enough questions."

Bright laughed. "What are the cones for?" He held his palms up. "I'm with Frog. I've been ordered to intervene."

Bright told Kyle and Swin what they were carrying, where they'd left from and when, and that they had a map of each state in the glove box. He explained that they had little choice about their immediate futures. They would work under Bright, at a park. Frog had cut a new loop of clients and Bright would run these deals. He'd known Frog for years, he told them, since he'd stopped one of his trucks lost in the park.

33

"Try not to look like deer in headlights," he told Kyle and Swin. "Look angry or bored or something."

Bright, Kyle, and Swin left the flatbed and the gun with someone in Austin and headed north toward the park in Bright's Bronco.

"I about blew you away," Kyle said.

Bright raised an eyebrow. "You trying to convince someone?"

"No, I hate guns. I'm saying it's not smart to fuck around with somebody you don't know."

Bright leaned around, looking at both boys in turn. "You're Kyle Ribb and you never killed a man. You're Swin Ruiz and you never killed a man. You're dependable, you're a project."

The air rushed thinly over Bright, who, guiding the Bronco up the highway with a thumb, felt a looming ease. He wouldn't have to do park labor. He'd hardly have to take trips anymore. He had a couple of charges who would long for his wisdom, who would pretend to ignore him but later, alone, would parse his words and file them away, shuffle and study them in bed at night. They could have family dinners. They could drink whiskey.

Bright's foot slipped off the pedal, causing the Bronco to rock. He felt Kyle looking over at him, but kept his eyes on the road ahead. The bones. He hadn't thought of the bones in a long time. The first time he left the house, Kyle and Swin would go poking around. They'd pick through the attic. But Bright couldn't get rid of the bones; he couldn't do that.

On his way south all those years ago, he'd stopped in a bad part of Raleigh, looking for a man who wanted the remainder of his Manchester speed—$1,100 worth. Bright had the drugs in a thin vinegar bottle which he'd shoved down the back of his jeans, under his draping purple shirt. The bottle made striding difficult, and Bright tried to turn his discomfort into style, a down gait, the bottle wedging and wedging. He ambled the block twice. The address, along with the fish shop to which it corresponded, did not exist. Bright knew he should get right to his car and continue toward the sun. He pressed a long blink and then a black dude wearing sandals and a cutoff shirt was coming straight at him. The dude had slats shaved in his eyebrows, a slant for a mouth. Bright slipped his knife from his pocket and opened it behind his leg, never losing his hangdog look. The black dude's strut ceased and the slant mouth was about to open. Dude could've been after a light, or Bright's uptown shirt, or he knew about the speed. Bright wasn't that concerned. The first stab fell into the chest too high and got caught up on the collarbone. The eyes went soft and there were those teeth. The knife went under the ribs three times. Bright cleaned the blade on the dude's khakis. The windows of the buildings were empty. Bright wanted someone to scream at him so he would flee. He stepped away from the body without looking down at it, then hurried around a corner to his car and slid the vinegar bottle under the seat. He couldn't help feeling he could do what he pleased. This neighborhood wasn't curious about him and would spit him out in a good direction no matter what road he took. He pulled up to the body, which had detached from its sandals and looked like a black and pink joke. The bloodstains were fast around each wound, as if the guy had been near-dead already, decaying, wanting Bright to finish him off. Bright knew he should get lost, should put distance between himself and this brand-new corpse, but he wanted it. He couldn't help himself. He felt greedy. He was not afraid of death, was not creeped by limp, flopping limbs or the exaggerated weight of a human body with no soul to lighten it. It took a full minute to get the body in the Dodge. Bright wasn't worried; he owned this body. Moments ago it had had ideas and rhythm and now it was Bright's possession.

The next night, a ways north of Vicksburg, Mississippi, Bright had driven over acres of leaning grass to the edge of a swamp. He wasn't sure what to do with the body in his trunk. He made camp and took a look around. There was nothing wrong with the swamp; he could've submerged the body in a few feet of stagnant water and rolled a log or two on top of it. He didn't, though. He wasn't ready to part with it. He built a fire and sat against a tree, his mind gone with hunger and fatigue and the strange feelings he had for his kill. He kept going over it in his mind, picking out new details from that Raleigh street. He carried more wood to the fire. More wood. Twigs and vines and whatever he could find. He didn't stop until the flames almost reached the sagging branches above. He took a few slugs from a bottle of brandy in his backseat, then heaved the body from the trunk, stood it up against himself, danced it over to the fire, and flopped it on, face up, feet hung safely out on the dirt. He imagined that when the flames touched it, the body would awaken. It would jump off the fire and say, "Whoa, now. You one crazy motherfucker." Its shirt went up in smoke while its pants burned onto its legs. The skin wasn't skin after a while. Liquid bubbled out of its eyes. The hair made a different-colored flame, and Bright could smell it over the other smells. He kicked the feet into the bottom of the fire, bending the knees backward. Bright paced around and around the body, knowing he should be worried about the pungent clouds he was sending up through the brush. The feeling from Raleigh hadn't dissipated. No one would come near. No one was interested in Bright. He sat down against his tree. He wouldn't need more wood. Bright did not sleep, but he wasn't sure he was awake, either. He was aware that the torso had fallen apart, had dripped onto the coals like pork fat and sizzled. He was aware that the smell had gotten terrible and then subsided, the fire shrinking and regaining its quaint campfire aroma. Later, when the flames had no lick left, when they were a pulsing blue lining along the floor of the fire pit, when Bright had grown stiff against his tree, he got up and examined what was left. There were bones of all sizes, some with gunk baked onto them, some brittle enough to break when Bright poked them. Bright fetched a flashlight and, when it didn't help much, realized the sun was coming up. He had no idea why he'd burned the body, why he'd slept outside—not slept, really—rather than dumping the guy and finding a motel. And he still didn't want to leave. What was wrong with him? When he'd taken the life out of that body, had he fallen in love with it? He went back to the fire. He couldn't stop himself. He extracted the big bones, the cleanest ones—the thigh bones, upper-arm bones—and set them away from the fire to cool. He would wrap them up and stash them under his backseat, sandpaper them smooth whenever he got where he was going. The bones would make him formidable as he waded through these shady states at the bottom of the map. He stoked the coals and the other bones around and got more flame to spring up. He ripped the carpety lining from his trunk and burned it. Burned the sneakers he'd been wearing and his purple shirt.

For years now the bones had sat in Bright's attic, buried in a corner in a lamp box labeled X-MAS STUFF. Maybe the bones would be good to have around. Maybe these kids didn't know who they were dealing with and would give Bright a lot of guff. Maybe he'd show them the box in the attic first thing when they reached the house. No. No, best to let it wait. Best if they stumbled onto the bones themselves.

He turned to the boys and informed them they would have nine-to-five covers as park peons—maintaining the grounds, directing lost SUVs.

"We get paid for that, too?" Swin asked.

"The checks come to me and I burn them. Your names are Robert Suarez and Ed Mollar. I got you licenses and park IDs."

"We have to take out the garbage and shit?"

"Sure you do."

"I don't do well with a boss," Kyle said.

Swin leaned up between the seats. "I never had one."

"Everyone has a boss," Bright said. "Frog probably has a boss."

"So you met Frog?"

"I spoke to a man on the phone that I believe was Frog."

"What led you to believe that?" asked Swin.

"He said 'This is Frog' before he started talking."

Bright's house had once been a school for woodworking. It had a huge main area and three yellow, bare bedrooms. Swin and Kyle wouldn't be staying with Bright. They would have matching trailers on the other side of the park. They would each keep two bags under their beds, one for their clothes and one for what-have-you. For their cars, which would be sold, each would get five thousand dollars.

In the big room of Bright's house was a white TV, a cabinet stocked with plastic bottles of bourbon, and scattered tables loaded with books about nature. Bright chose a bottle and fetched three short glasses. He filled one and handed it to Swin, who set it down on a book of essays about the boilerplate rhino.

"I don't really drink," Swin said.

"You don't, huh? You're a strange one, aren't you, Swin? You fancy yourself a genius?"

"Genius is a bit much. I could've been an intellectual, though."

"Intellectuals are white and they don't work out."

"They jog," said Swin.

"When you first meet someone and he offers you a drink, you damn well drink it."

"Not trying to be a dick."

"I have a feeling that's your line," said Bright. "Mine is, 'May you dream of offered tits.' I say that once in a while."

Swin picked up his glass and brought it to his face. "Nope. I can't."

Bright handed each of them a key, a map of the park, a handbook for state employees, and a pamphlet on national wildlife reserves. "You two go cuddle up with these. And may you dream of offered tits."

Kyle's trailer reminded him of a bad motel room, with its crooked AC unit and fake wood paneling. He was comfortable in it. He felt as if the trailer had been built especially for him and had sat empty a number of years. Its low, bug-trap windows were perfect, as was its indoor/outdoor carpeting and musty odor. Kyle felt concealed, like the trailer was a cave that blended into a mountainside.

Kyle wouldn't have to drive to Little Rock because he owned no personal effects that couldn't be replaced at a drugstore. In his wallet he carried two pictures of his mother, but he had refused to take any of her things with him when she'd died. And he'd never had a use for yearbooks or trophies—in fact, no use for school or sports.

Kyle's mother had raised him in a duplex. She'd been a receptionist on the social-funding floor of the county building. She kept her eyes and ears open and mastered the welfare systems to the tune of a half-dozen small checks each month. She'd always been there to see Kyle off and welcome him home. She made sure he always had sneakers to wear and meatloaf to eat. During Kyle's adolescence, she did not pressure him to get good grades or hang around with his classmates. She loved porches and had one added to the duplex at considerable cost even though she didn't own the place. She put up a swing and set out potted cacti.

Kyle was seventeen when his mother was electrocuted in the basement of the duplex and put into a coma. She'd been attempting to put floodlights on the old lady's side of the house, throwing breaker after breaker in the rusty, cobwebbed, gunked-up fuse box, trying to get power to the back corner of the building. At least this was the old lady's best account of it. She'd found Kyle's mother lying on the basement floor, her legs in a damp spot. The old lady's power had been out for an hour before she remembered that Kyle's mother was doing something electrical that day. Kyle got no phone call at school, just the old lady waiting on his porch, saying she'd told his mother not to fiddle with that box, telling him how to get to the hospital, telling him his mother would be okay in a couple days. Kyle called a cab. He took $50 from his mother's emergency stash. He put a stack of her photography books in a satchel. He stood in the basement a few minutes, staring at the spot where she'd fallen. There was nothing else to look at—a bare bulb, a washer and dryer, a tiny window.

Kyle's mother had good insurance and was set up in a cozy room with cable television. Kyle often left her bedside to take meandering walks through the downtrodden streets surrounding the hospital. These neighborhoods were not dangerous. These men—tethered to crumbling stoops, sharing cigarettes until they couldn't be pinched—had given up to the point where they wouldn't get off their asses and steal. Kyle despised them, and fought back urges to tell them so. His mother held on for five weeks. Besides Kyle there were three witnesses to her burial, two secretaries from the social funding office and a backhoe operator.

Rhoda, one of the secretaries, was going to take Kyle in until he could find a job and a place. She drove him to the cemetery. She enjoyed the drama, enjoyed being put upon. She had on a new pantsuit and a sparkly chain hung from her glasses. One thing she couldn't tolerate, she liked to say, was closed-mindedness. Rhoda often got irate about little things, like the way people chose their fruit or the way they waved people on in traffic. She lived in a good part of Lofton, in a villa on a man-made canal. Her villa was decorated with a safari theme. Kyle knew he wouldn't stay with her long. He'd thought of everything that would be left in the duplex when he skipped town—his mother's clothes and shoes and jewelry and makeup. Books. Soup and crackers and peanut butter. Vases and cookie jars. Pictures. Plants. Christmas ornaments.

Kyle remembered the funeral, if he'd call it that, in flashes. He didn't cry. His head felt like it weighed fifty pounds and was going to snap off of his neck. The backhoe operator was flirting with Kate, the other secretary, who held a container of olives in case anybody got hungry. Kate kept humming, kept smirking at the backhoe operator. Rhoda had her manly hand on the back of Kyle's neck, making his head even heavier. She kept saying his name to no one in particular. Kyle was speechless. Fast clouds rushed shadows over him. The backhoe operator had a huge gut. He said when you worked overtime it didn't build your check up; it cut it. He said he was allergic to olives and gum.

The chores at the park were not usually taxing, but they were very boring. Kyle and Swin took turns sitting in the booth, wearing brown shirts with embroidered badges, collecting day-use fees of three dollars per car and handing out maps and pamphlets. The garbage cans on the grounds would've taken weeks to get full, but had to be emptied daily because of the critters. Kyle did some raking and weed-whacking and Swin put out birdseed. Bright opened the gate in the morning and Kyle was responsible for locking it at night. Swin went for jogs along the park boundary to get out of his trailer, and this gave him occasion to run off a teenager or two, kids sneaking a can of beer or letting off bottle rockets. One day a kid in a tweed blazer was wandering around with a fishing net, nowhere near the pond. Swin yelled at him and the kid looked at Swin like he was a Martian and began holding forth about nude beaches. He'd been on a family vacation somewhere and had come back disillusioned. He described the world as a prude masquerade.

"I'm on something," the kid explained. "Something my brother brought back."

Swin drove Bright's Bronco to Little Rock and packed up his dumbbells, protein powders, elastic training cords, wrist and ankle weights, and all his fat gold herringbones and ropy bracelets. He was grateful to escape Little Rock. Swin's building was surrounded by puny trees, fences, and sleepless dudes who carried knives. It was a lonely place. He was glad to have a new face, Kyle, and even to have a boss.

Swin went to the closet and reached up to the highest shelf. There was a paperweight in the shape of a hamburger, a finger painting of the moon, and a miniature saddle that fit in his palm—items he'd received from his sisters when he left for college. He wished he had something from his oldest sister, but he would see them all soon enough, somehow. To him, a day without women was a tedious, droning march. He was a sucker for his sisters and he knew it. They could double his strength or cripple him. And they needed Swin. A young girl's life was a minefield; she needed someone—someone she could trust, not some strict, pale interloper— to nudge her this way and that as she strolled through that minefield. Swin had to make sure his sisters didn't turn against one another. He had to make sure they didn't get taken in by romantic notions about suicide. He had to keep them from getting beached on the rocks of intellectual shallowness. Eating disorders. Self-mutilation. Swin had to make sure one of his sisters didn't get pregnant from some guy in a dickhead ska band with white teeth and expensive boots who tells her about the big city and says his band might open for Green Day.

Swin approached the window-mounted air conditioner, raised his leg, then kicked the thing until it dislodged and fell two stories to the concrete below. The insulated crunch and after-tinkle lightened his heart.

The sun was high by the time Swin neared the park. He slipped off his shirt in order to catch the rays coming in the window. The blues station played a scratchy tune about a guy who had everyone in his goddamn business. At Bright's house, Kyle sat on the porch with a mug.

"You look like those guys on the do-it-yourself show," Swin said.

"Do *what* yourself?"

"You know, grout."

"What'd you go get?"

"Valuables."

"Like CDs?"

"And other stuff. Too bad it's summer; you could wear a nice turtleneck sweater."

Kyle stretched his legs and set down his mug. "You got quite an interest in my appearance." The coffee cup read THIS IS MY GOOD MOOD. "You're giving me that good-natured ribbing, right?"

"Now you do it back."

"It feels like flirting."

"It's very much like that."

Kyle's eyebrows spread. "Plenty of coffee," he said, gruffly.

"None for me. Makes me bored."

"Caffeine makes you bored?"

"Mugs and steam do. Just watching you drink that brings a malaise. Where's the boss?"

"Vacuuming."

Now Swin heard it. The noise had been blending with countless birds and rustlings and sways. "The shavings?"

"I can't see them. He says they're there."

"Wonder if he's tried it on blow."

"You think there's any chance Bright *is* Frog?"

"None," said Swin. "It's fresh thinking, though. An original yet dumb thought."

"Where do you think Frog lives?"

"You mean, what city?"

"You think he lives out on a ranch somewhere?"

"You don't get to be a crime boss by being solitary and contemplative; you get to be a crime boss by double-crossing and scheming and inheriting, just like on Wall Street."

"I don't believe you know much about crime bosses *or* Wall Street."

"Not firsthand."

"The guy must have *something* figured out, to go that long without getting caught or killed."

Swin scratched the back of his neck. "We'll have to work in this company for a long time before we find out anything true about Frog."

"I heard he has a pool shaped like a lily pad."

"That's what I mean. For a long time, we'll only know things like that—inconsequential falsehoods."

They waited until the vacuum shut off and went in. Bright began putting away dishes.

"Sleep well? All nested in?" Bright paused, a pair of tongs in hand. "Would either of you like to call me sir?"

They looked at him.

"Because you can if you like. I won't think it's corny."

Bright kept unloading until the drainer was empty, then sat down at the dining room table, which held a stack of newsletters about bobcats.

"Your first trip is Florida," he said. "I think the Panhandle." He picked his eye. "There's two things you got to hear before I settle in for my Premier League. First, there's a particularly do-goody cop named Cooper—Cooper the cop. He'll invite you guys out for beers and leave messages on the phone. Now that you all are here, he'll be off *my* ass; you're closer to his age. He's harmless. What I do is every once in a while go pal around with him—some charity field day or bake sale or some shit. Second, my park boss could show up at any time, probably today. She's due. Pretty little thing with a huge nose—wears pink all the time. She knows about us. She takes a cut."

Bright said he'd have dinner ready around eight, and for lunch he gave directions to a Hardee's, a barbecue pit, and a Japanese fast-food joint. There wasn't a proper town nearby, only a cluster of trailer parks and a large walk-in clinic.

"I'm going for a jog," Swin said. "Like the modern intellectual I am."

As he got up, a European car glinted past the front windows. Bright peeked outside.

"See this lady for yourself."

The woman knocked, then walked in the house. She had a bow in her hair and a pile of bracelets on each wrist. She was indeed wearing pink. Her hands and elbows looked raw, but her legs were smooth and lightly muscled. She sat at the table without seeming to notice Kyle or Swin, then rummaged through a soft briefcase, jerking out banded stacks of brochures. Bright offered the woman coffee. He poured it in a heavy mug adorned with Irish family seals and set it down in front of her, slipping an envelope underneath.

"The boys?" she said.

"Oh, these two. Don't be rude, guys."

"I can tell they're from your Frogman," she said. "What are their names?"

Kyle and Swin told her.

"Bored, I bet."

They shrugged.

"Mr. Bright's one of the boredest people I know. I'm lucky. I've got my painting. I couldn't stand this hobbyless camping." She shook like a wet dog, rattling her bracelets. "Not that painting is a hobby."

Bright dumped the coffee pot out in the sink, shook water in the pot, then dropped it in the drainer. She watched him, doing something with her nails.

"Do I need to check the papers?"

Bright shook his head.

This woman, Bright's boss and therefore Kyle's and Swin's, looked Kyle up and down, craning her neck to get a profile view. "You really stand at attention." She clicked her tongue at Kyle. "Can you believe you're here?"

"Yes," Kyle said.

"I sure as hell didn't want to get promoted so much. I'd have a show in SoHo by now if these parks suits didn't adore me."

"You look fantastic," Bright told her.

"I'm having a good eye day. They're really expressive. That's important when you got a honker like this. I've got something for you boys to do, which is a blessing in this place. Put ten each of these in the booth." She tapped a sheaf of brochures about wild boars. "There were four attacks."

"Injurious pigs?" Swin said. "I thought those were fiction, like Babe the Blue Ox."

The woman huffed.

"Why do you always wear pink?" Swin asked her.

"It began as a joke, but then I realized that it is, in fact, the prettiest color. It's the prettiest color for women to wear." She smoothed her collar.

"Every single day?" Swin asked.

"Every day." She glanced at her watch. "I bought a book of quotes by painters and I memorized them all. I'd like to share one: 'Your life should always be arranged just as if you were studying theology, or philosophy, or other sciences.'" Bright's boss in pink stood and pulled the strap of her big case over her shoulder. She'd only had a sip of her coffee. "'Eating and drinking moderately, electing light and wholesome dishes and thin wines; saving and sparing your hand, preserving it from such strains as heaving stones, crowbars, and anything else that would weary it. There is another cause which, if you indulge it, can make your hand so unsteady that it will waver like a leaf in the wind.'" She winked. "Which painter said that?"

"One of the naturalists," Swin guessed.

Bright grunted.

"Cennino Cennini. You boys, I imagine, indulge the hand six, seven times a day."

"Six or seven when we have the flu," Swin said.

The boss in pink made her exit, pinching Kyle's cheek as she passed, her bracelets brushing his stubble. Once the sound of her car had blended in with the forest noise, Bright took a deep breath. He explained that she came about once a month, and was supposed to examine all the paperwork and approve the appearance of the place. No one really checked up on state parks, particularly this one, Felsenthal, which was small and not cursed with a waterfall or dying species. The boss in pink wasn't greedy. If it wasn't for the greed of criminals, Bright said, cops wouldn't have a leg to stand on. He told the boys that if they ever got that itch, they should come talk to him about it. Just say "sir" and he'd be listening.

That afternoon, Kyle repainted the yellow lines of the parking area. This took patience he did not have. He had to get down on his knees and drag the brush impossibly slowly with two hands. Before he put the paint down, he had to sweep each line. Twigs and leaves kept blowing into the wet paint. He dropped the brush a few times. His can ran dry and he had to walk back over by Bright's house and lug over another one.

As soon as he got into a rhythm with it, a middle-aged guy in an unbuttoned shirt started talking to him about an endangered toad, asking where he could get a glimpse of one.

"The far end of the pond." Kyle pointed with no conviction.

"I thought they didn't like water," the guy said.

"Not usually," said Kyle. "They've been acting confused."

"I heard they come out when the scrub laurels bloom."

"Yeah, they love those."

"When do they bloom?"

"Any time now."

When Bright's dinner was almost ready, he started complaining that he had no radishes for garnish, so Swin volunteered to hit the grocery. He wasn't about to eat whatever pork and squash concoction Bright kept sniffing. That big pot of food reminded him of his mother, who used to freeze tons of runny casserole. Swin and his sisters would choke down the nuked mush while Swin's father ate a pressed Cuban twice a day. Swin's father, when Swin's mother left the house, would heat up all the casserole portions at once and call the neighborhood kids over. He'd line them up single file and slap a clod on each one's plate, calling the kids the wrong names. The guy did everything slowly, as if nothing was worth getting excited about. The only thing that pleased him was watching the Gulf. The beach was the same for Swin's father as it was for the millionaire condo-owners—same glare, same shells breaking again and again in the surf. Swin used to sit with him while he smoked his cigars to nubs. He'd never once felt close to the man, never accepted a puff or found a way to impress him. Kyle, Swin knew, would eat Bright's food and drink his liquor and become the darling.

The open-air grocery was crowded with barrels of nuts and peppers. Swin eyed a black-haired nurse with a fake tan while she filled a bag with chestnuts. The nurse wore blue scrubs and thick glasses. Something about her full bottom lip made Swin believe she must dig sex. She cracked two nuts together and put them in her mouth, and Swin went over and asked if she knew where radishes were. She located Swin's forehead through her bottle lenses and swallowed.

"With the vegetables? That's an educated guess."

Swin leered as if she'd said something naughty. "New in town," he said. "Name's Swin."

"Your name's about as dumb as mine: Johnna."

Swin conspicuously looked this nurse named Johnna from sneakers to barrettes. She had big yet uncrowded teeth and polka dots of blue polish on her nails. Her high breasts barely tented the front of her scrub shirt.

"There's no telling how long I'll be in the area," Swin said. He leaned against a barrel of fragrant chilis. "I'm a freelance government auditor."

Johnna was blushing through the brown of her cheeks, which created the effect of a blown disguise. She adjusted her glasses.

Swin said, "Let's get this courtship under way."

"I'm on shift tonight."

"Tomorrow night."

"Church."

"I'm out of town this—church?"

"You should try it."

"I have," Swin said. "We all have."

They agreed to meet for lunch on Thursday, right before Swin's departure for Florida. Johnna touched Swin's elbow and squeezed past him, maneuvering her hips through the barrels toward the checkout. Swin stepped into the produce room for the radishes. When he returned, Johnna was hissing at the clerk, a hairy individual with a thin neck. She ran down a list of his failures in life, which included community college, carpentry, and a run at the county board. Swin hoped she'd never had sex with this overall-draped dude. He wasn't fighting back. He totaled her order and made change. Johnna put the bills in her back pocket and told the clerk to feel free to die. Swin was convinced this woman had profound appetites. He slipped the radishes in his pocket and followed her outside. At her car, she turned on him with a stern look.

"What's with all the little muscles?"

"I stay ready to perform."

"It's creepy. The radishes and the tight shirt and the Duracell tattoos."

"Do you like creepy?"

Johnna unlocked her door and Swin opened it for her, ushering her with his arm. She started her car with much gunning of the engine, then traded out her glasses for a pair with tinted lenses. "You can't so much as kiss me for five dates."

"Then what?" Swin asked.

"Then you can."

You always think of Ken Hovan as the same person, while Froggy often changes. He has gone from a roofer to a bouncer to a man who squats around his store, wondering when he'll change again, watching dust float through light, making his eyes ache with coffee.

Testament is clockwork with his bootlegs—shipments every third Thursday which sell out in two days. Like before, you begin socking money away. The kids who buy the tapes also buy speakers and cigarettes. Sometimes you give the cigarettes away. Ghetto mothers start buying the tapes to give as presents. In the winter, on a day of jagged wind that finds its way up through your store's flooring and down through its attic space, Testament says the tapes are over. You tell him it kept up longer than you expected. You ask, with a nod toward a worn leather bag hanging on his shoulder, where he's headed. Illinois. But not with the bag. Either you take the bag, he says, or it's in a dumpster. It contains nineteen pounds of PCP and the phone number of a man named Buttons who, though he will not pay well, will not shoot you or steal from you. Testament is in a hurry. You shrug and take the bag, then stash it under a loose corner of the floor. The winds from outside pour in until you stomp the floor flat again. Within five minutes of Testament's departure you know you will sell these drugs. For the rest of the week you dust and mop and scrub your store. You peek once at the leather bag. You buy a pair of potted plants for the front window.

On Sunday you call the number and the name "Buttons" is spit into the other end of the line. It's him. He's black and his voice is not impatient. There's a game on in the background. You say that Testament has given you a suit and it turns out it doesn't fit. "Maybe it's more your size," you tell him. "You sound big." He tells you he's skinny as fuck, that he sounds this way because he's been smoking pot since age seven. You agree to meet him that night, a block north of Frayser High School. You wonder if the PCP was stolen and why Testament was fleeing, but you can't pin down a thought long enough to finish it. You have the eerie feeling of being in a movie, of having wandered into a movie. You don't know your lines. You don't know what happens to your character.

That night, when you pull up next to Buttons's car, a fat white woman gets out of the passenger side and passes you a JCPenney bag with a mess of cash in the bottom. You hand her the hefty leather satchel, resting it on the door frame so she can look inside, then she's back in the car and the car is leaving. The driver, who is probably not Buttons because Testament said he has bad glaucoma that makes his eyes look like bird shit, doesn't even glance at you. You sit there a few minutes, to dare this menacing slum. There are no dogs barking. No sirens. You have an impulse to sit there until morning, then walk into the greasiest diner in Frayser and buy everybody breakfast.

The next afternoon, Testament is on every local news show. He's been chased by cops onto the bridge, has gotten out of his stolen Maxima and perched himself on a railing high above the Mississippi River. The experts employed by the news shows agree that because Testament, identified as Nat Terrance Nailon, has been on the bridge for hours now, he is unlikely to jump. He's confused and wants attention. He throws his coat off into the wind and later tosses his T-shirt as well. With each passing minute, because of hunger, thirst, and fatigue, the cops have a better chance of talking him down. The news shows broadcast their shot of Testament serenely rocking, shivering, sometimes whistling, on a delay. If he jumps, they won't be allowed to show it. The picture cuts back to the studio and a somber anchor informs you that the experts have been proven wrong, that Mr. Nailon was not just looking for attention.

Kyle and Swin drove a brown Volvo to Florida. They didn't know what they were hauling or where on the car it was hidden. Kyle took the first driving shift and Swin slept for five hours while Kyle chugged the unwieldy wagon down Interstate 10, stickers for sappy rock bands and politics all over his bumper. There was no notable change in the surroundings until Pensacola, where every building had a deck and the air stank of burning tires. Swin awoke and demanded they stop in Panama City for dinner. He assured Kyle that the one-time Panhandle backwater had surpassed Daytona as the beach party capital of Florida.

Low, spiky palms. Neon. Gift shops giving away three T-shirts for five dollars. Kyle and Swin ate in a shotgun building with sand on the floor, a place that offered endless beers from California and turned muggy any breeze that passed into it. They walked up the strip asking about wet T-shirt contests and got only chuckles and stares. Where were the women? Kyle asked. A dude wearing boots with shorts? What were those three guys doing?

Kyle and Swin gathered that something gay was happening in Panama City. Swin cornered an older man who seemed the same beige race as himself and found that they'd wandered into a convention of elderly homosexuals. Every man in sight—fat, foreign, disabled—was gay. Swin asked if Kyle wanted to hold hands. Kyle, sick of Swin's joking, reached down and seized Swin's nuts, causing him to backpedal and stumble over a curb. They stared at each other a long moment. Kyle, satisfied, extended his hand to Swin, who looked at it skeptically before taking it. Swin had scraped his arm and gotten his pants dirty. He put on his best smirk, took a couple peppy steps.

"I'm surprised your hand fit around those boulders," he said. "You're lucky you didn't break your fingers on those cannonballs."

"Always with the jokes," Kyle said. "Jokes, jokes."

"What's really lucky is that the old skin cannon didn't go off." Swin's ego was almost fully intact again, that quickly, snapped back like elastic. "People have been maimed."

Most of the land on Highway 19, covered with dry oak trees and vines, was being sold off in parcels of five to twenty acres. There were no streetlights. The later it got, the hotter. By ten p.m. Kyle and Swin were running the air full blast and getting headaches from the bit of beer they'd drunk. The Volvo labored. They stopped at a gas station for high test and cold water and popped some Excedrin. Kyle said this state wasn't meant for white people and Swin answered that the whole country wasn't.

In Crystal River they passed a nuclear plant, then many signs shaped like manatees, some waving a flipper. Swin said the only two animals in the world with no natural defense were from Florida: manatees and love bugs. He detailed the accidental invention of love bugs, which were meant to be mosquito killers. Kyle told him that was fascinating and to get out the map and directions because they were close. They watched for a service station shaped like a dinosaur. They were in Hernando County. This newly populated stretch of the highway contained half a dozen strip clubs, one named Mom & Pop's. Kyle waited for Swin to suggest stopping at one so he could tell him no. The clubs had no signs, just names painted on the stucco.

"A place like that is where my sisters will end up." Swin tapped the window.

"How many of those you got? Like ten?"

"Their titties are plumping this very minute."

"That tends to happen."

"They don't have their real father around and their stepdad is overly strict. Sounds like a stripper recipe to me."

Kyle used his T-shirt to mop his face. "You can never tell."

"Did you know that one in four women would agree to be abused if it meant they could eat anything and stay thin?"

"If they agree to it, it's not abuse."

"I mean they'd be willing to have it happen."

"Abused how?" Kyle asked.

"Does it matter?"

"It would to them."

They left the Volvo in the lot of the abandoned movie house, walked to a nearby Dunkin' Donuts to use a pay phone, then waited in an adjacent pine clearing. Kyle paced about and came upon a chain-link enclosure with two huskies inside. They didn't even bark at him. They panted a mile a minute and blinked their cloudy blue eyes, reclined pitifully on their sides as if shot. Kyle put a stick through the fence and pulled over the empty water bowl, then went into Dunkin' Donuts and got several cups of ice, which he carried out and poured in the bowl. The dogs rolled their heads and stared at Kyle, not understanding.

Soon a dump truck full of pineapple palms bumped into the lot. The driver got out and, as he'd said he would, began smoking two cigarettes. Kyle and Swin shouldered their bags and emerged from the pines.

———————

Johnna was pawning a scooter with a wooden body that she'd found abandoned near a railroad crossing. The pawnshop was a cement-block building that rested at the bottom of a muddy hill. There was no way to tell if the place was open. Johnna told Swin to make noise getting out of the car, so he slammed his door and loosed a yawn. He didn't know if Johnna was counting this as a date, but he was. He banged the scooter, which had no seat and was painted all over with bumblebees, up the stairs onto the porch, where Johnna rattled the screen door. Soon a man in a ball cap stepped into the doorway. The man said he was barbecuing shrimp, making dinner for breakfast. Johnna said she wasn't hungry. She pulled the scooter inside, then leaned it on her leg and touched it here and there, like someone showing a dog. The room was crowded with poetry books and packages of socks.

"A hundred," Johnna stated.

The man removed his cap and looked inside it. "Does it run?"

"You don't ride it. Thing's a curiosity."

"But it's wooden."

"Which is curious, right?"

"I guess it is."

"What if you *had* to buy it?"

"In that case, I'd give you fifty and sell it for eighty."

Swin raised a finger. "You're able to turn a profit with books and socks?"

"I don't have to turn a profit."

Johnna huffed. "This sucker's hand-painted."

"The bees don't look real. They're smiling."

"This scooter is a piece of America."

"I don't care about America. I care about listening to the St. Louis Cardinals on the radio." He checked his watch and was startled by what it said. He left the room.

Johnna was stoic behind her glasses. She explained that this man had moved to the area several years before with enough money to open a shop, fill it with useless shit like books, and never make a transaction. All he did was cook breakfast and listen to the radio. He was mean. With all that money, he wouldn't give you ten bucks for a Rolex. He came back with a plastic-wrap-covered plate of sticky shrimp.

"I'm sorry, dear," he said. "You two can take some poetry with you."

Johnna sighed. "Tell you what I need is a saw. Handsaw."

"Just a minute."

The man left the room once again. Johnna rolled the scooter onto the porch and Swin followed with the shrimp. The air was hot and crowding. Swin told Johnna that if she needed money, he had some. She shook her head, said she simply wanted to be able to sell something she'd found, to rightly trade an interesting object for U.S. currency.

When the man returned with the saw Johnna let the scooter tip over, sat Indian-style beside it, and went to work on the handlebars, savagely yanking, a layer of sawdust forming on the porch floor, a droplet of sweat clinging to her glasses. Despite her strain, she wasn't cutting through the wood. Swin and the man looked at one another and the man winked. For a moment, Swin thought the man knew what he was thinking, that Johnna's current hotness and frustration were indicative of other hotnesses and frustrations, and that she was looking forward to their fifth date as much as he was.

———

Lightning flashed, followed by a barrel-filling rain. Bright said it would last all night, that the trails would flood. He told Kyle and Swin if they didn't start the mile-long walk to their trailers now they'd be stuck with him until morning. Kyle said he'd wait it out; Swin, cracking open the door and peering outside, nodded agreement. Bright told them to do the dishes, then settled in front of his TV to watch tennis, mumbling against a young American who faked injuries and walked like a peacock. After a couple commercials for stock funds, Bright's cable cut out. He kept looking at the screen for several minutes, a patient man or a man in denial, then he lobbed the remote control into a corner of the room, where it broke into pieces. He got himself up and cut off the pot of coffee Kyle was brewing. He snatched two glasses and opened his cabinet. Half the plastic whiskey bottles had been opened, all drunk down a different amount. Their labels read FILED TALON.

"As the English say, let's push on through till dawn."

Swin said, "Dawn?"

Bright stopped what he was doing. "Why don't you hit the sack, Abigail? Sleep in my bed if you want."

Bright handed Kyle a whiskey, the last thing Kyle wanted. Since the ride home from Florida, he'd had heartburn.

The phone rang and Bright answered it. After a few moments, without speaking, he hung up.

"Got to pick up the new orders."

"That was Frog?" Swin asked.

Bright sighed. "That was Her. She calls herself 'Her.'" This was a black woman who lived in a nearby trailer park and always called with the orders. Bright hoped Kyle and Swin would get to meet the woman, but often she left a packet outside her door and sat inside, ignoring any knocks. Kyle and Swin were to go to her trailer day after next, in the afternoon. They were to park down the block and walk. One reason Bright didn't go out much was that Her refused to leave phone messages.

"Why does she call herself 'Her'?" Kyle slugged more whiskey.

"She thinks if someone infiltrates the company and wears a wire or taps the phone or something, all it'll be is someone saying 'her' this and 'her' that, and 'her' could be any woman at all."

"Hmm," Kyle said. "I *guess* so."

"It's slightly more vague than a regular alias," Bright admitted.

Swin yawned demonstratively. "Got a radio?"

"I do not. Got some CB equipment in that closet that I never took out of the box."

"You said we'd get rifles," Swin said.

"You will. I still need to dig them out."

"I hope you never find them," said Kyle.

"I wasn't sure what to do with that birdseed," said Swin. "There's like three different kinds, I think for different seasons."

"The rest of the chores need to be done right." Bright sat down on a footstool next to his cabinet and reached up for a bottle. "Far as the seed goes, I don't care if you dump it in the pond. Now, you want a real chore, try getting all those damn wood shavings out of the bedrooms. They breed."

Raindrops pinged off the awnings. Swin slumped to the floor and did a set of push-ups, then crawled to the corner and reassembled the remote, snapping circuits together, pressing tight-bunched wires into place, finding the batteries. He did not try to turn the TV on, to check his work, just set the remote on a table and perused the short stacks of books scattered about the room.

"*Journey of the Snail*. This'll do." Swin got back in Bright's chair and flung open the book cover. "I predict this snail will overcome adversity. Slowly."

Bright replaced the whiskey bottle in the cabinet and turned the label square out. He let out a petite cough. "Let me say something here about boredom. Boredom is a beautiful thing. A bored criminal is a good criminal. If you ever catch yourself complaining about boredom… well, you'd rather look for something to do than have something to do find you."

A heavy scratching came at the front door, cutting Bright off and causing Swin to jump up.

"You get that when it rains," Bright told them. "It's only a dog."

Swin looked out the window. He clicked on the porch light. "It *might* be a dog."

Kyle slurped some whiskey, then joined Swin at the window. He tapped the glass and the animal looked up at them. It was certainly a dog. They opened the door and a fat bulldog mix with black teeth and bright blue fur tottered inside. Someone had dyed the thing. Swin offered it a bowl of baked beans with a hot dog cut up in it, but the dog would not so much as sniff this meal. He wandered to a window with open blinds and, like an old prisoner, coolly stared outside.

"Do we have to call him Blue?" Swin said. "Or can we do like the Romans and name him after a Civil War hero?"

"Your dog," said Kyle.

"Bedford," Swin called toward Bright. "Dog's name is Bedford, okay?" Swin set water down beside Bedford and he butted the bowl, spilling on the carpet.

"Give him time," Bright said. "Being beige is no picnic, but imagine being that color."

Over the next hour, the rain somehow got harder. It was near midnight. Bright and Kyle drank and drank. Swin asked if Bedford could sleep in Bright's bed and Bright said he'd sooner have the dog in there than the owner. A feisty, inconstant wind picked up, adding to the noise of the rain, lashing it against the windows. Swin prepared a fruit salad and shared some with Bright and Kyle. After Bright had eaten his fill, he threw himself into telling his story. It seemed the right time for a story—no cable, rotten weather, middle of the night. Swin came over and he and Kyle looked down on Bright, perched on his footstool.

He told them he'd struggled a good while in Arkansas before renting the garage of a man who owned a tree service. The guy didn't need Bright's money but his wife had died and he needed to talk to another bitten man. Bright knew, even before he'd gotten a taste for this man's whiskey, that listening to his laments could improve Bright's position in life. Bright started going out with the tree crew, he told Kyle and Swin, volunteering to sit in high branches and convincing customers to get more trees removed than they'd planned on. One guy in the crew, a kid with beefy knuckles and the hair part of a news anchor, made a comment about what lewd favors Bright must be doing for the owner in order to earn his keep. Bright asked the kid to clarify what he'd said, then grappled him to the ground and drove a knee into his ribs.

A three-month job began at the park. Bright's landlord put him in charge, promoting him with the title Crew Chief. The important thing with tree-service work was not to act unsure. If an operation turned dangerous or created a mess, Bright would act as though he'd set it up that way so they could have some fun. The kid Bright had beaten up made a big show of holding no grudges and remained on the crew.

The head ranger, a friend of Bright's landlord, had a huge family and had pursued the ranger position in order to secure a vast play area for his kids. These children loved Bright. They handed him gifts of glittered pine cones and paper birds. After the park job ended, the head ranger, who was the type of man who could disarm you with the enthusiasm of his greetings, created a position for Bright at the park—Landscape Coordinator. This was the only time in Bright's life that he'd enjoyed legal work. He didn't have set hours and was free to destroy nature.

After the birth of his next child, the head ranger was called to a cabinet position under the new governor. Bright was promoted. He thanked his former landlord by giving him unnecessary tree work in the park and still sometimes getting drunk with him. The man had died a few years back and had left Bright most of the books that now rested on every flat surface in his living room.

"Then what?" Kyle asked.

"Then Gregor got lost and pulled into the park and the rest is history."

"Gregor used to be a driver?" Swin asked.

"Until that night."

"I'd like the gig he has," Swin said. "Sitting amongst disassembled tubas, reading the newspaper. I don't mind the solitary life. Of course, I would wash my hair."

"Being a holder is punishment." Bright made a sound in his cheek, then belatedly laughed. "Maybe you'll screw something up, then you can be a holder too."

The next day, the boss in pink, Associate Director of Parks Operations—Southern Arkansas Region, dropped by with more pamphlets. She'd gotten a massage from a deaf woman in Hot Springs and felt beat up. In her rose suit, she drifted from window to window in Bright's house, then announced that she'd found a gray hair. Being an old biddy, she would officially never become a renowned painter—would, in fact, never again touch a brush. The last thing she'd do was make painting a hobby. She had another quote. "'Do the light and air change? The passions of the human heart? I will not change with my century. Because my neighbor does good, must I? Because he misunderstands, must I? Having no more of sophistry is my crime.'"

After she left, Kyle found himself wondering how soon she'd return. He pictured her driving her little car with the windows down, singing along with the radio, and wished she were not his boss's boss, that she didn't know he was a criminal. A woman like that would consort with criminals but she wouldn't date one. Oh, well. If she ever became his girlfriend, it would be a matter of days before he got bored with her. And her with him.

"What's sophistry?" Kyle asked.

Swin said, "It's when something seems reasonable enough, but it's full of evil."

In the afternoon, Bright showed Kyle how to make his "muck," which was a sort of unspicy chili. He said one could substitute any meat. Swin, watching the two of them bond over onions and dried herbs, became depressed and thought he should learn to drink. He got a bottle of Bright's whiskey, picked up his lethargic dog, and went to his trailer. He mixed the whiskey with apple juice and downed cup after cup, careful to use less juice each time. Bedford begged for some juice and Swin gave him a bowl. The thing loved apple juice. Swin felt this was the time to teach the dog a trick. He said, "Sit, boy. Sit." He demonstrated sitting, whispered the command then nearly screamed it. Swin tried to make Bedford beg, roll over, shake hands. All dogs liked to fetch. Swin grew unsteady on his feet and felt a generalized sense of nostalgia, perhaps for events that hadn't happened yet. His mouth was profoundly dry. He had no ball for Bedford to fetch, so instead he threw paper plates across the trailer like Frisbees. He got much drunker all at once and collapsed on his side with a bag of organic vegetable chips. He chewed one for minutes without swallowing.

At dawn, Swin awoke to his first hangover. He stood, hunched, and put one foot in front of the other until he reached the tiny refrigerator, where he drank a gulp of skim milk and vomited effortlessly. He called Johnna, then slumped at the table and had a dream where men in overalls removed his entire brain, assuring him that his peripheral nerves would compensate. The brain was not strictly necessary, they told him. Swin drove himself home from the surgery and, despite their explanation, felt sluggish. What was that? Johnna was knocking. Her mouth was lovely. Her arms were full. She set Swin up on the couch with a cold eye-press shaped like the Lone Ranger's mask. She had a system for hangovers and was happy for a chance to use it. One liter lukewarm water. Cold shower. Orange juice. Eye drops and lip balm. Then, a liter of *cold* water. *Steaming* shower. Bagels and coffee. Stretching. When Swin felt better, they made several slow laps around the trailer for fresh air. Swin's eyes welled. He told Johnna he missed his sisters, then said he didn't want to talk about them. Johnna said she hadn't asked him to talk about them.

"Want to know something?" he said. "One in four women would trade having their husbands cheat on them for the ability to eat whatever they want and stay thin."

"Might as well stay thin," Johnna said. "They're cheating anyway."

"I'm curious to see how wonderful this stepdad is when they start showing up pregnant with their credit cards run up and needles in their arms."

"He's *your* stepdad, too."

"But they listen to him. They're impressionable."

"I'm sure they miss the shit out of you."

"I hope they cry over me."

Johnna stroked Swin's head for a few minutes, until his eyes grew calm. She vetoed his idea that a morning of medical care counted as a type of date. She had to hurry up and go tan before her shift. Swin said *that* could be a date, if he went tanning with her.

"In progressive cities, men tan and women cultivate their paleness."

"For it to be a date, you have to pay."

"Anything you ask for while you got those scrubs on."

"Need to feed that blue dog?"

"Oh, yeah," Swin said. "I got a dog. His name is Bedford."

"I like when people call dogs Steve or Dwayne."

"He's been Bedford for twelve hours. If you get along with him, you can have him. He hates me."

Kyle and Swin did not get to meet Her. They navigated the trailer park with Bright's lousy directions, watching the unit numbers jump about with no rhyme or reason, until finally, there was 56. They backed up a ways and parked, then stalked through a light rain, past all variety of small statue, flimsy fence, and colorful flag. An old man with sunglasses pushed up on his head stared at them, the stream from his hose sloshing into a birdbath. The sharp-cornered yellow packet rested on a tray table under Her's carport. The packet contained a map, the meeting time, instructions to take the payment, how much, from whom. They would hand-deliver the drugs and receive cash, which led Kyle and Swin to believe they must be gaining the trust of Bright and Frog. They looked at the map, turned it right-side up: Louisiana.

The delta dawn of Memphis beams through the front glass of your shop. It's harsh in your eyes, warming the bag of money. You now have a modest nest egg—nearly twelve thousand dollars, plus another ten you'd already saved. You drop the bag under the floorboard and spend two customer-free hours in a haze. What you need is a breakfast that comes on several plates. Newspaper. A cigarette. You stand, but here is your first customer, a black guy with braided sideburns and long teeth. Buttons sent him and you have to give the money back. The PCP was bunk. You can't give the money to *him*; he's just a messenger. You have to take it back to the spot of the transaction, tonight, two in the morning.

"How do I know he isn't lying?" you ask.

"Probably is. Between the two of y'all."

"Tell him to stop by here."

"I done all the telling I got to."

"Just tell him I won't be there tonight."

"All I'm telling is the chicken man two thighs."

He leaves and you know you've done something stupid. Your appetite is gone. Buttons wants you back in Frayser to kill you. You will start carrying a revolver. Your days as a shop owner, you know, are over as of this moment, your inventory lost. You say goodbye to Froggy's. Buttons will have his people trash it.

You go to a hotel in Germantown to think. The clerk says it's too early to check in, and you tell him to charge you for yesterday, too. Over a period of four or five hours, you flip through the nine channels repeatedly. You should be able to sleep by now. Nothing is happening in the world—no earthquakes or celebrity deaths or medical breakthroughs. People on game shows are doing silly things with food, urging one another. You're starving. Though you've chosen to pay double for this hotel, you refuse to be fleeced for a room-service hamburger. You walk down the street to a barbecue restaurant full of pictures of celebrities in bibs—Merlin Olsen, Ed McMahon, Steppenwolf. You get a pound of pulled pork and a half-order of beans and stroll toward the hotel, over a retired railroad track and past a day spa and a political headquarters. In the hotel parking lot a vintage Buick cuts you off and the driver shows you a pistol. You get in the passenger seat and a big black dude with a sharpened gold tooth asks for your gun. He works for Buttons. Surprisingly, he's alone. You hesitate and he tells you not to play. You hand over the .22 and then try to appear composed, opening the Styrofoam box on your lap and digging in. You offer the guy some and he says he's on a strict diet of Hennessy and ass. He's driving down the narrow lanes of Poplar Avenue, stopping at a light every ten feet, another police cruiser at each intersection. You suggest he cut up on Mendleson and he does so. You begin on your beans.

"How'd you find me?" you inquire.

"Followed you since you left the shop, you dumb shit." He chuckles.

"I'll give you five thousand dollars if you let me go."

You see his breath catch, his head twitch, weighing the risk and reward. He starts to smile, something cute to say. You launch yourself on top of him, pinning his gun arm with all your weight, bust his nose with the top of your head, find his eye with the tines of your plastic fork and plunge it in. He jerks the wheel. The Buick bucks a curb and flattens a fence. You waggle the fork in his eye socket and keep butting his nose and mouth. You don't know where the car is going. There is the neat pain of his filed tooth against your scalp, and you notice there is no noise. When the Buick slams into an oak tree, your revolver, which had been tucked under the driver's seat, thunks onto the floor. There is noise now. You roll out of the car and shoot the man in the torso three times. You are on your side in an azalea thicket, baked beans smeared across your shirt. You open the driver door and allow the man to fall out. You back over the fence and down off the curb and drive the Buick to Darwin's Recovery, where Darwin gives you two grand for it. He looks at the blood on your sleeve and collar and the bean stains on your chest and says, "That was some food fight."

The walk back to the hotel is a blessing. You feel an insidious cramp of love for everything you see—the wily children with their schemes to get cigarettes, the river-colored haze hanging in the sky, the twenty-year-old pickup trucks that have been waxed until they gleam. You love the Mississippi women, dragged here by their husbands, the thick-accented women who will never understand why people want to live in the city. You love the old people who have watched this place go to shit. You love your .22. It's accurate, doesn't kick, doesn't jam, has a marble grip, and you can get cheap ammo for it anywhere.

You will leave Memphis now.

Pine Bluff, Arkansas—craggy and pretty and shrinking. There is always fog in the troughs of Pine Bluff's hills, and you enjoy walking down into the fog and emerging on the other side like a rising spirit. There is a tiny university and there are many rednecks. There are small buildings shaped like different foods, mom-and-pop lunch joints. You play the part of a user for a couple weeks, always getting what you want but always in a small quantity. The bars of Pine Bluff are big on amateur competitions. You sit in these bars, stoned or hopped-up, watching people try out jokes and pull things from their sleeves. At times it seems everyone in Pine Bluff is in an altered state; they are a little slow and too even-tempered.

Your dealer is an older man named Almond. He is also from Memphis. He has black hair and thin gaps between all of his teeth. Almond believes the world is becoming morally atrocious, that individuals of low quality are overrunning the planet. As long as you stay on the correct side of his moral-quality line, Almond will be a friend. You tell him you didn't always have muscles, that you got picked on as a kid, that having to talk your way out of things made you into a salesman. This impresses him, and he gives you a shot selling for him. You pop from bar to bar, watching spindly girls croon and bald guys do impressions, becoming known, becoming the man to make eye contact with. In a matter of days, everyone knows where to find you, your prices, what you have. You gain confidence as a drug dealer. You've seen the business from the viewpoint of a bouncer and a buyer and a man on the run—a man who escaped with the money of one of the sizeable bosses of Memphis—and now you see it from Almond's perspective. Almond is a fastidious, careful man, a man who steadily and quietly monopolizes a tiny city. Almond counsels you often. He wants to show you the right way to do things. He doesn't want you to disappoint him. He doesn't realize your time with him is merely an apprenticeship; he thinks you'll be with him for the long haul. Sometimes while he's making his coffee, which he drinks with one Sweet'n Low and one sugar, he stops and stares at you, regarding you with you-don't-know-what. Almond strikes you as the kind of man who, in a fight, would expertly and quickly break someone's nose, then take two steps back and just stand there.

Almond owns a sign-making company that he uses as his laundry. He spends about twenty hours a week in the workshop, and much of his remaining time goes to his sister, who is fifteen years his senior and has severe health problems. Her brow is always furrowed and her fingers won't bend. Almond has all kinds of adaptive equipment for her: mechanical beds, wheelchairs, customized toiletries, creams and balms and powders. Videos and toys. Almond will not take her to a nursing home. He processes her food and deposits tiny spoonful after tiny spoonful into her quivering lips. You offer to sit for her. Though Almond refuses the offer, this fully convinces him that you are a high-quality person.

Almond has a nemesis, his former brother-in-law, a man they call Hink. Hink, twenty-one years younger than Almond's sister, divorced and abandoned her when she became ill. Hink still lives in Pine Bluff. He wears an anklet and flip-flops. He has a girlfriend in her thirties who wears high heels that are too big for her and sprinkles glitter on her arms and shoulders. Almond and Hink never go near one another. Almond is too smart, he says, to let himself go to jail for killing Hink. If Almond goes to jail, he says, his sister will be alone. Almond considers Hink a dog, not a man. Once, when a bunch of Almond's signs were vandalized and everyone assumed Hink was responsible, Almond grew so irate at Hink that he had himself locked in a garage for twenty-four hours.

Almond lets all his other sellers fall off. You sell what he gives you in three or four days, before the weekend even hits, but he won't buy more because it would be bad for the users and because it might bring trouble near. Almond has a ton of rules that are meant to keep him out of trouble. Apparently, they work. If you stretch one rule, he says, all the others are useless. Never cheat the customer and don't allow yourself to be cheated. Find your volume equilibrium and stick to it. Have one middleman and one middleman only. Define your farm area and don't stray.

Almond's rules are appealing in the abstract, but after five months in which you earn the same meager commission, you grow antsy. Some guys aren't careful enough, but Almond is *too* careful. You lead him to believe you're fully on board with his program. One night, in a great show of esteem for you, he brings you along to his middleman's house for a buy. The middleman is surprised to see you. He wears a T-shirt and a suit coat and has a fridge full of light beer. You and Almond and the middleman square away the evening's business and then the three of you settle in and watch a movie featuring testy exchanges on balconies and women throwing their earrings. The middleman wants Almond's car to sit in the driveway a few hours; he doesn't like people pulling in and pulling right back out.

You understand that pleading with Almond would be useless and would make him suspicious. You understand that he is too meticulous to steal from. What you have to do is set him up to be caught by the police and make him think Hink is behind it. This is not a good plan but it's the only thing you can do. You drop gossip around Pine Bluff about Hink wanting to end Almond's self-righteous feud once and for all. You bust up a few signs. You type I KNOW THINGS on a postcard, put Hink's name on it, and slip it in Almond's mailbox. You look Almond in the eye and offer to take care of his Hink problem. A few weeks later, when things are settling down, you pull up next to a pay phone out by the mineral plant and call the police station and tell them that between nine-thirty and ten-thirty a gray Thunderbird with several bricks of cocaine in the trunk is going to cruise down Stringer Avenue and make a left on Tornbore Lane.

Almond is denied bail. When you are finally allowed to visit him, when you saunter across the room with a fake look of outrage on your face and pat his shoulder, he tells you not to fucking touch him. He knows it was you. He grips the edge of the table with white knuckles, his face locked in a twitch. You slide your chair back before you sit. It takes a great effort for Almond to speak quietly. He tells you that you will take over his responsibilities as a man. If you don't, he will have you killed.

"Responsibilities as a man?" you repeat.

His face darkens, overrun with ire, wanting you to make light of what he's said so he can spring across the table at you. You haven't seen anything in your time with Almond to suggest he knows a hit man. He doesn't deal with junkies, isn't the type to farm out dirty work. Still, who knows what friends he's making in prison? Still, you *do* owe him. You respect him. Although he was bound to be usurped, if not by you then by some guy like you, you respect him.

Your inherited manly duties, Almond tells you, are to kill Hink and to put Almond's sister up in the Rissler House, the finest old folks' home in the area.

"One condition," you say. "I want your middleman. I want the dude with the light beer and the HBO."

Almond turns his chair so he is not facing you and enjoys a deep breath. He seems relieved to be among such blatant immorality, to not have to worry about immorality sneakily encroaching.

"Have him," he says. "Have him and be cursed."

So you do what he wants. You put the sister in a tower of the Rissler House, a converted Victorian mansion where the residents eat shrimp cocktail and filet mignon. Hink's girlfriend goes to visit her family in Mississippi. On Friday, you break into Hink's house and wait for him to return home from bowling. You don't bring your gun because it will be too loud. You didn't want to go into a store with a small-talking clerk and a receipt reel and maybe even a camera and purchase a baseball bat to use on Hink. The best thing is to use something of his. You survey and rummage, under beds and in closets, unable to find anything to use as a weapon. You check the garage. No baseball bat, no golf club, no tire iron, no fireplace stoker. The most suitable thing Hink has is a hefty casserole dish, and this is the object that brings him death, possibly at the first blow, while he is passed out on his couch, still wearing his two-tone shoes.

In jail, Almond quickly grows into the old man he is and one morning fails to wake up, a weight off your shoulders. You are eager to move to Little Rock. You're not like Almond, satisfied with being small-time. You want to go somewhere with less familiarity, somewhere you won't have to hem business in. You've been in Pine Bluff six months and already everyone knows you. More than all that, Pine Bluff gives you a cloudy feeling. It sullies your meanness, this trusting, foggy burg.

Once in Little Rock, you make trips back to Pine Bluff every couple weeks to meet with the middleman and check on Almond's sister. After eighteen months, she too passes away. Soon you establish your own middleman in Little Rock and squeeze the Pine Bluff guy on price until he tells you to fuck off. You're glad. You don't need him and you're tired of driving down there and you want to, once and for all, sever all connection with Pine Bluff.

One day your Little Rock middleman offers to sell you his wholesaler. The middleman is desperate. He asks for one hundred thousand then quickly accepts your offer of sixty-one, which is all you have. You may get screwed, but you have no choice but to hold your breath and roll the dice. This is the part at which you excel, the point where you have to register fear only with your brain and not let it invade your guts. You do the same thing with frustration and discouragement; they can never really touch you. You can acknowledge injustice and the absurdity of life while never getting weighed down by these things.

You make the middleman watch you put the cash in a locker. You make an envelope out to him, put the key in it, and drop it in a mailbox. If the plan is to screw me, you tell him, you better change it to shooting me. You drop him off and turn your thoughts to meeting the wholesaler. You will wear a suit. You will arrive not a minute early and not a minute late. It will go smoothly and your next problem will be that you need people. You drive through a frail moonlight that settles like dust, knowing that your problems from here on out will be the kinds of problems you *want* to have.

You cannot get people. You wait outside a Labor Ready until you see a pair of prison-looking dudes, tough and lazy. You ask if they want to work for you and the question exhausts them. They say, "Naw, man." You run a vague ad for delivery drivers and it is answered only by high-school kids and graduate students. You ask around at a biker bar on the edge of town and the owner tells you his customers have a hard enough time keeping out of trouble, then he drops a glass ashtray on the bar, where it wobbles to a stop.

You are not going to be the only game in town. You will not be familiar. You will not be predictable. You will not get caught. You will spread yourself thin. Your deals will have no routine and will pepper the entire Southeast. It will be too much driving for you alone. You want two guys, two guys to start with, to bring in on the ground floor. They will drive only until other drivers are added, and then they'll be management. These two will be your heirs, the keeper of your story. You never asked for your life to become a great story, but that's what's happening here. This is a lot to plan when you haven't even met these two, when it seems you may never find them, when, before they do any of this, they'll have to sit around in bars and work the streets and hone themselves like you had to.

The next trip was short. Kyle and Swin were to cross into Louisiana, barely into the swamps, and drop off a net bag of soccer balls filled with pills. They drove a Ford Taurus with digital dash meters and a CD player for which they'd brought no CDs. Kyle was sick of words, even his own.

"No more radio," he said.

"There's a lot of good stations around here," said Swin. "This is a musical area."

"Not today it isn't."

Swin picked at his door handle, a nuisanced look on his face. "What, are you going to contemplate the nature of the ever-expanding universe and man's place in it?"

"Doubt it. But if I do have a thought, I'll hear it."

"Sure," Swin said. "*If* you have one."

"I feel one coming on."

"Maybe you should pull off."

"Nope. Nope, false alarm."

"So now let's turn the old radio back on."

"Tell you what," Kyle said. "Find something with no words in it."

"But I'm in the mood for blues. I want to hear that one where the guy says it's nobody's business if he wakes up crazy and kills his baby."

"Take a nap."

"Hey! Welcome to Louisiana."

Kyle checked his watch.

"You ever been to Mardi Gras?" Swin asked.

"I'm not sure."

Many towns whizzed past. Lots of churches. Lots of food stands. A black man with no shoes holding something that was on fire.

They pulled up to the trailer and honked four times. The door cracked open and an arm waved them in. Kyle lugged the balls in like Santa Claus, and a swarthy guy in slippers cut the bag open and began puncturing the underinflated spheres one by one, his knife tearing through the glossy vinyl.

"In my country," he said, "is rude not to study something you buy. You like Capri Sun?"

Swin said, "Sure."

"We buy bulk. We're sick of them. Poking that straw is an American stupidity. The juice, it squirts out."

"We?" said Kyle.

The man stopped tearing up the soccer balls. "My nephew." He called the name Nick. "Bring juice pouch this minute."

A kid about high-school age appeared and tossed Swin a Capri Sun. The kid shook his head, as if daunted by the thought of getting rid of all the Capri Sun in his stewardship. He had close-set eyes and slicked hair, like an old-fashioned immigrant. As he left the room, he grunted something in Greek that caused his uncle to fly off the sofa, knife still in hand. Kyle stood and said, "Easy." The man looked at the weapon in his hand.

"Look how rude. I wave this thing. Nick, speak English in front of friends. You know only curses, anyway. Let them see you or they get nervous. They don't know how harmless you are."

Nick doubled back into the room, leaned on the wall, and began messing with the wristbands he wore on each forearm. Kyle told the uncle not to worry so much about being rude, but instead to hurry up and check the balls and bring out the money. This main room of the trailer contained a sofa, on which the uncle sat, two folding chairs, on which Swin and Kyle sat, several mason jars of pennies, and a stack of license plates. The floor was scattered with slippers.

"His poor papa drove a tow truck," the uncle said. "The least noble profession of the world. Even police are sometimes noble. Or teachers or singers. Not tow-truck drivers."

Nick shook his head. His uncle broke a pill open and dumped it in an ashtray. Using a turkey baster, he doused it with a pink liquid.

"His papa told me what great comfort it was he could kill himself. When life was hard, he thought of this. A strange egg, as Americans say. As a child he paid another boy to partake in the carnal act with a dog. Small dog."

"Dogs enjoy sex with humans," Swin said. "It would be like you having sex with a super-hot alien."

Now Nick smiled. Maybe he was slow. Swin held up his empty Capri Sun and Nick took it from him and disappeared. The uncle had two balls left. He sighed, put the knife in a drawer, and brought out a different one.

"What county of Arkansas are you from?"

"Tell him to bring in the money," Kyle said.

"Sorry, rude question. All these customs."

"Don't say the word 'rude' again. It's in my power to pull the deal."

The guy yelled for his nephew to bring in the bag.

"My plight is horrible one," he said. "I only ask what county because I once designed water towers. Fifty-one towers for Alabama, Mississippi, Arkansas. Now the fashion changes. No new towers. Now I'm not noble. Now I am threatened by men in my home."

Kyle nodded. "Could be worse. If he doesn't get that bag out here in a hurry, it could get worse."

The man called out again and Nick came in with the bag and gave it to Swin, who opened it and took a look. Nick's grin was amused. He wasn't slow. In fact, something about him was condescending. As Kyle and Swin left the trailer, the uncle said, "No hard feelings."

Kyle replied, "No feelings at all."

Swin drove. Kyle reclined his seat and wondered about Nick, about why someone would subject themselves to such shit. It was a matter of time, Kyle thought, before that kid offed his uncle and ate him. That head shaking was pure maniac. Swin said whoever was driving made the rules about the radio, then tuned in a folk station that was begging for donations. Kyle wondered about the nation of Greece, about the field of water-tower design, about what it would be like to have an uncle. He drifted and had a dream in which he tried to relax in a breezy place. A resort. He didn't know the name of the drink he wanted to buy for an older woman.

It was not easy for Nick to follow the Taurus in a Datsun hatchback with an 85-horsepower engine. Several times, he had to scream his roller skate of an automobile and close in on the Taurus to see the stuffed Razorback in the rear window, wearing a #4 jersey. If these two dudes from Arkansas knew he was trailing them, they weren't going to let on. The blinkers of the Taurus flashed only when the car moved from right to left, and its speed was sporadic. Nick was burning up, his insides cramping. He calmed himself with the thought of having enough money to move somewhere rugged where he would get a certificate to be an X-ray tech, keep a clean trailer, and head down to the bar once a week with fresh fingernails. People would say he was a regular dude—run-of-the-mill, good dude. Nick didn't know why he hadn't been able to kill his uncle before he left. He suspected his uncle had some kind of slave grip on his mind. The guy had told everyone in their town that Nick was lazy and stole, preventing him from getting a job at the mug factory or the outfit where they put ketchup and mustard in packets. He talked Nick's father down at every turn, though Nick's father had supported him for years while he was out of work, before he found his way into the drug trade. For a solid year, until he got bored with it, Nick's uncle had called Nick "Prickolas." Nick wasn't quite eighteen. His uncle had reminded him every day that if he left he'd be reported missing, tracked down, and dragged back in disgrace. On this outing, though, Nick would have the means to get as far away as his Datsun would take him. By the time anyone found him, he'd be the lawful owner of a nice adult life. Because of his maturity, folks would know he'd been through something. It was common knowledge that women liked a dude who'd been through something.

Two hours from home, Nick realized he'd never driven this far. He should've brought a tape player because the radio in his Datsun didn't work. A voice in his head sang bits of the song "Honesty" at a sped-up pace. How was the word "honesty" easy? Easy to spell? Easy to do? The rhythm of the song conformed to the bump and hum of the tires against the road, and Nick couldn't shake it. His face was sweating. He'd already rubbed his forehead raw against his wristbands. Deep breaths were what was called for. Nick wanted coffee. He hadn't drunk it since he was a kid, since his father gave him sips from a metallic thermos. The Taurus was never going to stop for gas. It had settled in behind a semi in the right lane. Nick thought of his uncle's gun in the glove box. It was tarnished black and prone to kick down and left, but at short range it would get the job done. He imagined getting pulled over, having his gun confiscated, getting returned, in cuffs, to his uncle's trailer. He banished the thought that he'd be relieved.

The Taurus broke onto a two-lane county road and suddenly Nick wasn't anxious. He felt himself to be a natural detail of the place. Dawn was starting. Nick was surrounded by broken-top hills. The Taurus pulled into a park with a funny name and Nick parked outside the gate and killed his lights, tossed his sopping wristbands on the floor. He had a sixteenth of a tank of gas. He shut off the engine. He had a book bag that had been given to him by a charity which had also given him a set of rulers. He put his gun in the book bag, which already held a hammer and a tangle of thick shoelaces, and waited about five minutes, giving the dudes from the Taurus a chance to feel safe. Nick didn't know if they were going to camp in the park or if they had a meeting scheduled or what, but this park probably had only one entrance, so they wouldn't be able to leave without Nick knowing about it. He entered the park on foot and headed down a path blocked off by a gate with a sign that read PARK EMPLOYEES ONLY. He scaled a dry hill scarred with stump holes. From the top, he saw a Bronco and a low, expansive house. No sign of the Taurus. Lights on in the house. Nick descended the hill and hid behind the Bronco. He needed to observe, to find out what was waiting in there. An old lady with a bunch of sons? A Confederate militia? There was nothing inside the Bronco—no music or food containers or corny objects hanging from the rearview. There were, however, fresh tire tracks up the drive and back down, and a set of footprints to the porch and back. After about two minutes of observation, Nick felt like a sitting duck. He scaled the porch steps without creaking them and positioned himself outside the front door. TV. An announcer who was maybe Scottish was explaining the financial straits of some rugby league. As far as Nick could figure, the dudes in the Taurus had dropped something here, whether it was his uncle's money or something else of value. Nick would've rather had cash, but a good amount of drugs, if that's what it had to be, would work. When he went inside and encountered this dude, whether it was some thorny chief runner or pumped skinhead or just some loser like Nick's uncle, Nick wouldn't let on that he didn't know what he was looking for. He tried the door handle and the lever yielded to his thumb. He unzipped his book bag and removed the gun, pressed it against his thigh. He nudged the door open an inch, his body snug against it, and took a moment to breathe—not stalling. He wasn't going to stall. He put his eye to the opening and saw part of a large room—books everywhere in uneven stacks, the television. Nick let the door open another foot and yanked himself inside. He was stopped short by the sight of a hulking cabinet stocked with dozens of identical liquor bottles, all half-empty. He shut the door behind him and slipped into the nearest room, weapon at the ready. The room was blank, yellow, with no closet and a fan in the corner. Nick peered down the long hall before taking the next room, also yellow, matching the other except that it held a shiny vacuum with countless accessories. The machine was like an injured animal, plug hanging half out of the socket, tubing draped about like maimed limbs. Nick was scared to turn his back on the thing. He paced farther down the hall and halted at the next open doorway. In the same glance, his eyes found the stack washer and dryer, trisection laundry basket, cardboard box full of light bulbs, lopsided hill of pamphlets, and the bald man down on one knee, holding a broom and dustpan. It took what felt like a long time for the man to transfer his attention from the floor to Nick and his pistol. When he did, his eyes lit up.

"I don't mean to die before I whip these shavings."

Nick was out of his league, but the man didn't know that. Nick instructed him to empty his hands and remove his boots and socks. The man did this, yawning, then cracked his toes. Nick put him on his front and tied his wrists behind his back with shoelaces, led him to the first bedroom, the one with the fan, where the man got back down on his stomach without being told.

"Fetch a couple chairs from the kitchen," he said. "I ain't heading nowhere."

Nick got one chair from the kitchen, put the man in it, tied his ankles.

"Time is a consideration," the man said. "Go ahead and tell me what you want."

"I'll decide what's a consideration," Nick said. He pulled the hammer from his bag.

"I got seventy bucks in my wallet."

Nick swung the hammer at the man's abdomen, stepping into it, and though no jarring shock seized the handle, a loud crack was heard, the man's hip bone. The man sucked air through his teeth. Nick swung again, not aiming this time, and the hammer thudded into the flesh of the man's upper arm. This time, his grunt had a higher pitch.

"My name is Bright." His feet were shaking. "It's only decent I tell you, I'm a state employee."

"This hammer is a Craftsman. If I wear it out, I can trade it in for a new one."

Nick was impressed with himself. He went to the kitchen to brew coffee and found the maker already set up. All he had to do was flip it on and wait for the first drops to dink in the pot. Nick found a mug that read I HATE THE LONGHORNS FROM THE TIME I WAKE UP. He knew he couldn't indulge the situation too far. In the past minutes he'd found something he was good at, something that came to him. He felt smart. When the coffee maker quieted, he poured some. It was like sludge. He added a lot of milk and tasted the bitter stuff, dumped it in the sink and turned off the pot. At the far end of the hall he found the master bedroom, got a wire hanger from the closet, and straightened it. He strolled back into the room with Bright.

"I don't lie to folks in the business," Bright told him. "I'm expecting guests for breakfast."

"I can tell that's not true."

Bright was slumped in the chair now, favoring his battered hip. He was focused but distant, like he wanted to fall asleep with his eyes open. "Done in by an adolescent," he said.

"When your father dies, you're no longer a kid."

"My father died young. I was happy about it, though."

"Well, I wasn't."

"Where you from, son? At least tell me that."

"Castor, Louisiana."

"Castor?"

"I followed the dudes in the Taurus."

"You followed them? Who was driving?"

"The shorter one."

"The beige one?"

Nick nodded.

"You two worked something out, huh? You worked something out with Swin, didn't you?"

"They didn't know about it."

"Don't bullshit me," Bright said. "Swin couldn't face me for the dirty work."

"This is *my* dirty work and I wouldn't do anybody else's."

"Kyle's over there snoring and Swin's lying in a pool of sweat, straining to hear a pop."

Nick paused. "They live in the park?"

"What's the state of things when a person like me can be disgusted?"

Nick felt it slipping away. Bright didn't seem hurt anymore. Nick had lost his mystery. He bent for the hammer and turned with a low, compact swing that shattered his captive's shin. Bright's body twitched from its core.

Nick waited for Bright to settle a bit, then he brandished the hanger.

"Don't you think Swin has the money if he's producing this picture?"

"I don't want to hear Swin or the other one's name one more time. I know you got a stash in this place and you're going to give it to me."

"So you can waste it on junior college? You wouldn't know what to do with my stash."

Nick wet one end of the hanger and palmed Bright's bald head like a volleyball. He tapped around the inside of his earlobe with the hanger.

"You're not bluffing," Bright said.

"You figured that out?"

"I've never been tortured before."

Nick felt resistance and pressed the hanger in, causing Bright to gasp and jerk his head. The hanger tinked across the floor.

"Nowhere near the other side," Nick said.

"I've had enough. Jesus, I've had my fill. I'll give you what you want."

Nick hurried to the kitchen for a glass of water and dumped it on Bright's head. He asked where the money was and Bright's answer was ready: the attic. Inside an air duct. He could fish it out with one hand, but nobody else would be able to, even with instructions. About fifty grand.

In the hall, Nick pulled down the staircase and held Bright steady as he scaled it, wincing with each step on his wrecked leg. Nick then secured his gun in his waistband and climbed up and sat Bright down on a rafter. Nick was hunched over and could barely breathe the brittle air. On first glance, he saw no air duct. There was one light bulb and no windows. Bright told him to free his right hand and tie his left to his belt loop behind him, and to move a box of pink flyers and the terra cotta pots.

Nick saw his future, saw himself crossing leaning wheat fields, the Rockies coming into view, sunflowers behind him and snow ahead, stacks of hundred-dollar bills in his book bag. He leaned farther over and took Bright by the arm to turn him, and then they were stumbling. Nick felt a beam smack the back of his head. He landed on his ass, groped to get the gun from his waist. Bright managed a sideways lunge and his weight fell on Nick's legs. Nick squeezed the trigger, the gun kicking wildly. Bright was bleeding all over Nick's lower half. Another hand was on the gun. Bright's arms were loose, though one was pinned beneath him, and with his free hand he twisted the gun to crush Nick's fingers. Bright had the barrel. Nick wanted to catch him in the face with an elbow, but he was inches out of reach. The gun was wrenching Nick's fingers, breaking his will to hold on. He hoped his knuckles had a plan of their own, but no. There was a second of relief when the steel slipped free, and then warmth coursed through Nick's shoulder. He wondered what he'd do next, was surprised to see his arms extended, pinning Bright's hand, the gun fast against the floor. Bright had fired twice. One bullet went into Nick and one bore a perfect circle in the roof, through which light poured in and rested on Bright's bald head.

"I always thought I'd die outdoors," Bright said. "I don't know why. Just a feeling."

"We're not dead."

"Oh, no?"

"We're okay."

"That's the rest of your life talking."

Nick kicked and tried to roll Bright off, but the two of them were wedged between rafters on a bed of insulation. Their blood was mixing. It felt to Nick like he was pissing his pants. He couldn't feel his arm, couldn't feel anything but his heart, which kept forcing its red leak. Maybe Bright would die first. Nick waited. He watched the blue hole full of light. He grew comfortable with the itching, dozed off. At least an hour passed. Bright's eyes were shut but he was still breathing and was still intent on his death grip. It seemed he was going to speak. Nick resolved not to answer him. Bright opened his eyes long enough to find Nick's and mumbled something about dreaming of tits.

Most of Little Rock is a rotten maze.

To clear your head, you drive to Hot Springs on a sticky interstate in your spanking new Nissan sports car, listening to a radio show about the act of laughter. You check into the second-best hotel in Hot Springs, into a room that is not fancy but is twenty-five yards long. A balcony runs the length of the room, looking out into the side of a mountain. The mountain is so close, you can't decide if it's blocking your view or if it *is* the view. You walk to the other end of town, to see if you can take the waters. The women's baths are cramped and have exposed pipes, while the men's are colorful and full of statues. There are secret pathways that go nowhere. The baths are abandoned, the towel racks empty, the pools dry.

You return to your room and flop open the thin phone book. There are no listings under Escort Service or Adult Entertainment. Massage has its own two-dozen-page section, but there's no way to tell which are massage and which are *massage*. You go to a restaurant called The Faded Rose and eat a trout covered in almonds, then you drink at a karaoke bar, listening to the finest duets you've ever heard. In two hours you lose all respect for professional singers.

Drunk, you wander the streets. Until you have people, you are an amateur criminal. Some guys con people into sending their sons to slaughter, and you can't even convince skid-row losers to peddle drugs. You go back up to your room and watch people on TV pretend to be dumb and stare at snack food. They are acting stoned.

In the morning you shave and drink hot tea. You get back on the interstate, wanting a long meal before you get back to Little Rock, a Southern lunch with many side bowls. Magnet Cove will do. The town stores are set in an oval around a crumbling fountain. There are flags everywhere—U.S., Razorback, Confederate. A tanning shop. A shop for benches and swings. Here's your restaurant, The Heartland Fryer. Is this the heartland? You take the biggest table and order the barbecue platter. You browse a real-estate magazine full of cabins, taking a bite after each page. The old waitress shakes her head. "Nobody expecting this one. Another crazy drifter." You laugh, but reckon that you *are* a crazy drifter. You're alone and no longer have a set residence. It's fair to say you are living on your wits. You have killed a man while he sprawled sleeping and probably killed another, the man Buttons sent for you, with a fork and a .22.

After finishing the last of your greens and stopping at the fountain, which houses a family of cats in its basin, you head down a soundless alley toward your car. In the parking lot of an old service station, two boys swing a metal ring which hangs from a string, wanting it to catch on a nail they've hammered into a post. They take turns. They're tall, with thick arms and legs, baby faces—stunning in their pale expanse. They notice you and turn their abundant heads... Jesus, those faces. It's not a memory at all. It's a presence in the brain, that moment—a buried planet that casts a pall over everything else.

"That your slick two-door?"

"Paid for," you say. "Free and clear."

"Bet you just hit the high spots in the road."

"This you boys' station?"

"We're full in our rights to use it."

The one speaking has a red earring. The boys might be twins.

"How much for an oil change?"

The brother with the earring burps alertly. "No charge."

"Has to cost something."

"We don't need money. We live with our aunt."

The brothers go in the garage and step into overalls big as tents. You pull in. You stand aside while they raise the car about a foot off the ground with a lift.

"How old are you boys?"

"Guess."

"No idea."

"Yeah, that game's boring. Seventeen."

"You both?"

They nod.

"Twins."

The one with the earring shakes his head. He identifies himself as Tim and his brother as Thomas. They were born eleven months apart and this month they happen to both be seventeen. You say people call you Frog and they don't inquire about the nickname, just prop the hood and get to work. They may be the largest teenagers you've ever seen.

"Your aunt know what you do all day?" you ask.

"She believes anything we tell her."

Thomas gets under the car, his legs and boots sticking out.

"What if you told her you were off to college?"

"Sad to say, she'd go hook, line, and sinker."

"You two could play fullback for the Razorbacks. Fullback's a good position for corn-fed white boys."

"We don't like sports. We like games."

"I happen to be in the black-market game. Happen to be looking for some help."

"He's trying to impress us," Tim calls down to his brother.

"Ain't working, is it?"

"Sure ain't."

"How long you been out of school?"

"We can read," says Thomas.

"We can read plenty."

"It's hard to find gainful employment without a diploma."

"We got the one oil here. It'll have to do."

Thomas, still under the car, warns that whatever you want from them, it better not turn out to be sweeping and rearranging. Every job turns out to be sweeping and rearranging.

"You're squatting on this place?"

"We're trying out being mechanics, to see if we like it."

"What do you think so far?"

"We think it isn't going to work out."

Thomas squirms out, dragging a shallow bucket of used oil with him, and gets to his feet. He hands new filters to Tim, who puts them in place and lets the hood fall closed. They lower the car to the ground.

"So, what do you say?" you ask. "You guys want to try working for me?"

"What's the official title?" Thomas asks.

"Oh… Senior Distribution Executive."

"Senior," Tim says, seeming to like the ring.

"Executive," adds his brother.

There's a pause in which the brothers don't say anything or even look at each other, each giving the other an opportunity to protest. The moment passes.

"Won't your aunt come looking?" you ask. "You're not really college types."

"It don't matter," Tim says. "She thinks not believing someone is un-Christian."

"You ever meet anybody truly wants to be like Jesus?" Thomas opens a steel cabinet and pulls out some small boxes—Life, Four Corners, Jenga. "She don't keep jewelry or decorations. Prays for people she don't like. When she goes for groceries she calls it a 'journey.'"

"Does she do carpentry?"

"She tries," says Tim.

Now the brothers look at one another. In unison, they shrug.

"Pop the trunk," Thomas tells you. "For the games."

The boys load in the boxes and some tools and a bottle of fancy garage soap. They say they'll return in half an hour with clothes and toilet supplies.

"Don't you want to know where you're headed?"

"Sure."

"Little Rock," you say. "Ever been?"

"No."

"What weapons you got?"

They shake their heads.

"No guns?"

"Never shot one."

"All right. Get your gear."

In less than ten minutes, they return. They load themselves into the backseat, each holding a canvas sack on his lap, and you pull out of the garage, speed up the interstate ramp, and explain things to them. You are the boss. They may never quit, may never refuse an order. If they ever run off, you will hunt them down and kill them, no matter how much you may have grown to like them. Things may move slowly at times, you say, but they may not complain or second-guess you. You are a killer, they are not. You are smart, a city slicker from South Memphis. They may not tell a soul what they do or who they do it with. They are not allowed to drink or get a side job. They are not allowed to bring girls around. Tim will no longer wear his earring. You will get a condo for the three of them, and in a year or so, if things pan out, you'll move out and give it to them. In time, they might take over the operation, cutting you in for a percentage.

They sit stunned in the rearview like harvested crops, realizing they are different people now that they've ducked into your car and been spirited out of the hills and onto the groggy plains of Arkansas, the flatlands, where there's no place to hide.

PART TWO

THE BODIES

It was after ten before Kyle, Swin, and the blue dog, Bedford, got themselves together and strolled to Bright's house. Bedford, drunk on the scent of rotten plants and critter tracks, would not use the trail, opting for the dried mud and patchy new grass of the forest floor. The house came into sight and Bedford jogged toward it. He scratched at the door, then turned loops. Kyle knocked. When he got no answer, he tried the knob and found that it wasn't locked. They went inside, where Bedford cocked his head and whimpered, then arranged himself in Bright's chair. Swin said Bright must've gotten into the old whiskey.

"Nothing in the sink but a coffee cup," Kyle said.

"He doesn't take walks."

"No." Kyle turned down the long hallway toward the bedrooms and almost smacked into the hanging attic stairs. He called to Bright again while Swin checked the rooms.

"Book bag, but no books," Swin said. He stood in the hall, suspending the backpack from its top loop. Inside it were shoelaces and loose bullets. The smug look was gone from Swin's face. His eyes were wide. Kyle knew that whatever had gone on might've *just* happened; last night, when Kyle had put the bag of cash in the dryer, all had been normal. That was only, what, eight hours ago?

He told Swin to stay put and keep a lookout, then scaled the short ladder until his top half was in the attic. Nick? The kid from last night? What was he doing here? He was dead. Bright was dead. The deceased men appeared to have fallen asleep cuddling. Kyle got to his feet and saw the blood-soaked insulation. One of Bright's cheeks was bunched, pulling his mouth into an ornery smile. Nick looked as though he had something left, like a battered snake that could still strike. Kyle got the unwieldy pistol from the two of them and noticed a quarter of light on Bright's pant leg. The roof had been shot. Kyle wondered if Frog was involved in this, or if Bright had a side deal. Did Bright know this kid? Where was the goddamn uncle? Kyle heard whistling wind. He was surrounded by boxes of holiday crap, old exercise devices, an ironing board made of PVC. Kyle realized the noise he heard wasn't wind, but the whistling of his mind. He felt rushed. He had to listen hard to hear anything over the buzz in his skull. What had to be done first? He heard Swin calling him, then saw his partner's face pop into the attic.

"It's not as bad as it looks," Kyle told him.

Swin made a noise.

"Nothing but a busy day. We thought we had the day off, but we have to work."

"Can I hold the gun?"

"Sure you can. Keep the safety on."

Kyle handed Swin the gun and Swin tucked it in his pants.

"Cold."

"There's two rounds in it."

"We can't keep it, can we?"

"Nope."

Swin stared at the embracing men and Kyle let him. Swin needed something horrid in his guts, something to chill his blood, something that would help him think in terms of alive or dead, breathing or not breathing. After a minute, Kyle took him by the elbow and told him to lock the front door and bring up a pad and paper. Kyle dictated, making up his directions as he went. They had to untangle the bodies and bring them downstairs in plastic bed sheets, shower and scrub them, then put them in fresh sweats from the dime store down the road. Did that store sell sweats? They had to turn the AC all the way up and fix the hole in the roof. Right? Turning the AC up couldn't hurt. It would keep the bodies fresh, keep Kyle and Swin from sweating all over them. Wipe down the door handles. Clean up that bedroom. Rip out and replace the drenched insulation. They had insulation at the hardware store by the clinic. Kyle knew that. Burn the dead men's clothes and shoes.

They did all of this wearing gloves and hats and long sleeves. They buffed the hammer and clothes hanger until they shone, tucked the kitchen chair back in its spot. Bedford yelped, not willing to leave Bright's chair. Swin washed the coffee mug and set Nick's wallet and keys on the table. The money from Nick's uncle was still in the dryer. Kyle didn't know what to do but leave it there. He searched the park, found the gate locked, found Nick's Datsun. There were his stupid wristbands. Nick had followed them last night. While Kyle was asleep and dumbass Swin was at the wheel, Nick had tailed them for two hundred miles. Kyle backed the car into a dry grove and returned to the house. He told Swin that his sole duty for the rest of the day was to not let anyone near the house.

Kyle was speeding east toward the Louisiana border in Bright's Bronco. The whirling in his mind had died out. He could hear the ticking tin roofs of the roadside shacks, the panting of hidden dogs. He smelled the insect carcasses deep in the oak trunks. His memory felt sharp. There were a lot of details from particular days of Kyle's life that he hadn't known he still possessed. There *were* days that, for better or worse, meant something.

In middle school, Kyle's counselor had forced him to apply for something called State Camp. She'd kept stressing that grades weren't very important to the application process; character and potential were. Only one boy from each middle school could attend the camp. It was an honor. It took place in a well-to-do suburb of Atlanta, at a community college. The boys all brought razors and displayed them prominently on their sinks, though few of them needed to shave. Kyle's roommate had a box of cigars he kept talking about smoking but never did. Mornings at State Camp were spent in an auditorium, listening to officials with odd titles like Comptroller. In the afternoons, the campers endeavored to set up a mock political system. Each boy was supposed to either run for an elected position or claim a support duty, but Kyle knew no one would elect him and didn't want to be anybody's assistant, so he did neither. He avoided the meetings. He stayed in his room doing push-ups or wandered down to a rushing stream that ran through campus. The second-to-last day, while Kyle was sitting off by himself in the courtyard, he was pelted by an orange. It hit his forearm and exploded onto his shirt, one of five dress shirts he'd brought for the five days of the camp. He looked in the direction the orange had come from and saw only a roving mass of laughter and slick hair—no way to tell which one had thrown it. The mass of boys tripped around the corner and was gone. Kyle stared into some tree branches awhile, then flicked the shards of pulp off his arm. He peeled off his shirt and went to the laundry room of his dormitory, dropped the quarters in, and propped himself in a chair. Not a minute later, two boys in the next room started talking about the orange-throwing. Kyle could hear every word through the vent. They referred to Kyle as "that weird dude." They exaggerated the distance the orange had flown. They said the orange had hit Kyle in the head, not the arm. Most important, they said the name Brent Hodge. That night, Kyle eased open the door of Brent Hodge's room. Brent had the bottom bunk. His mouth was wide open and one arm was flailed off the bed. Kyle went to the closet and poured orange juice over all the clothes. He poured some in the shoes, poured some in the sock drawers, and used what was left on the spare sheets and blankets. He rested the empty juice carton in the sink. He turned, but couldn't take a step toward the door. The mission was complete, but he couldn't leave. He kneeled beside Brent and listened to the catches of his breathing. All he had to do, Kyle thought, was stop those slight noises, stop that push and pull of air. It was much too easy to kill a person. Kyle knew it was only the hassle it would create that stopped him from fetching Brent's unused razor from the sink and slitting the kid's throat.

He turned onto the country road, minutes from Nick's uncle. Here were the falling mailboxes, the tree with fishing net strung in its branches. Here was the trailer. Kyle shut the engine off and stepped down from the Bronco. He pushed the screen door open and stepped inside, where he saw Nick's uncle at the sink in his slippers, back turned to Kyle, sudsing spatulas and skewers and piling them in a hubcap. The soccer balls had been flattened out like hides and stacked. The uncle shook his hands off.

"Here is prodigal nephew."

When he turned around, Kyle shot him twice in the chest and watched him come to the ground, looking here and there like he didn't recognize the place. He left the world in thought—confusion, anyway. He'd underestimated them. Well, he'd estimated Swin correctly, but he'd underestimated Kyle. He hadn't known Kyle was a person who would clean a mess thoroughly, who would not allow someone who killed his boss to live. Kyle knew the uncle had given the order. That fat Greek couldn't be allowed to let his nephew and Bright die, then proceed larkily with his scumbag life, filling his trailer with close Mediterranean aromas, waiting for another chance to be a scumbag. He was a spider, and Kyle had squashed him.

Kyle measured his steps back to the Bronco and drove. He turned on the radio and listened to a patriotic story that was told over brush drums. Bright was dead. Just like that. Nick: dead. The uncle: dead. Was it over? Would this storm blow out to sea now? Kyle, unable to stop himself, imagined Swin dead, imagined finding him cut up and bled dry on the floor of his trailer. There was a specific feeling the thought of a dead partner should bring, Kyle knew. He could sense the feeling was near, but couldn't grip it. It was a wily eel that was slipping around Kyle's heart, teasing it, knowing it wouldn't be nabbed. Kyle's heart was fumbly.

Kyle saw that Swin was right; Kyle hadn't cared about his mother. He'd been angry when she passed, had felt the furious disbelief of awful luck, but no part of him had gone into her coffin. Her death was mere verification to Kyle that the world had no intention of offering him a worthwhile life. If his mother were alive, Kyle knew, nothing would be different. He would have left Lofton, left *her*, would've gone from Athens to Little Rock, would've ended up a fake ranger with a dead boss, and would've shot some Greek guy who'd just gorged himself on kebabs.

On a vista that overlooked the pond and wouldn't flood, they began digging. Kyle started about eight feet from Swin and they worked toward each other. The mosquitoes had their fill, then moved on. The sun set. Kyle and Swin had decided that Bright and Nick should not be buried together, that, in fact, Nick should not be buried on the park grounds. There seemed to be a lot of vague reasons having to do with staying out of trouble, with distancing themselves from Nick and his uncle, to take Nick's body elsewhere, but mostly it was Kyle's insistence that it wasn't right for Bright's killer to be buried in Bright's park. Kyle had other plans for Nick. He knew a spot.

Kyle's grip started to go, so he tossed aside his gloves. He was making headway twice as fast as Swin, who had taken off his shirt and was treating the creation of a grave as exercise, glancing down at himself after each shovel fling. At midnight they rested, drinking RC Cola, listening to the grebes in the pond squabble. Swin complained of his blisters and said six feet was only a custom.

"That's true," Kyle said. "And it's a custom we're going to follow."

By two-thirty they were nearly banging shovels, so Kyle told Swin to hop out and let him finish. His shoulders were mush and his fingers wouldn't straighten, but his mind was in better shape than his partner's, who was pacing unsteadily and spitting.

They had to lug Bright three hundred yards, one holding the arms and one the legs, Bright swaying like a man in a hammock. They stopped to rest several times, never having to speak to know it was time to let their plastic-wrapped load meet the ground. By the time they reached their vista, the sky was losing darkness. Kyle told Swin he didn't want anything said. They would spare Bright any stupid words they could come up with. They ate some bananas, then picked up their FSP shovels. The filling took only two hours. They covered the area with twigs and moss and looked over the tan pond. The grebes had calmed.

"I forgot to check if anyone was following us," Swin said. "I take responsibility."

"What good does taking responsibility do?" asked Kyle.

"Makes me feel better. Makes me feel civilized."

"I already know it was your fault. You don't have to tell me that."

"And you don't have to be a dick. I'm apologizing; it's what people do."

"It's not what I do," Kyle said. He turned at the waist, running cracks and pops up his spine. "What you don't get is that it has nothing to do with paying attention. You should have *felt* someone following you."

"So-called 'gut feelings' come from your brain. I was thinking about something else. I got distracted."

"Thinking about what?"

"I don't know *now*. I think about shit all the time. I spent my life training my brain to race, and now I can't get it to stop. That's why you're good at this shit—your brain is manageable."

Kyle stayed still. He thought he might laugh. He thought he might shove Swin down the hill, into the pond.

Swin looked away. "Why didn't we run away as soon as we saw them dead?"

"In whose car, Bright's? With whose money, Frog's? Headed where? Back to Athens and Vanderbilt?"

"But we didn't even consider it."

"I did," Kyle said, and kicked a clod of dirt off the embankment. "You ever *consider* that if we run off, it looks like we planned this? It looks like we have a reason to run?"

"Maybe it does, maybe it doesn't."

"Someone's going to show up wanting an explanation and we're going to tell them the truth. Except about being followed. They'll assume the uncle knew where we were going and sent the nephew."

Swin sniffed, half-convinced.

"I'll try to get in touch with Colin, too. It'll be better to tell the story ourselves than have it trickling up the chain of command."

"Bad metaphor. Things trickle *down*." Swin dropped his shoulders. "Sorry," he said. "It's not me; it's my mind. My mind is a stickler. My mind is a real asshole."

Kyle nodded his agreement. "I'll try Colin first. If that doesn't work, I guess Gregor."

"Yeah, I have someone I can try—the guy who referred me."

"It works," Kyle said. "It'll work out."

"Even so, don't you think maybe it's time for a gun? I've pretty much gathered Bright was lying about having rifles for us."

Kyle flexed his hands, wincing. "Bringing in guns doesn't settle a situation down."

"What if just *you* had one? You trust yourself, right?"

"The answer is no."

"Do you think it makes you tough to be unarmed?"

Kyle turned his head but didn't look at Swin. "Which one of us recently shot someone?"

"Knew that was coming."

"You did, huh?"

"You were taking care of business and I was minding the nest. Who cares?" Swin rubbed a hand over his face. "I don't get you. Nobody would know if we had a weapon hidden somewhere."

"If Frog wanted us to have guns, we'd have guns."

Swin could not concentrate on the music. He stayed quiet and held Johnna's hand, and she seemed to like him this way—preoccupied. They watched a band from Canada composed of four children who made self-deprecating jokes between songs. These children believed they were hot shit, which, in Canada, they likely were. Songs came and went, and Swin attempted to force the dead bodies from his mind. He saw Bright and Nick stacked in the tub, saw the hopeful expression on the kid's face, saw Bright's wrists and ankles worn raw from Swin and Kyle carrying him across the park. Swin wished he would've gone with Kyle to kill the uncle. He felt like he had had no say. Maybe Kyle was right and things weren't so bad. Maybe it was best to do nothing, to stay put. To lifelong criminals, a couple guys getting killed wasn't an enormous deal. Maybe Swin was only freaking out because he was new to it. Maybe in this life, when a couple guys dropped below the surface, it barely made a ripple. Bright didn't seem like a guy that wouldn't make a ripple, though; he'd do a cannonball. Swin tried to convince himself to quit worrying so much, to let it go, to hope for the best and let the universe take care of him. Swin believed the universe was fond of him, even if the universe didn't always show it. The universe might mess with Swin, but it wouldn't kill him or put him in prison. He and Kyle should simply remain in their trailers and act normal. They would get in touch with someone and explain themselves. They would stay calm. A drunk man leaned on Swin and tried to focus his eyes.

"I met you about a month ago," the man said. "If I was an asshole, I apologize."

"No. You were terrific."

The man, who Swin had never seen before, chuckled, then ambled off. The children onstage began a song that went, "You ain't a Nova Scotian if you don't like fish," in which they listed dozens of seafoods they enjoyed. These kids could not have imagined that someone in the crowd, a subdued young man holding a nurse's hand, hated their guts.

For this concert, Swin and Johnna had driven to the next county, to a town named Feston whose citizens had erected a cinder-block bandshell on the banks of a reservoir. Feston held shows each weekend. Swin and Johnna had been handed a flyer of upcoming events, which included a canoe-fashioning lesson and a tribute to Earl Scruggs.

Swin was glad when the show was done. He felt calmer when he was moving. He and Johnna got in her long, low car and left the reservoir behind. Johnna unfurled herself in the passenger seat, making a show of being relaxed. She said one of her favorite things was getting driven around out of town. She didn't drive out of town herself because she always got lost and fell into a rage.

They passed through a cluster of houses that still, or already, had up Christmas lights. Johnna took out a squat brown flask and suggested a shot. She threw her head back, then passed the empty flask to Swin. He held it upside down over his tongue and felt something prickly drip out.

"I want to stand in the middle of a sunflower ranch," Johnna said. "Biggest one they got. I want to go over a ten-mile bridge. I want to go where it snows in the summertime."

Swin gathered that Johnna was nervous. He should've been too, but all he could think of was digging. Drowning Bright in dirt. No priest or family or agent of the law—no buffer between the dead man and the black forever. All he could think about was the fact that he'd been involved in something that was very bad for a lot of people and, against his instincts, was not running away. Staying was the right thing to do. Swin trusted Kyle. He did. For some reason, Kyle had the ability to think through matters of crime more clearly than Swin could, and if Swin believed in anything, it was that people should defer to superior expertise. Anyway, this mess had to be good for *someone*. Maybe Frog had wanted Bright dead. Maybe Frog wanted Kyle and Swin to take over. It was a simple promotion. You're assistant manager and the manager dies: promotion.

Swin and Johnna crept onto the park grounds and Swin brought the car to rest next to his trailer. It was still strange to Swin that he lived in a trailer. Trailers were for unwashed white people, not Ricans who did okay for themselves. Swin didn't like the space between the trailer and the ground, or the undersized kitchen appliances, or the smell of wet cord that lingered inside. This was no place to bring a girl back to, but Johnna had been raised in trailers. Plus, Swin already felt that Johnna was his friend.

They went inside and Bedford was stretched out on the table like a luau pig. Johnna went over and shook his paw. The dog had begun to grow roots. Johnna said to wait about a week, then shave him. She put the apple-juice bowl in the closet, then shut Bedford in there as well. "All right, then," she told Swin. She opened the futon and punched the mattress. Swin was not in the mood, but he knew it didn't matter. This was the moment that had been chosen for him. He had to meet it.

Afterward, Johnna tripped away from the futon and leaned in a corner. She talked under her breath and hummed. Swin's frayed nerves had caused him to last nearly an hour, during which Johnna had handled all the writhing and bouncing, talking herself through it, assuring herself it would be okay if she came now or came later, okay if she slowed or sped up, okay if she took a moment to shake her hip out.

She returned to the futon and stretched out without touching Swin. They could hear Bedford pawing around in the closet and the scrape of a tree branch on the roof. Swin was thirsty and weak. Somewhere in the past hour he'd lost the illusion that he had control over his life, that there was any use in wondering why he did the things he did—why he'd founded a fake club and stolen a bunch of useless jewelry and sacrificed seeing his sisters to his stupid pride and bought an enormous pickup and then agreed to sell it and fallen in love in this redneck nowhere and convinced himself he was a criminal and not noticed a car trailing him for hours on end on the way back from Louisiana. A Puerto Rican park ranger.

"I played baseball for one season," he said. "That's what Latinos are supposed to do. We sold stickers door to door to buy uniforms. People were really snapping them up, so I stole all the stickers and quit the team."

Johnna set her fingertips on Swin's head.

"Took three years to sell out. I always spent the money the day I got it. Nine hundred thirty dollars."

Johnna cleared her throat. "I used to steal pennies from my grandpa's jug and buy candy cigarettes. Guess that's not so bad."

Swin rolled and clung to Johnna's arm.

"I can't see my sisters." He immediately regretted saying this. It felt good to say it, but it was a stupid topic to bring up with Johnna. He didn't want her to try and make him explain *why* he couldn't see his sisters: because it would be terrible if they knew what he was doing, because he'd run off from Nashville with a bunch of people's money, because he was embroiled in a couple of *murders* at the moment, because he was possibly in danger and anyone he associated with was possibly in danger.

"I'd rather have none, like me, than not be able to see them."

"There's too many. There's no way all their lives can turn out well." Swin couldn't help himself. He said their names: Rosa and Rita and Luz and Lizzie. They all had long legs and weighty black eyes. They were a squad of serious, beautiful women who loved Swin no matter what.

"Where are they?" Johnna asked.

"It doesn't matter. Might as well be on the moon."

Johnna made a face.

"The other day, I couldn't picture Luz," said Swin. "I could see her teeth and that's it."

"Don't you have pictures?"

"No, I have little toys. I wouldn't want pictures."

"Pictures are pretty good," said Johnna. "Especially with writing on the back."

"I hired an investigator." Swin squirmed against Johnna. "I had him check out our stepdad, the Blond Baron."

Johnna moved her head so she could look at Swin. "You paid some scumbag to dig stuff up on your stepfather?"

"That's what I did."

Johnna seemed to take this in without much difficulty.

"I don't think he's that scummy," said Swin.

"Your stepfather?"

"The PI."

"How much did he cost?"

"I had money from selling my truck."

"Did he find out anything bad?"

"Not even close."

Swin and the PI had patched the story together this way. Swin's stepdad had been born in Virginia, in 1951, to parents who were never U.S. citizens. His father soon returned to Europe, after which his mother got sick and died. Swin's stepdad grew up in a Catholic shelter, then got a full ride to a mostly black college in Alabama, where he double-majored in social work and finance. He volunteered all over town and became friends with an old woman who was involved in a lot of service clubs. When this old woman died, she left him some money, which he donated to her favorite charity. A short time later, so it seemed, another old woman died and *she* left him money—more this time. He kept enough of it to found an insurance company that catered to low-income families and single mothers. He became expert at securing grants. He built this insurance company up and then handed it over to his underlings, then spent six or seven years managing trusts and endowments for nonprofits, never accepting much pay. Now he worked as a consultant.

He'd gotten in trouble twice, once in college for scuffling with repo guys who were trying to take a poor family's refrigerator, and once, later, for screwing a plastics and oil corporation out of six hundred thousand dollars and redirecting it to aid groups. He'd done a few months in jail, during which he organized a program where inmates raised dogs so they could learn love.

Swin remembered how his mother and stepdad had met. She had a gig cleaning offices overnight and he'd been working late in one of them. He helped her finish her work and then took her to brunch at the Don Cesar. When she'd come home, four hours late, she was giddy and drunk and took a nap right on the living-room floor. When she woke up, she ran out and bought a dress she couldn't afford. From that day forward, Swin had felt he couldn't wholly trust his mother.

The PI said Swin's stepdad was not in debt. He wasn't having an affair. He drank a lot of milkshakes. He exercised by keeping his hands in his pockets and jumping as high as he could.

"That's the story," Swin said. He assured Johnna he was done with the PI, but he knew he wasn't. He'd have to know about his sisters. He'd have to get a cell phone soon. The only pay phone was at the market, where there were always people around. Kyle would go nuts, Swin knew, if he found out Swin was sneaking calls to a PI on Bright's house phone.

"Aren't you *glad* he's a good guy?" Johnna asked.

Swin shrugged.

"Could be a lot worse." She bit his shoulder. "Let me ask you something. What the hell do you spend nine hundred dollars on when you're ten?"

"Fat shoelaces. Swatch watches. Pop music. Though I suppose all music is pop music."

"How so?"

"It's hard to explain."

Kyle, in Nick's Datsun, headed toward a swamp outside Little Rock where the government had tried to grow rice, public ground no one went near. He checked the rearview for Swin, who was following in the Bronco. Swin had Nick's body in the back, covered with whiskey boxes and coffee crates and fishing gear. The interior of Nick's car smelled like tarnished silverware and bad fruit. The seat would not recline at all; it forced Kyle into the posture of a responsible citizen who trimmed his azaleas and bought cleats for needy punks. The Datsun was loaded down with cement yard doughnuts, riding low. Kyle skirted the old section of town and led Swin onto a built-up clay lane, then onto a service road.

They threw the cargo off Nick and tethered cement doughnuts to his arms and legs. Kyle realized they should knock out his teeth. He found a lead sinker the size of a grenade and brought it down over and over on Nick's face. The boy looked older with every blow, his jowls widening and lips splitting. Kyle plucked a handful of teeth out of Nick's mouth, rinsed them in the swamp water, and dropped them in his pocket. Swin was pale and looked off to the side as they dragged Nick to the swamp's edge and lowered him in. They took the Datsun about a mile away, to a part that looked deep, shoved it in, then stood aside and watched the bog eat the car with the even appetite of a trash compactor.

They headed south in the Bronco, back on the interstate. Kyle fastened his seat belt and tried to hold seventy-one miles an hour.

Swin rolled his window halfway up. "It was my fault this shit happened, but it doesn't mean I'm taking a demotion. I'll let you be leader, but I want to be consulted on everything."

"Don't worry, I don't want to be anybody's boss."

Swin rolled his window the rest of the way up and chewed his cheek.

"Just don't argue with me," Kyle said. "I'll listen to you until you start arguing."

"Takes two to argue."

"I've never argued with anyone in my life."

They passed a parking lot full of teenagers, mostly Asian kids wearing visors. Kyle dug Nick's teeth out and tossed them in a ditch. He and Swin agreed they would keep quiet and wait. They would get the packets and go on the trips. Soon enough, they would have their chance to explain all this. And if Frog's people thought Kyle and Swin had killed Bright, let them think it. If they thought Bright ran off, let them think it. There was a chance Frog himself was dead. There was a chance Nick had been a cog in a hostile takeover, that one of Frog's guys had usurped him. Kyle and Swin had to show they could run the Felsenthal operation. If they did that, whoever was in charge wouldn't care that Bright was gone. Bright was friendless and without family. The unease came from the forty-four thousand dollars. It was supposed to go somewhere other than Bright's dryer. Forty-four thousand dollars didn't get lost in the shuffle.

"We'll get a little perspective," Swin said. "All you do is present your mind with the facts, then get plenty of sleep and protein."

Kyle closed his eyes sluggishly, then reopened them, ignoring Swin. "I left a message with Colin. I got the number from the guy who originally introduced us."

"Who introduced *us*?"

"Introduced me and Colin."

"What did the message say?"

"That a few things had happened that he probably ought to know about."

"And to call us back?"

"I thought that part was obvious."

"Well, we don't want him coming to the park, do we?"

"Why not?"

"I don't want to see any of them face to face right now, to tell you the truth."

A far-off look passed over Kyle's face. "Shit, you're right."

"We're not in trouble, though," Swin said.

"He might think we're luring him out here."

"We wouldn't do that."

"He doesn't know what we would do."

A bunch of cows appeared in the headlights. They were off to the side of the road, jostling one another. Kyle slowed as he passed them. They'd escaped through a big gap in their pasture fencing and now they didn't know where to go. They couldn't manage to get back into the pasture. When he'd cleared the last cow, Kyle sped back up.

"What about you?" Kyle asked. "Any progress getting in touch with anyone?"

"Nada," Swin said.

Kyle waited a moment. "Nada? That's it? That's your contribution?"

"Yeah, it is."

Kyle squeezed the steering wheel and pushed his arms straight, sort of stretching, sort of venting frustration. "I don't know what you been telling that nurse, but it better not be the truth."

"Nothing."

"She must want to know what you do."

"Doesn't seem like it. I'm being mysterious to no effect."

"You need a lie you can stick with."

"Lying is a strong suit with me."

"And don't think about running away," Kyle said. "If the time comes to run, we both have to run. Don't take Bright's Bronco and leave me here with no emergency transportation."

"Where am *I* going?" Swin said. "What, I'm going to work in a factory and buy a Saturn and read science fiction?"

"I don't claim to know what you might do."

"Me neither," Swin said.

"If you get spooked, talk to me."

"You sound like Bright," Swin said. "I wish you'd calm down. You're speeding."

It was hard to calm down while talking to Swin. Kyle turned on the radio and let the seek drag through every station, no intention of sticking with one. Tacky music. Tacky opinions. News about an unprecedented filibuster. There was always something unprecedented. What Kyle wanted to hear was a woman close to his age, with no accent, reading complex instructions. God, he was tired.

"Tomorrow we'll reopen the park and make sure everything's spotless."

"I'm opposed to spotlessness," Swin said. "The park should be a natural ecosystem—nature on its own with no meddling from us."

"Prepare to meddle."

Swin yawned. "In case your honey shows up."

"That's right." Kyle picked something out of his molars, trying to remember the last time he'd sat down to an actual meal. "We'll tell her Bright's on a trip."

"That'll only work for so long. That lie has a short shelf life."

"I'm sorry I don't have ten-, twenty-, and thirty-year-plans mapped out for us."

"What if the boss in pink asks you to run away with her?"

"Yeah, she'll probably do that. She's probably got that in her day planner."

"She's waiting for you to make a move," Swin said.

"Make a move," repeated Kyle. "She'll make a move if she finds out Bright's dead. Fire us at the very least. Shut the park down and hold an internal investigation. Possibly just freak the fuck out and call the cops."

"There's no way she could get us in touch with anyone, anyway."

"Please," Kyle said. "She doesn't know anybody."

Swin concentrated a moment, and then released an amused breath. "Let's get this straight. Bright went with an Indian... to Oklahoma. And that's all we know."

"That's it?"

"You throw in a couple details, but you don't care if the listener believes the details. It's the apathy of authority."

"Oklahoma with an Indian."

"Don't make up a name for the Indian," Swin said. "Like 'Overhears With Disdain.'"

Kyle got up early and searched Bright's house for the guns the ranger had promised, not so sure Bright had been lying about the rifles and not wanting Swin to find them first. He ended up in the attic again, staring at old fitness machines that utilized rubber stoppers and planks. There were garden pots. Bright owned Christmas decorations. He had reindeer heads for the door handles, a nativity scene in which the holy family appeared to be Samoan. Kyle opened a box and found a lumpy tree apron full of bones—almost blackened human bones. The femur was smooth and knotted, like treated pine. Kyle lifted it and was surprised by its weight. The bones seemed old enough to be called remains. Kyle flattened out on his back and looked up at the bullet hole he'd patched and caulked, a skin-colored nickel that stood out from the wood. He laughed. He lost his breath but kept forcing out the syllable "ha." Then he was quiet for a time. He made growling noises, pushing gurgling snarls up through his throat.

He heard the front door and heard Swin coming up to the attic. Kyle knew he should hide the bones, but didn't feel capable of quick movements. He got himself to a sitting position. Swin came over and blinked into the box.

"I like to watch my calories," he said. "You *can* go overboard with it."

"Who the hell was this?"

Swin just shook his head.

"It was a fluke Bright died. He was a badass," Kyle said.

"Yeah?"

"Somebody that doesn't need the right situation to be tough."

"You might be one of those," said Swin. "Little old you."

Kyle got to his feet.

"These would burn up your modem on eBay," Swin said. "Think they'd let you sell bones?"

"Maybe we *can* look into a gun." Kyle covered the bones back up with the tree apron. "As long as there's no way it can be tracked back to us."

"I know a pawnshop that might be worth a try. It's not a shop, really."

"I'm an idiot," Kyle said.

"A *live* idiot." Swin tapped the box. "This guy here's a dead wise man."

Waiting outside the pawnshop door, Kyle noticed a wooden scooter and a lantern made of bronzed feathers. The shop was an old house, with no sign or anything. The owner opened the door, his mouth cocked upward, puffing steam. He held a beer stein full of stewed cherries.

"Not Halloween." He swallowed with effort. "So why these kids at my door?"

"Halloween's for Baptists," Swin said.

The shop owner pulled the door all the way open and stepped aside. "Suppose that's true."

"Remember me?"

"I do."

"This is Ed. We need guns."

"For what?"

"*A* gun, singular," Kyle said. "We work over at the park and we got our vacation coming up. What we like to do to relax is shoot targets, but all we have at Felsenthal is rifles. Our boss said we should try here for handguns."

"Ranger Bright said you should try and get guns from *me*?"

Kyle nodded.

"He respects you," Swin said. "Says nothing mystifies you."

The shop owner slouched in thought, then spooned up more cherries. He slurped them around and got them to go down. "Shit, hang on." He fetched a small radio from the kitchen and put it on the coffee table. The man on the radio described a fat pitcher the St. Louis Cardinals had acquired in a trade from Seattle. The kid was decent with every pitch, but didn't excel at a single one.

"Why don't you go to Memphis?" the shop owner asked. "It's out of state."

"I got a real problem with city guns," said Kyle. "I want a gun from out in the sticks that somebody's dead daddy owned."

The man set down the stein of cherries. "What's the plan for you two? You know, in life."

Kyle and Swin looked at each other.

"We try to keep the meat on the bones and keep the bones moving," answered Swin.

"Because it's not too late to get in the raft and float downstream. Bad things are in store for those who don't pay the community fees."

"You're a little nutty," Swin said. "I like that."

The commercials ended and a man on the radio said St. Louis had as good a shot as anyone to win the division. He rattled off a bunch of statistics that backed his assertion. The shop owner held out his hands as if he'd proved a point. "As good a shot as anyone." He shut off the radio.

Swin crossed his legs and looked at his fingernails. "It's fair to say you trade in underground goods. How much could one get for a set of human bones?"

"With the skull?"

"Say, without."

"Depends on the person. Bill Clinton or an infant, you'd do okay. Now, a live person you can sell easy."

Kyle stood. "Will you sell us a gun or not?"

"I will not. In your line of work a gun is as likely to get you killed as protect you."

"What line of work is that?" Kyle asked.

The shop owner frowned. "Rangering."

"What's *your* line of work?"

"I guess I'm a ranger, too. I guess we all are."

Kyle opened the door and waited for Swin, who shook the shop owner's hand and slapped his shoulder. Kyle didn't look at the guy. He didn't appreciate receiving double-talk advice from a stranger. Kyle didn't *want* a gun from this guy.

Swin wasn't sure he had a *plan*, but he saw a possible picture of his future. He would never again be a college student, but there was no reason why, in time, he couldn't be a college professor. They gave a certain number of professorships away based on nothing but intellectual merit. One could write a book or make a discovery and leap, overnight, from nowhere to tenure. For the true stars of thought, there were no ladders to climb, asses to kiss, or background checks. In ten years, this stuff with Kyle would be ancient and Swin could live in a big-windowed loft in a college town, where he would teach young girls how to have good taste. His shady past would give him a mystique. Eventually, a memoir: *Mule to Emeritus, My Story*. If this was a plan—to one day use his Arkansas experiences as some kind of academic bolster—then all his time here, every single thing that happened to him, was part of that plan.

Johnna showed up at Swin's trailer half-drunk, glasses crooked, clasping a plaid thermos to her chest. She had on a pair of clunky headphones. She kissed Swin, then sat on the edge of the futon. Swin went back to his tiny kitchen table, which was smothered with graphs, testimonials, and photographs of pleased people. He was choosing a cell-phone company.

"Texas is ours this time," Johnna announced. She pushed the headphones tight to her ears. "They can't stuff the first-down run."

Swin squinted, trying to look impressed. He knew nothing about football except that the Arkansas Razorbacks and the Texas Longhorns hated one another, and that Arkansas was a constant underdog in this rivalry. He flipped through the brochures. Minutes packages. Rollover. Roaming. The Cingular company, for some reason, stressed originality. If you had their phone, you could be an individual. Swin waved his arms to get Johnna's attention. He mimed drinking, then made a puzzled face.

"Brandy and diet," said Johnna. "Tie game." She flipped the sipper on the thermos and sucked on it, then tipped her head down and shut her eyes.

Swin gazed at her and in a soft voice said, "Let's stay together till we die. I'll never tire of looking at you when the sun hits you through a window." He watched her for what could have been a long time, enjoying the range of her facial expressions, then she pumped her fist and said it was halftime. Her team was up a field goal. She removed the headphones and took another slug of brandy.

"That outfit for me?" Swin asked.

Johnna had on scrubs and white sneakers. "I'll be hung over in the morning and I don't want to slog home and change. Lot of people say use a sick day, but

I ain't used one yet. I got seven weeks. There was this RN retired a year early."

"You're staying here tonight?"

"That's the plan."

"You should drink some water and maybe come back to the alcohol later."

"I only got a couple swallows left."

"We could make love *now*."

"You should know this about me: the Razorbacks come first."

Swin had a disgusting vision of an entire football team lining up to get a turn with Johnna. He had no idea how many guys she'd slept with. Could be two or two hundred. She rooted through the pantry and pulled out a box of croutons, shredded a wad of cheese, then mixed the two up and spooned it all down. She went into the bathroom and emerged with Swin's electric clippers, calling for Bedford. Swin told her to hang on while he put down a sheet. Bedford came to Johnna, who was kneeling now, and sniffed her. Johnna whispered to him and let him sniff the clippers, and when she started it buzzing, Bedford jerked but didn't try to get away. Johnna soothed him with one hand and scalped him of blue with the other. He yelped, but it was false; he was enjoying himself.

"Now you won't look like a punk teenager," Johnna told him.

Bedford's natural color was a nutty red. When Johnna finished, the dog looked athletic—no longer a vagabond. He rubbed himself against the wall, then went into a series of pre-nap stretches. Johnna checked him here and there for missed patches. She cursed, groping for her headphones.

"Already?" she cried.

Texas had scored on the second-half kickoff. Johnna solemnly poured the rest of her cocktail in a tall glass. Swin gathered the sheet by the corners and shook it out the front door, sending wavy blue clumps tumbling over the grass. He tossed the sheet in the hamper, then randomly selected a wireless company, sliding the rest of the ads into the trash. He sat at the table and took another look at his life: a mobile home, a refugee dog, a redneck nurse, a deranged white boy, and a shithole park with a Jewish name. Seemed like a good book, but right now Swin was *living* it. He had to subscribe to some magazines or something. Maybe he would mail a picture to his sisters, a shot of himself and Johnna and Bedford looking pleased like the people in the phone brochures. He could ask for pictures of them in return, to be sent to a PO box up in Missouri somewhere belonging to a Mr. Suarez. If something bad had happened to his sisters, his sisters wouldn't say. They would send winning pictures that showed them living their dreams and Swin could choose to believe these pictures. Swin didn't want his sisters to think he was dead and, in an unconscious attempt to replace him, become slutty.

Johnna stomped. She was red in the face. Swin could tell things were going to pieces for the Arkansas football team. Interceptions. Personal fouls. Johnna shouted to herself. Arkansas's quarterback was too well-rounded a person to lead a Southern team into battle. He didn't get insulted, didn't want to step on anybody's neck. The Texas quarterback was drawing roughing calls even though he'd run for over a hundred yards. Their fullback was bigger than our tackle, and so on. For a time, Johnna called the Longhorn offense, seeming to know everything they'd run. She finished the brandy and produced her flask, which she emptied in three gulps.

"We ain't got one screen in the playbook?" she asked. "One goddamn screen pass."

She dialed off the headphones and detached them from her hair, then turned to Swin sweetly and said that what she'd like to do was dump off a few rounds at a tree stump. She held up her flask and said they could try to put holes in it. She didn't want to talk about the game or about anything. She wanted to safely take target practice with her good friend Swin.

Swin was ashamed to own no gun. He and his partner, Kyle, he explained, had visited the shop where Johnna had tried to pawn the scooter, but the guy had played dumb about guns. Next, Swin said, they might try a flea market inside the Texas border that was sponsored by a bulletproof-vest company. Some guy who owned a tackle shop had told Kyle about it. Johnna had stopped listening, stopped blinking.

"That shop-owning son of a bitch. Moves here from God-knows-where. He's a rotten Yankee if he wears socks."

"He's seen *me* for the last time," said Swin.

"Not me, by God."

"If he wants to be despised, that's his right."

"And I got a right to collect tax when sons-of-bitches come down here from Michigan and treat everybody like shit."

"I believe he's from Memphis or St. Louis."

She was already outside, her keys glinting in what daylight was left. She fell inside her car and revved the engine. Swin let the trailer door slap behind him and hopped in the passenger seat.

"I'm sure he's closed at this hour," he said.

"He ain't ever open," Johnna said. "Greedy bastard."

"I don't know that he's greedy, exactly. I think he's kind of content."

Johnna bumped onto the paved road and used her eight cylinders, gripping the wheel at ten and two.

"Who said he can come down here and be content?" she asked.

Here Swin was, a man who'd traded hundreds of thousands of dollars' worth of narcotics, lecturing a nurse who wanted to scream at a stingy shop owner. He decided to let Johnna do what she wanted, to simply watch that she didn't hurt herself. She was driving steady as a train, doing seventy. Swin saw an object in the glow of the headlights but couldn't say anything. Johnna gasped. It was an owl. It thumped against the bottom of the car and Johnna eased to a stop, then went in reverse. She and Swin got out and kneeled by the carcass. It had arresting, still eyes. Its talons were mangled.

Swin touched Johnna's shoulder. "If you didn't hit it, someone else would've."

"It was plumb crazy."

"Animals get brain tumors, too. Particularly birds."

Johnna hoisted the owl by its legs and nested it in her backseat. For the remainder of the trip she muttered under her breath about owls, shop owners, the director of nursing where she worked, and the dime defensive package. When they pulled into the yard of the shop, Johnna killed the lights and stopped short, skidding in the mud. She flopped her hand around in the glove box and came out with a box of matches, then strode to the front door, Swin lingering behind. She knocked harder and harder, then realized she could turn the knob and push the door open. Swin flew up the steps and slipped inside and almost slammed into Johnna, who was already coming back out with an armload of jacketless books. The poetry.

"This is how you get shot," Swin said.

"Ha." Johnna dropped the books in a heap and they seemed to splash. She passed Swin on her way back in.

"Let's try again when he's here," Swin said. "Then you can tell him off face to face."

"You could help, you know."

Johnna's next load was too ambitious and she spilled books here and there, not bothering to pick them up. In and out she went, the dormant pyre growing. Swin went to the back room to make certain the owner wasn't there. It was a dim room with big windows. Baggies of dried fruit rested on board games. A wagon? Swin brought the wagon to Johnna. He propped himself on the porch railing and smiled at her as she worked, keeping one eye on the road.

When the mound of poetry was the size of a compact car, Johnna held a match under a flutter of pages. The flame flared, then disappeared. It whispered around inside the mound and suddenly flexed, licking toward the sky, spitting out half sheets marked with words like "bellicose" and "truncate." Johnna sat in the mud, yawning. Swin went inside and got two glasses of water and a frosted cookie. When he returned, Johnna was asleep, her cheek on the soft ground. He slipped her glasses off and hung them from his collar, wondering what the pawnshop owner would think when he returned to a pile of smoldering books in his yard. He would think somebody really hated poetry, more even than most people, or that some teenagers had had a good time at his expense, or maybe he'd *know* what had happened, that a local had finally gotten sick enough of him and his sham shop to do something about it.

Swin carried Johnna to her car and gently unloaded her onto the passenger seat. Johnna was one of those people who looked like a saint when she slept. A hellion awake, a saint asleep. Sexy with her eyes open, innocent with them closed. Swin felt he could spend a long time at Johnna's side. He felt he could stay fond of her for the rest of his life.

The next day, Kyle and Swin did park chores. They'd fashioned a sign that said TODAY: FREE ADMISSION, which they used to keep them out of the booth. There was no one to *make* them do the chores, no boss anymore, and this made the chores seem all the more important. There was nothing productive to do *but* the chores. The weed-whacker had been out of gas for some time, and Kyle had been lazy about figuring out what fuel/oil mixture its testy two-stroke engine took, but now he found himself digging out the manual, finding a funnel. Once he began weed-whacking, he didn't want to stop. He ran the thing for an hour and a half, up and back along the edges of the fire road, before he ran the tank dry. Meaning only to drag away a few branches that had fallen in the road, Kyle and Swin ended up clearing more than an acre of the forest floor, building a kindling pile that stood taller than they did. They could do nothing about the mess of death they'd been drawn into, could do nothing to figure out where they stood in Frog's eyes, but they could clean the damn park. They raked and policed, watered and mowed. Kyle, for his part, felt an unexpected pang of possessiveness toward the park. He'd never felt, as people said, "really at home," had never felt beholden or grateful to a certain place, but he knew that for the time being, until he was told different, this was *his* park. It was his lair.

Kyle and Swin put a message on Bright's phone that said he was away on business. They planned, when the paltry day-use fees were due, to estimate the total and pay it out of their own pockets. They kept doing chores. They kept, whether they wanted to or not, thinking things over.

Kyle ended up with the owl. He had the owner of the produce market clean it, then he cooked the bird into Bright's muck. It tasted similar to every other meat Kyle had eaten in the muck. He ate the owl muck for six straight meals, then started on Bright's reserves—instant mashed potatoes, candied nuts, frozen bananas. He and Swin, against Kyle's better judgment, spent several mornings lounging in Bright's house.

One day, a UPS man knocked on the door and handed them a padded envelope from the boss in pink. It contained papers about revenue, temperature and precipitation, incidents, pamphlet dispersal. Swin gleaned that these papers were due once a month, and that each quarter a more involved report would be expected. The forms required Bright's signature, a model for which was easily found in a kitchen drawer packed with forgotten or miswritten forms, and Swin claimed he'd have the signature down cold with a half hour of practice. The package also contained a sheaf of pretty paper covered with pictures of cotton. At the center of each page rested a mournful verse about the days of the boll weevil. The boss in pink had enclosed another quote: *I would call that man an artist who from the beginning is endowed with an ideal that, for him, replaces the truth. His life's task is to realize it completely, and set it forth for others to contemplate.*

"Drivel," said Swin. He carried all the papers to Bright's chair and began arranging them.

"You just don't understand it," Kyle said.

"Everything I understand, I partially disagree with." Swin pulled a book in front of him and began signing Bright's name all over it.

"Then what's your ideal?"

"That no one own or achieve anything except through random luck. An all-encompassing lottery system. And she's right: I do wish everyone would contemplate the ideal." Swin set the book down and flipped on the TV. "*Yours* is that nobody speak to one another. You want pointing and nodding and, when necessary, grunting."

"I wouldn't mind having an ideal," Kyle said.

"You don't want one," said Swin. "I can tell. You *want* to want one."

Kyle didn't know what to say. "Why don't you turn the TV off till you finish learning that signature?"

"My schedule's wide open." Swin's face was gleeful. He'd found the public-access channel, on which a tall man with a rattail haircut argued for the abolition of all insurance. Insurance went against God, he believed.

Kyle started a pot of coffee and chose Bright's FUCK GOSPEL SINGING mug. While the coffee brewed, Kyle warned Swin again not to let Johnna in on anything. He told Swin he'd seen her over at his trailer a lot lately. Swin replied that Johnna was closer to Bedford than to him. She'd begun taking Bedford to work with her, to cheer up the sick people.

"Looks like the only bill we'll get is for cable," Swin said. "Bright gets reimbursed. The rest of it goes straight to the department. Cable bill should come any day."

"We can't get a checking account."

"We can pay cash at the place."

"That'll look weird." Kyle poured his coffee and sat down with the phone.

"Money order?"

"Answer's no."

"We won't survive winter without cable."

"You just started watching it this week."

"You should try it. It'll make you more normal."

Kyle dialed the number of Gregor's shop. Gregor was the only person left that might give up some useful knowledge. It was a long shot. Gregor was a grub, half-crazy, his interaction with the world pared down to unlocking and relocking his door and reading the classifieds. Gregor probably knew less than

Kyle, but Kyle had left more messages with Colin and had heard nothing back. Kyle had stalled on calling Gregor because it was a last resort and Kyle didn't want to be down to a last resort. He knew nothing good would come of calling Gregor, but here he was, calling Gregor.

The phone rang and rang. Kyle redialed the number and waited ten rings. Nothing. But Gregor never left his shop—he could be in the bathroom, or in a deep sleep. Kyle drank his coffee. He told Swin they would cancel the cable the next day, and this sent Swin into an impassioned rant about learning and discovery and history and connection with the outside world. The show he had on now was teaching a dance that glorified camels. Kyle pressed the numbers again and could not hang up. The phone rang thirty, forty times. Kyle smelled his coffee and stared at his watch. On TV, the dancers were stomping out a crude beat. The voice on the other end startled Kyle. It wasn't Gregor, but a cheerful man who was opening a store for all things spicy. They'd have seven hundred hot sauces. This man didn't know Gregor personally, but he knew Gregor had been a slob. "Had been?" said Kyle. The man said the cops had come pounding on the place and Gregor wouldn't open up—had a bunch of inch-thick deadbolts and wouldn't answer their bullhorn. He holed up for hours until they blew a hole in the door and climbed through, then Gregor burst from a closet and took a leap at them. "Still got the door," the man said. The cops had wanted to ask Gregor about some car they'd found in a swamp. He didn't even have anything illegal inside. He had filthy magazines and a periscope, but nothing illegal.

Kyle hung up. He absently emptied his pockets on the table, then looked over to see his partner flipping through the channels with a daffy grin on his face, signing Bright's name on the book over and over without looking. Kyle thought of Bright's X-mas bones. He hadn't buried them like he'd told Swin. The bones were in a deep, covered tray, underneath the kitchen sink of Kyle's trailer. Kyle saw his park ID jutting out from a flap of his wallet. He'd forgotten all about it. He was Edward Mollar. These identities, Kyle knew, these names, Mollar and Suarez, weren't intended to help Kyle and Swin. They were insurance for Frog, in case Kyle Ribb and Swin Ruiz were wanted for something. Frog didn't want anyone who might be tracking down Kyle or Swin to find them while they were working for him. The names were just something to put through the background check at the Parks Department. Kyle examined his picture, next to this strange name that he didn't even use. Someone could probably yell, "Ed!" for twenty minutes and Kyle wouldn't answer. He wondered if Frog thought of them as Kyle and Swin or Mollar and Suarez. He knew Frog didn't care one way or the other what happened to them, what happened to Gregor or Bright or even Colin. Frog had things arranged in a way that kept him unconnected, untouchable. He would stay low awhile, then have them all replaced.

"Gregor's dead," Kyle called toward Swin. "Cops killed him at his shop."

Swin didn't flinch, didn't ask for any details. He stared thornily at the TV screen, no longer amused by the dancers.

"He's dead," Kyle said, in a softer voice.

Swin looked stupefied. The dancers on TV had no music to guide them. They didn't look to one another to keep the beat. Most of them had their eyes closed.

"Hear me?" Kyle asked.

Swin's head stayed just where it was, his expression barren. "I'm employing a little well-timed denial. I'm not up for more death at present, so I'm defending myself with old-fashioned denial."

Kyle watched Swin for a full minute, during which Swin did not take his eyes from the dancers.

"Fair enough," Kyle said.

He slipped his photos of his mother out of a fold of his wallet. In one, she was surrounded by dunes, wearing a colorful dress and a hat. In the other, she stood in front of a brick building, her face made up. It was from the day she got her government job. Kyle wondered what his mother had been thinking that day, what she believed that job would mean for her. He wondered what she thought having a son meant, what she'd wanted for Kyle. He wondered what, if anything, dying had prevented her from doing. What was her unfinished business? Kyle heard Swin telling him to answer the phone before he heard it ringing. He said, "Felsenthal Park. How can I help you?" It was Her, the woman from the trailer park who handed off the trip packets. She said the bake sale was a go.

To show that the debate throughout the South over whether church services should be held on Saturdays or Sundays was beneath them, Johnna's church alternated. This weekend the service was on Saturday, and the Razorback game had kicked off at eleven a.m. Johnna had already missed seventeen minutes of the action and the pastor showed no signs of wrapping up. To make things worse, it was the day of the monthly potluck. All the heavy dishes had to be brought out, plates and silverware and cups set up. They'd say grace. They'd have a chitchat session referred to as "fellowship." They'd say another grace, thanking God for the chance to *have* fellowship. The whole first half was shot, if not part of the third quarter.

The pastor had a thin, orange beard, and held his Bible aloft when he quoted from it. He'd started the day warning of the evils of jealousy, and was now musing about meekness. Johnna felt bad for the pastor because his children were sad cases. His son shot bluebirds out of trees and entered arm-wrestling competitions in whatever slight weight class he belonged to. The pastor's daughter wanted to be a slut, but due to her tender age and buckteeth, she had a tough time finding willing boys.

"What does the Bible mean when it says, 'Inherit the earth'?" the pastor said.

It seemed to Johnna that the people in her church didn't care if a sermon made sense, so long as it was lengthy and animated. First off, jealousy was *needed*; without it, everyone would be swingers. And who were the meek? Meekness as an actual human trait was absurd. None of the famous Christians Johnna knew of, past or present, were meek. Johnna thought of God as a wiry, black-haired man who found amusement in leaving just enough justice in the world to give people hope. Once in a while rich people got in trouble. Once in a while there was no fine print. Once in a while a mechanic didn't screw you. Slot machines paid out. Once in a blue moon, Texas got called for holding.

When the pastor came down from the stage he seemed surprised his audience was comprised of real people. He waded into the greetings as if not sure what his hands were made of, gripping the women by their upper arms, full of an affection that was infused with arrogance. The crowd was full of florid, fat ladies who could sit around for a month pointing out examples of moral foulness in movies and TV shows. All modern entertainment was devised as an attack on these ladies, and these ladies were the reason Johnna had to stay for the entire service and the entire potluck, why she couldn't be the first to leave. Once the old ladies judged you, you might as well switch churches.

There were also a couple of skinny families with numerous sons. These sons had melodious faces, did yard work all day, and made straight A's. These sons didn't care for candy. They didn't let their eyes drift to Johnna's chest when they spoke to her. They hung around with the pastor's son out of charity.

There were a few farmers. There was a lawyer. There was a gaggle of retired military. There was a contractor of some sort. There were those who switched jobs often.

Fifteen minutes after the sermon, this group still hadn't herded itself into the front room, where the food waited. The pastor had started preaching again. He didn't understand that when you harped on something too much, it became a joke. In her mind, Johnna cursed the fat ladies out. She made a wish that they would break their heels and fall. Outside the window there was even, bronze sunlight. The branches swayed. Johnna drifted toward the main hallway, a lid on her breath, exhilaration swimming inside her. She slipped into the front room, filed several squares of cornbread into her purse, and escaped to her Oldsmobile.

The air that tossed her hair around smelled of honeysuckle. The wildflowers were bright. Johnna would catch some of the second quarter. She waved at an old man with orange gloves who was walking his bike up a hill.

It wasn't just the Razorbacks and the weather and defying the fat ladies that was making Johnna's heart smile. Johnna's heart was full of Swin. He made the world off-kilter. It always tipped toward him or leaned away. There was island magic in his grin. He was a dopey professor. He was rambling, ambitious. It had startled Johnna, having one of these odd boys pursue *her*, rather than the other way around. It was good to be pursued, good to be the frightened one.

Johnna was two days late. Two days was no big deal. Two days plus the fact that they'd had condom problems their first time. The thing had been bunched up and hard to get on, then it kept slipping. And they'd gone for so long. Afterward, Johnna saw the condom in the trash and it looked lacerated and gummed. Condoms were tough, though. Back in high school, to prove that boys were lying if they said they were too endowed to wear one, the nurse had stretched a condom onto an eggplant. The nurse had filled one with a gallon of water.

Your condo in Little Rock has a bungled Frank Lloyd Wright bathroom. Because the only light in this bathroom comes from a secret window and the floor of the shower stall is on a slight incline, you get the condo cheaper than you should. It's on the fourth floor, overlooking a river park with dead grass.

When Thomas and Tim have worked with you for a full year without incident, when the country in them has been sufficiently choked out by the city, you tell them to establish their own farm area, that you will cover the old strip of bars. Nightly, you settle into dim booths, your pockets plump with twist-tied baggies of cocaine, and nurse a beer. At first you run from bar to bar, but soon all your customers come to you, to a basement lounge whose decor centers around the golden age of Hollywood. Sometimes they screen movies and you have to sit by the door and catch your customers before they walk in and disturb everyone. The crowd at this bar is a bit older than at the others. You blend in. You sit under a poster of Humphrey Bogart and watch people get trashed on martinis and manhattans. When the bartenders realize what you're up to, you cut them in. They require only a thin cut, and some take their payoff in cocaine. The owner is a woman who lives in the country and shows her face at the bar every other weekend. She has inherited the place from her brother and doesn't know the bar business. You dread the day when she gets wise and freaks out and calls the cops, so instead of waiting for that day, you request a meeting. You explain to her that if it wasn't you, it'd be someone else, someone flashy, someone belligerent—some asshole. You've caused her no trouble and you never will. If you ever get busted, you tell her, she just acts dumb and nothing happens to her. It's best if she doesn't take a cut, best for her to stay clean, stay out with the crickets. You can guarantee you'll be the only dealer in her place, and that you won't have slobbering junkies in there. You are an honest man, you admit. You finish your coffee and say you have to run.

Your neighbor in the next condo is your best customer. His day job is carving cedar elves. A big company bought him out of his copyright, but they still sell a select line of elves hand-carved by the inventor. This man hates sleep. He hates to let time pass while he's not watching, and does not want to say, one day, that his life was short. He measures time in elves.

The city council offers incentives for certain types of businesses. Soon after you establish two more volume clients, you open a small bakery that also sells art—paintings you get for ten dollars a pop at flea markets. You price the paintings anywhere from five hundred to fifteen hundred bucks and claim to sell half a dozen a week. Your bakery is rarely open, so no one notices that the same paintings hang in it for months. You put your neighbor's elves up as decorations. You buy raw materials for baking and throw them out, turn the lights on and read the paper every few days. You enjoy owning a shop again, especially because you don't have to sell anything.

The clients you drum up are nothing compared to the volume Thomas and Tim do at the University of Arkansas branch. They get plugged in to pot parties, church outings, folk concerts. They are novel because of their size and the fact that they don't drink. You make them get separate savings accounts and they watch the accounts grow. You buy a VCR. On nights when none of you work, you watch comedy movies and sometimes a Charles Bronson. You look forward to the day when the daily operations move into the boys' hands and you move to the sticks.

At some point the monthly letters are not enough. The boys' aunt comes to visit. You clear your schedule and treat the aunt to ribs and steaks and bacon-wrapped shrimp. The boys' clients are happy to lend them books and, when the aunt is present, stop by to borrow notes or set up a study group. You are the boys' sponsoring professor, the man who chose them for their scholarships, a feared critic of Canadian poetry. The boys say they're sociology majors. They want to learn other languages. Studying makes them whole. For them, there is nothing like thought. It's fun, lying to a person who would believe anything you say. You even fire up the ovens at the bakery so the boys can have part-time jobs.

Her's trailer had plush carpet. Blankets were hung over the windows and in one corner stood a bare coatrack and empty umbrella stand. Kyle and Swin sat on metal folding chairs, happy to have finally gained entrance into Her's little fortress. She presented them with a tray covered with dry crackers.

"I don't care for these Ritz." She rested the tray on the floor. "Go ahead and stare for ten seconds."

Her had sponges lashed to the soles of her feet and squares of egg crate taped to her palms. Kyle didn't know if he was supposed to stare at that or at her face, which was gracefully aged and bewitching.

"Cheekbones like frozen waves," Swin said. "Lips like rosebuds. Eyes the color of a sheik's camel."

"Ten seconds is up," she said. She explained that she suffered from a disorder that made her hands and feet sensitive. As a child, her mother had taken her to specialists who'd tried to toughen her so she could compete in pageants and appear in commercials. No one could diagnose the problem. Some said it was all in her mind, to which her mother would reply, "Then fix that."

"Very little pain is in the mind," Swin said. "Possibly none."

"It's not all that bad," she said. "Basically, I'll never work in a factory or play handball."

Kyle and Swin ate a few crackers. Her went to the kitchen and brought back plastic cups of warm milk. Swin said he wanted his put in the fridge awhile, which Kyle thought was rude. Kyle muscled down a couple gulps. It wasn't that bad. He wondered when they'd get the packet—if there was a password or some other bit of protocol they didn't know.

"I like boys like you," Her said. "That don't get hung up on having a long life."

Kyle and Swin said nothing.

"I can't wait to die, but I'm not going to hell. It'd be a lot simpler if I could kill myself, but I ain't going to hell. I want the *Lord* to strike me down."

"What does your family think of that?" Swin asked.

"Mother's dead. Never had kids. Husband, I divorced him." She pointed at a porch table in the far corner, which was laden with books about accidents, chaos, suicide. "You can't be expecting it. You can't wait for a storm and then go to the middle of a field and set a hubcap on your head."

"So," Kyle said. "That packet."

Her cast two tan eyes on him. "Don't be rude."

"Don't be rude," Swin said. "There's a proper way to treat a lady."

Swin asked if there was anything Her enjoyed about life. Of course, she said. She liked watching animals hunt and mate on TV. She liked her husband's blowtorches, which he'd left in a shed behind the trailer when he'd gone to Mississippi.

"And how does such an arresting complexion come to be?" Swin asked.

"A Swede owned one of my ancestors." Her pulled aside her sponge and pressed areas of her foot. "Some get illnesses that take them to the grave," she said. "And I get this." She looked upward a moment. "Where's the ranger?"

"He went with an Indian," Kyle said. "Over to Oklahoma."

"What kind of car did the Indian drive?"

"I think it might've been a Kia."

"You're lying."

"No," said Kyle.

"Just say, 'How the fuck should I know?'"

"It could have been a Hyundai."

"Stop that," Her said.

Kyle nodded.

"Here." Her tugged the packet out from under her chair, where it had been taped, and handed it over.

In the morning, Kyle found a note on his trailer door that said Swin had come down with the flu and had gone to Bright's to sit in the big chair and recuperate. Kyle didn't like them to hang out at Bright's, but if Swin would be there, he figured, he might as well go, too.

He walked over, dug fish sticks out of Bright's freezer, and slid them into the oven on a cookie sheet. Swin drank tea with lemon wedges and swallowed a few smelly vitamins, then watched a black comedian in a red vest make fun of the way white people sold things, responded to danger, and shopped for shoes. Swin said he didn't know why all black guys didn't become comedians. Kyle asked what he meant, but before Swin could answer there was a knock at the door. Kyle strolled to the window, pulled aside the curtain, and said that he'd known the nurse would become a problem. He sat at the kitchen table and watched Swin theatrically prepare to stand, tossing sections of the comforter this way and that, scooting his teacup and lemon carcasses, muting the black comedian. The knocking came again. Swin blew his nose. He pulled a roll of mints from his shorts and chewed one, then sauntered over and opened the door. Johnna guessed he'd be sick, she said, because *she* was sick the day before—a twenty-four-hour bug. She'd brought a broth of saw palmetto, which would help Swin pee. She explained that Bedford had wobbled up to her just as she'd given up knocking on the trailer, and he'd led her back to the house. On cue, the dog came out from behind the door. Johnna took a load off near the whiskey cabinet. She looked around herself, at the ceiling and moldings and appliances. What a nice house, she said. Jesus. It was the nicest house she'd ever been in. Except it was plain. It could really use some touches, but wow.

When the fish sticks were done, Johnna got sauce from the fridge and ate a few, dipping with no delicacy, just speed and intention. She started asking questions. Who all lived in this place? Swin and Kyle could use it, but not sleep in it? Who else worked at this park?

"I knew you'd crack," proclaimed Swin, coughing. "I knew you'd become fascinated with me and my lifestyle." He told Johnna that he and Kyle worked for a private firm that had been hired to evaluate the state park system. They had deemed the ranger at Felsenthal unfit, and he'd been shipped to a remedial ranger school on an Indian reservation in Oklahoma. Swin and Kyle had to stay on and put things right until the ranger was replaced—no telling how long that would be. Johnna wanted to know what, exactly, they were putting right, and Swin said it was mostly record-keeping.

"The house?" she asked.

"Well, now that it's vacant—"

"We can't live in it," Kyle said. "Conflict of interest."

"But no one would know if we did," Swin said.

Johnna sized up the windows and peered down the long hall. "I could do this place up adorable."

Kyle set his plate in the sink and ran the water. "We only come here for meals. We were about to leave."

More knocking was heard at the door. Kyle shut off the faucet. He looked outside and saw a beefy guy with a backward cap. The guy was maybe thirty-five and had driven his SUV right up to the porch.

"An old frat boy with a 4Runner," Kyle said.

Swin turned up his palms.

The guy was talking before the door was all the way open, saying not to be disturbed, that he was looking for Patrick Bright, the head ranger.

"We're not disturbed," Kyle assured him. "Ranger Bright isn't available."

The guy's name was Barry. He was the son of the man who'd given Bright his break in the tree service, who Bright had lived with when he first landed in Arkansas. Barry's father, before he died, had spoken a lot of Bright, saying he was one of the good guys. Barry was on a cross-county trip, visiting his father's old friends. The park was just how he remembered it. Boy, was a cute nurse a sight for sore eyes. Hey, were those some of his father's books?

Kyle let him finish then introduced himself and Swin as Mollar and Suarez, junior rangers. He said Johnna was a friend of theirs.

"Junior rangers?" said Barry, eyeing Johnna.

"That's what I said."

"So the little nurse is only a *friend*."

"Sorry you came all this way," Kyle said. "He's at a convention in Tulsa—something about Native Americans."

"And he'll be back when?" Barry lifted his cap up and pulled it on tighter.

"They don't tell us. How about I take your number?"

Kyle picked up a pen and a stray pamphlet. He wrote the numbers Barry recited, set the pamphlet on top of the fridge, then went and held the front door open.

"I'd like to have *her* number," Barry said.

"We don't want any trouble," said Kyle.

"No trouble." Swin wiped his nose on his sleeve. "I invite alternative suitors."

Johnna perched on the arm of Swin's chair and tossed her hair, trying to look like a prize. Swin called out her age, weight, and height. He said Johnna was a spunky nurse who enjoyed collegiate football matches.

"Careful," Barry said. "I got no problem breaking up a happy couple."

Kyle sat at the kitchen table. He peered at the grain of the wood, flattened his palm on it. It was *his* kitchen table. Whether he and Swin spent their nights in this house or not, it was his house now. It was his living room. A stranger was in his living room, insulting his partner. This was the point when regular people called the police: when a sleep-deprived asshole barged in and tried to steal a woman.

"Let me try something," Swin said. "Who's Gertrude Stein?"

Barry shook his head.

"The Medici family?"

"Never had the pleasure."

"What nationality was Copernicus?"

"Not yours."

"I'm smarter than you, Barry. And younger." Swin pulled his blanket aside and lifted his shirt. "Girls like abs."

"I'm rich. And I'm not a *junior* anything."

Swin pointed vaguely toward the front of the house. "I could buy that pretty truck out from under you with hundred-dollar bills."

Kyle burst up from the table. "The fun's over."

He held Barry with a stare until the guy backed out onto the porch and down to his 4Runner. Kyle guided the door shut and Bedford belatedly hopped into sight and growled.

"That true about the hundreds?" Johnna asked.

"It's complicated," Swin answered.

"Junior rangers?"

He shrugged.

"I thought Bright was at remedial training."

"He is," Swin said. "It's all pretty complicated."

JOHN BRANDON

Another call from Her. Another packet. Another car.

Shuttling to Cape Girardeau in the spare comfort of a Mitsubishi Galant, Kyle did not feel easy or strong. He couldn't even enjoy an interstate run. The road followed the Mississippi up to Missouri, but never came in sight of the river. Kyle agreed to listen to singing on the radio as long as it wasn't in English, so Swin dialed up a Danish woman who belched out noises like a humpback whale. Swin called the music a "sonic landscape." When that ended, two guys came on and answered trivia questions about cars. Kyle and Swin ate lunch in a place where the waiters juggled rolls. They discussed Bright's Bronco. Maybe there was no need to get rid of it. Best to park it behind the house and put it out of mind. And it was about time, Kyle and Swin agreed, for them to get their own car. If they pitched in, they could buy it with their own money. They needed a way to get around town, to escape the park once in a while. And they trusted each other now; each felt reasonably confident that the other wouldn't drive off in the car and never come back. If an occasion arose that forced them to run from the park, it would be a surprise to both of them, and both of them would leave together, and *not* in Bright's Bronco. Registering a car under their park names would be a breeze—a lot easier than finding a clean gun. They could drop six thousand on a car without having to dip into the money in the dryer. They would hold that money, along with the bag from this trip, until someone came for it. Kyle had no doubt someone would come. Frog would be impressed if Kyle and Swin held all the money for weeks, months, and hardly touched it.

"He probably already counted it as gone," Swin said.

"How much do you think he knows?"

"Maybe only that something's not right."

"Or maybe he knows about every piss we take."

"Also a possibility."

"I wonder if he's a genius," Kyle said.

"Like most people, you have an elementary understanding of that word." Swin grunted. "I think six grand is low for a car."

"You do, do you?"

"If we get a clunker, we'll end up opening the bags to pay mechanics. My vote is for a late-model Saab."

"I don't believe we'll have a vote on it," Kyle said. "Maybe we can swing eight or nine, though."

At a gas station, Swin bought a scratch-off and won a dollar. He decided to keep the dollar instead of getting another ticket, and this annoyed the clerk, a small woman with lofty hair.

"You're no better than when you walked in here," she told Swin.

He and Kyle went out to the phone booth and found what street the pawnshops were on. They had time to stroll in and out of as many run-down establishments as they wanted, looking for a merchant who didn't take gun regulations to heart.

Kyle parked in a pay garage and he and Swin took opposite sides of the street. In the second place Kyle hit, he found the merchant he was looking for. The guy said he was the only one in town who dealt in orphans, and that he only had one, a .45. He was open about charging Kyle double, and insisted that Kyle never come back to the shop or send him any business. He took Kyle's bills, then handed him a heavy newspaper. Kyle retrieved the Galant and found Swin, who hadn't had any luck.

"People like their Ricans unarmed," Swin told him.

Kyle unfolded the newspaper.

"*Sledge Hammer!*" Swin said.

"What?"

"It's a spoof cop show."

Kyle held the monstrous gun. "You could drop it on someone's head."

"Or set it in front of their car," Swin said. "Block their getaway."

"It's like Dirty Harry's gun," Kyle said.

"That's what *Sledge Hammer!* is a spoof of."

Heading across town, Swin perused the envelope and found that the meeting was at nine, not six. He and Kyle couldn't remember how they'd gotten this wrong, whose fault it was, and this inability to lay blame seemed more indicting than the mistake itself. They stopped for sandwiches, ate sullenly, and still had well over two dead hours in front of them. They got back in the car and meandered into the suburbs, into the tamed hedges, where a Barnes and Noble loomed up.

The place was a labeled maze packed with women who were not quite good-looking. Kyle traversed the self-help section, head down, then found a table of books about exotic dancing. One was instructional, for wives—wives, apparently, who had fireman poles in their foyers. What kinds of faces was this lady making? He waded into the reference section and selected a volume called *Pillars of Statesmanship*, then sat in a bouncy chair to try and catch a snooze.

Swin went straight for the periodicals. He flipped through a magazine that dressed natural beauties up like plumbers, then he scanned the *Daily Girardeaun*, which featured an announcement that the sheriff's department was officially giving up on finding a certain murderer, some dude that bashed a girl's head on a root at a hair-metal festival. Swin got a green-tea milkshake and selected a stack of magazines for back in Arkansas: the *New Yorker*, the *Economist*, *Premiere*, one about Las Vegas, and one full of socialist art. He gathered whatever reviews he could get his hands on and stationed himself on an out-of-the-way bench. He had an almost physical hunger to be made aware of the merits and shortcomings of recent art. This was how Swin could make the most of his time at the bookstore, could cram the most odd, unnecessary, beautiful thought into an hour and a half: criticism. Nothing brought the mind to a brazen pump like criticism. Swin didn't understand half of what these people were saying about ironic use of shadow and callous formal barriers, but he could feel the words filling small fissures in his psyche. He felt like a stressed-out woman at a spa, reviving herself.

When the time came, he reluctantly located Kyle, reluctantly woke him up, reluctantly went to the car and off to the drop.

In the morning, Swin went to a cell-phone dealer. He didn't want to receive a bill, so he had to pay for a full estimated year of service right there in the store. It put a good dent in his emergency funds, but he considered it a small price for some sweet words from his sisters.

While a guy in a bow tie tried to sell Swin phone insurance, he indulged in a fantasy in which his mother and stepdad were dead—burned up in a train crash while touring Holland—and Swin swept through in the dead of night and took his sisters to his penthouse in, oh, New Orleans, and got them dresses and tutoring and all the scallops and banana pudding they could eat. They didn't ever go downstairs, and they waited with bated breath for Swin's return.

When they got back to the park, Kyle found a cassette in the mailbox. Richard Strauss (1864–1949), *Also sprach Zarathustra*. It was a promotion. The company must send out tapes randomly, he thought. Must've been random, because Bright didn't listen to *any* music. There was an order from, which Kyle balled up and threw out. If you liked Strauss, you could call and order his old buddies.

There was also a note on Bright's front door:

> Ranger Pat,
>
> There were gunshots reported a couple weeks ago. Just reminding you the boar poachers will be out soon. They start tracking the things fifty miles off and lose track of where the hell they are. If you catch any, you get some sort of citation. Don't mean to be such a stranger. Benson's elbow keeps hurting him from the surgery, so who gets the extra patrol? Like my back isn't killing me. Guess I need to complain more. Hey, tell those newbies to come out to Stumbler's on Wednesdays and play trivia.
>
> Lawfully,
>
> Cooper

Neither Kyle nor Swin had a word to say about this note. They both understood that before long they'd have to go to this bar and bullshit with cops. Kyle took Bright's modest ghetto-blaster back to his trailer and played *Also sprach Zarathustra*. Kyle believed Richard Strauss was not fond of life, but still had hope. Strauss was angry at himself for believing he could get caught up in life like other people. Kyle, he realized, was hearing himself in the music. He wondered if that was why the company had chosen this particular tape to send out, because people heard themselves in it. It was a dirty trick.

———

Kyle had a morning appointment with Straight Ralph at his dealership out near the paper mill. Ralph was the only used-car dealer in the area and his inventory was limited, so he would only sell you the car that most suited you. When Kyle and Swin arrived at the lot, Ralph was not in his office booth, so they waited in the Bronco. Kyle wondered how you got a name like "Straight" when you couldn't even show up for an appointment. Swin turned on the radio to a show about immoral football recruiting. A man with a drawl kept saying, "All comes out in the wash." Swin turned the radio off before Kyle could complain about it. The Bronco was heating up under the sun, its frame groaning. They opened their windows.

"All comes out in the wash," Swin said.

"We'll give him ten minutes." Kyle positioned his visor.

"What does that mean? It all comes out in the wash?"

"Everything that's hidden. Like if you had a nickel or a lighter in your pocket."

"Sure it's not the dirt and odors of your soul?"

Kyle craned his neck to look around for Ralph. "It's about judgment day."

"You might not know whose pocket something came from."

"You can usually guess."

"I don't know," Swin said. "This would be the whole world's laundry."

"No, just the hypocrites'. So my laundry wouldn't be in there."

"Mine *would?*"

"I couldn't say."

So what if Kyle was a truer criminal, Swin thought. Kyle was a simpleton. Swin was probably the smartest person for a hundred miles. One of the smartest people in this state.

"I've read more books than you've seen," he told Kyle.

Kyle spread his eyebrows as if he'd misheard, but Swin didn't repeat himself. Kyle wouldn't understand. He couldn't fathom the trials of an intellectual in exile. Swin needed someone better to talk to. He needed a modern gym, an internet café.

A breeze picked up, pushing the stale air out of the Bronco. Something smelled funny. More than funny. When the breeze turned to wind, it was laden with the scorched-urine smell of the paper mill. Kyle went into a coughing fit. He closed his window and Swin followed suit. Too late; the stench was in the Bronco. Swin breathed through his mouth until he felt he was eating the industrial stink. He and Kyle jumped out of the Bronco and hurried to Ralph's booth, which, surprisingly, wasn't locked.

"Must've got called away for an emergency," Kyle said.

"Probably never locks it. Nothing in here but forms and key chains."

In a few minutes, the air did not stink. That, or they'd gotten used to it. They agreed to take a look at Ralph's stock, then come back another day. There was an early-'90s BMW that Swin liked, an extra-cab pickup, a Honda with three hundred thousand miles on it.

"Finally," a voice called.

Kyle and Swin stood still.

"Around here, girls."

They rounded a minivan and saw an older man lying on the ground. He wore a maroon vest and was using his hat as a pillow.

"I lost my balance." Straight Ralph had been down on the gravel for two hours. He'd been checking the weather stripping on the back doors of the minivan and had slipped off the bumper.

"How bad you hurt?" Kyle asked.

"Whole left side, including the ear."

Swin scooped a flask from the minivan's shadow and gave it a judgmental shake.

"No, I don't drink strong liquor," Ralph said. "I carry that everywhere. Sorority sweetheart gave it to me. She liked me something awful."

Kyle nodded. "You paralyzed?"

"Back's locked up. I need a ride to the hospital in Sheck County, if you don't mind. Could I get that back from you?"

Swin handed him the flask and he tucked it in his vest. Ralph said he'd chosen the minivan for them because they could carry their friends around on the weekends, and it was a sharp color and had custom rims. He shared his view that a paper mill smelled worse than vulture shit, and that the best type of movie was a sorority horror flick. He'd lost his second wife, in part, due to his fondness for this film genre.

"We don't have friends," Kyle said. "And we can't take you to the emergency room. But we'll pay cash for the van."

"You don't have forty-five minutes for an old man?"

"Afraid not," Swin said.

They carried Ralph to his booth and propped him up to the phone. They counted out the money and Swin took the keys and straightened Ralph's hat on his head. Kyle had the gun in the Bronco. He was going to stop for ammo then meet Swin in an abandoned goat pasture on Route 12.

Once alone in the minivan, Swin saw that it had a small entertainment center drilled into the floorboards. There was a TV with a built-in VCR. Swin felt the urge to watch movies. He knew a video store/tanning parlor/candy shop not far out of the way. He went in and scoured the aisles. Class-clown comedies. Insufferable cop drivel. Cameron Crowe crap. To Swin's shock, they had a Woody Allen movie—*Manhattan*. Neurotic Jews were just the thing Swin needed. There were no Jews in Arkansas.

At the goat pasture, Kyle and Swin walked into a live-oak grove and Kyle loaded bullets into the gun's spinner. He lifted the pistol slowly, appreciating its balance and weight, then aimed at a shed roof that leaned against a tree. He squeezed the trigger tentatively, then as hard as he could. No blast came. Kyle frowned at the weapon and tried it with two hands. He unloaded the gun, cleaned it, reloaded. The thing still refused to fire. Kyle wasn't going to deny what had happened. He said "I got taken," wiped the mute hunk of metal hard with the cloth, and tossed it in some weeds. He faced the distance.

"Why do people keep doing stuff?" he said, talking to himself, it seemed. Swin hesitated.

"Wiping counters down and taking pictures. Cheating. Defending things."

Swin couldn't see Kyle's face. It appeared he was about to say more, then thought better of it. It seemed he was going to laugh or cry; of course, he was going to do neither. It was a moment of defeat, nothing more. Kyle looked back toward the woods, where he'd thrown the gun. Swin felt he had to speak.

"It's involved," he said. "Many schools of thought. In layman's terms, being the most sophisticated monkey makes you the most confused monkey. Taking action, any action at all, is a way to alleviate that confusion. You, you're one of the least sophisticated of us sophisticated monkeys, and therefore suffer less confusion, and have less use for the empty actions that alleviate confusion. I don't mean that as a put-down."

Though Kyle didn't move, Swin knew he was listening, knew the explanation was somehow helping.

A resolute knocking came at Kyle's trailer door. He eased to the window and aligned his eye with an opening in the blinds. Johnna. She knew he was home. He opened the door and she hoisted him a Big Gulp. She had one for herself, as well, which she now took control of with both hands.

"How'd you knock?" asked Kyle. "That didn't sound like kicking."

"Sharp hip bone."

Kyle stepped aside, presenting a small, round table. Johnna set her soda down and dropped her purse on the tabletop, causing the table to skid on the vinyl floor. Kyle sipped his Big Gulp, some orange drink, and watched Johnna yank bag after bag of candy from her purse: circus peanuts, Boston baked beans, blow pops. As Kyle was about to let the door shut, Bedford padded in and sniffed for a moment, confused. He'd never been in Kyle's trailer. No one had ever been in Kyle's trailer.

"I was hoping on giving out candy." Johnna sat and Bedford settled in under her chair. "Then I was like, Do I want to sit on the porch all damn night?" Johnna's face dulled in thought. "I really should like kids more."

She opened a chocolate cookie and ate it in measured bites. Bedford looked up at Kyle doubtfully, and Kyle thought of putting him in Bright's muck. When Johnna finished the cookie, she began nibbling a circus peanut. Kyle asked where Swin was and she said he was on a long jog. He'd strapped on his sun goggles, his ankle weights, and a little satchel of protein bars and trotted off.

"Can I help you with something?" Kyle said. He knew he should be having a hard time controlling himself in the presence of this sexy nurse. He knew he wouldn't come on to Johnna, but he wanted to be tempted. Her neck was firm, giving way to cleavage as it slipped behind her scrub top. Her ears were perfect, her arms and hands brown as a berry.

"I need to know how long you're staying," she said. "Don't say to ask Swin."

"Impossible to tell right now," Kyle said. "That's the truth."

"He doesn't tell me a thing. He won't even tell me where his family lives."

"At this moment we don't have any plans to leave."

Johnna's eyes bounced around behind her glasses, nothing to settle on but Kyle. She arched her back in her chair and looked at the ceiling, her breasts pressing their shape into her shirt, a strip of her midriff grinning at Kyle. She positioned her forearm and plowed the mound of candy toward him, but he shook his head. She was still working on the same circus peanut, guiding it past her lips tentatively. Kyle moved in his shorts and it gave him a start.

"You don't need to tell me anything exact, but how bad is it, what you two do? I mean, if you got caught, how long a sentence we talking?"

Kyle waited.

"Rangers in training? Park auditors? I'm not stupid."

"I should check you for a wire."

"*Right.*"

"I like you, but truth is I don't know you."

"Where would I hide a wire?"

Kyle knew he wasn't important enough to have to worry about someone wearing a wire. He tapped his chest. Johnna smirked then shimmied her shirt up far enough that Kyle could fully view her bra. Kyle felt like a bully, but that didn't stop him from pitching a tent. Flush with gratitude, he adjusted himself as slyly as he could.

"It's impossible to tell about jail sentences."

Kyle turned sideways in his chair and leaned against the wall. He hadn't felt this sort of want since coming to the park, since maybe back in Athens.

"Rapists get off," he said. "Potheads go to prison. Depends what kind of evidence, or who rats on you. Sometimes you can buy a way out."

"Still, I don't know if you're smuggling piranhas or baby girls."

Johnna tried to smile, but her eyes moistened. Kyle didn't know what was going on. He suspected he was confused because of his hard-on, which, with Johnna basically crying, was losing steam. Kyle had never seen this side of her, unsure and mired.

"What is all this?" he asked.

She drank her soda down to the bottom, jabbing at the ice. Kyle wasn't thirsty and his cup was sweating all over the table, so he carried it to the fridge. While his back was turned, Johnna said she was pregnant.

"I'm trying to figure out how to tell Swin. I could always make something up and dump him."

Kyle sat down gingerly. He was in foreign territory. He'd never had a female friend, had never been compelled to speak frankly to a woman. "You can't leave us," he said. "You have to face us." He wasn't sure what he was trying to say. "Should you be eating all that candy?" he asked.

"I just want to know where I stand," said Johnna. "I'm not scared of being a mother. It's the most natural thing in the world."

"I guess."

"A lot of people think parenting is impossible because *their* parents were lousy."

"I don't know anyone who had good parents."

"I didn't and I still turned out all right."

"Better than all right," Kyle said. "Way better than all right."

Johnna took the lid off her soda and began eating the ice doughnuts one by one, trapping them cautiously between two fingers.

It was a bad idea to tell Johnna anything, but Kyle knew he would—anything she wanted to know. It was beginning to seem to Kyle that his actions weren't of much consequence; trouble came from obvious causes or no cause at all, every once in a while or in a bunch. Kyle's life had been secret for a long time, one big omission, and now here was someone looking him in the eye and being straight. He told Johnna about his and Swin's trips, about what had happened to Bright, where Bright was buried. Johnna's eyes bulged but she kept quiet, not wanting, Kyle knew, to break whatever blabbing spell he was under. He told her what he'd done to the boy's uncle, and that he and Swin were now flying blind, taking the assignments as long as they kept coming and doing their best to save the money. If they were ever going to run away from the park, Kyle said, they'd have done it the first day, the minute they found Bright and Nick. They would've done an about-face and got in the Bronco and drove far away.

When Kyle stopped speaking, a pressure built in the trailer. He got up and opened the door. Bedford dragged himself outside to the dappling shade. Kyle tried to set the stopper that held the door open, but it kept slipping.

"Who am I kidding?" he said. "These trailers are pieces of shit. We might as well live up in Bright's house."

After three years of steady business in Little Rock, you are approached by a mouthpiece who wears the bad suit of an insurance agent. He is not an insurance agent. He tells you a conglomerate will buy everything you can get your hands on in the next ten days. You have no idea how much you can get your hands on, and he says to find out. You stay up all night and have your arrangements made in less than thirty hours—so many pounds of PCP and cocaine and marijuana that you have no place to store it but the kitchen of your bakery. You go to a sporting-goods store and wipe out their stock of gym bags. The salesman thinks you're a wrestling coach.

You barely sleep for six nights, dreaming of break-ins, raids, fires. Thomas and Tim volunteer to sleep at the bakery, but this wouldn't look right. Your bakery/art gallery has been ignored by Little Rock since its opening and will, you tell yourself, be ignored a few days more. You instruct Thomas and Tim to stay in. You will not take them to the deal because their size makes people nervous.

You are alone at the bakery when the guys pull up, in broad daylight, in an unconvincing FedEx truck. They wear FedEx hats and long shorts. Three load and one tallies everything on a tiny notebook like a reporter would use. The mouthpiece is not with them. The one with the notepad gruffly bosses the others. He asks what you think about stand-up comedy—whether you consider it the highest form of comedy, whether you consider it an art, a living art or a dead art. He's been performing on a semiprofessional basis for fifteen months. He has nineteen minutes that he's proud of. It's all delivery, he tells you. There are no new jokes left, no original wardrobes or catchphrases. You make affirmative noises and nod, hoping he won't tell any jokes. You are pleased at how fast the loaders work, and by the figures this guy is absently compiling. Punch lines are for hacks, he declares. Hacks and junior-high kids. You have to grab that crowd by the shirt and convince them you don't give a shit if they laugh or not. Half a dozen bags left. By now the loaders have slowed. While the last bag is loaded and the truck locked up, the guy reveals a formula for jokes per minute. He adjusts his JPM if he's doing an accent or a silly dance. His disadvantage is he can't talk about his job in his comedy, and he also gets along with his family. We could talk about this for hours, he says, then raises his voice in some code that utilizes bowling lingo. One of the loaders rolls out a suitcase. The comedian hands you a slip of paper and hops in the truck, and they bounce out of the alley and onto the avenue. On the paper is written the number *421*.

421. Damn near half a million dollars.

You give Thomas and Tim a share. For a joke, you tape up a roll of hundreds and put them on the toilet-paper dispenser. Lobster brunch. St. Louis for a couple Cardinals games. You leave a waitress with the sweetest smile you've ever seen a seven-hundred-dollar tip. Thomas and Tim are inspired. With their new buying power, they get exclusives all over town. This makes you nervous because any of these people could roll over on Tim and Thomas, especially with no one else to roll over on, but being nervous is part of the business. They have a woman at a three-story club, an old man who drives up into the Ozarks, and a company that owns radio stations throughout Texas. Thomas and Tim abandon the university, where everyone knows them too well.

Tim turns twenty-one, and you take the boys to the top of the Barnett building and have them look out over the brown neighborhoods, the cluster of honeycomb government offices, the four-lane road that leads to the suburbs, and beyond it all, the fields of twisted trees. Just the beginning, you say. You're trying to hand them managing power in an official way, to create a moment they won't forget. You touch their shoulders and tell them you will take your own place, a townhouse on the same block as the bakery. It won't be long before they will need their own laundry.

You clean and paint your new townhouse. You cook a little something each night and watch the local news. There's baseball to listen to, and radio hosts who believe the opposite of what you believe. Three times a week, you meet the boys at a place that makes everything a sort of dessert—bacon pastries and sweet-potato hash browns. The boys grow interested in real estate. They order videos through the mail, study textbooks, watch TV in the wee hours, subscribe to trade magazines. With their mouths full of honey-pecan sausage, they explain good debt and bad debt. They want to become level-six investors, true capitalists, poor-looking all the while—little hat, fields of cattle. They finance their cheap cars in order to build credit. They will own everything jointly and keep a separate account for T&T Enterprises, their laundry. To keep things from getting messy between them, the brothers agree never to get married. You laugh. You two can handle this business, you say, but you wouldn't stand a chance against women.

That's when you should've stopped treating them like the same person, when you should've shed the illusion that they had identical souls. But how could you have known? At that point, as far as you knew, they *were* identical. You should've made Tim the straight-business manager and put Thomas in charge of the dirty business. Other than hanging out in an unlicensed secondhand shop, selling stolen Michael Jackson tapes out of your back room, you didn't know what straight business was. You still don't trust it. You still don't think, for a drug dealer, there's such a thing as good debt. But you should not have forced Tim into a race he wasn't suited to run. Once it became obvious Tim wasn't what his brother was, it was too late. You weren't paying close enough attention. You can't treat brothers differently if they know the reason, if they know it's because one brother can't hack it.

Kyle was sick of people knocking at his door. This time he was in Bright's house, alone, and he knew who it was when he glimpsed the dusty Audi convertible. He could hear the jangling of bracelets in the knock. Kyle did not like to meet with people or attempt anything that might be stressful with bare feet. He slipped his socks and shoes on and pulled back the door. There were those eyes, shackling Kyle. The boss in pink was, today, the boss in purple. Kyle felt a familiar floatiness, like what he'd felt with Johnna. He resolved to masturbate, whether he wanted to or not, as soon as he got rid of the pink boss. He let her in and explained that Bright had gone to the University of Oklahoma with a professor of Indian Studies.

"American or Hindu?"

"I didn't see the guy."

"Well, shit. He already mailed me the paperwork, but I need my payment early. Won't be back this afternoon, will he?"

"I doubt that."

"I'm going to California for eight days."

"What part?" Kyle asked.

"Like, the boring part."

"Park stuff?"

"Old friend that wants to show off her husband and her baby and her shutters and, you know... her fruit tree." She leaned on the back of Bright's easy chair and stared at something. "You got nice wrists," she said. "You should wear dress shirts and roll the sleeves a little."

"I used to have a dress shirt. I spilled gasoline all over it and burned it."

"You should make some effort in your appearance."

"No one sees me."

"Am I no one?" She jutted out a hip.

"How much does Bright owe you?" Kyle asked.

"Four grand."

"I can get that for you."

Kyle went down the hall to the laundry room, to the forty-four grand still sitting in the dryer, and counted out forty fifty-dollar bills and twenty hundreds. He didn't like using any of this money, but he didn't have enough of his own to go around paying people off at four thousand a pop. He rolled the bills tightly and wedged them down in a thermos, then handed the thermos to the pink boss.

"My name is Wendy."

"Wendy?"

"Doesn't fit, right?"

"No, I think it does."

"Cali-fucking-fornia." She put her face in her hands and her nose poked through between her palms. "Last week I had to see this bitch from art school. Chicago." Wendy began berating a layout her friend had gotten published in a journal. The girl's work featured historic scenes drawn from a society of porcupines.

"Can I ask you to do something?" she said. "I want you to grab me by my elbows and jerk me around, like you're shaking sense into me."

Wendy stepped out of her shoes and composed herself, offering her arms reluctantly, turning herself in. Now Kyle was conscious of his wrists—pale and covered with tame swirls of hair. They were not muscular or bony. He wrapped his fingers around her elbows and tightened his grip until she made a noise. She was looking down as if ashamed, letting her hair cover her face.

"I deserve it," she told him.

Kyle moved her stiffly from side to side, feeling like Frankenstein. He steadied himself and pushed her forward and back, enough that her head couldn't keep up with her body and her lavender blouse fell from her shoulders. She made a halfhearted attempt to get free, and Kyle knew this was his cue. He shoved her back against the armrest of the chair, not letting her fall, then he jarred her about in a rhythmless way, tossing her hair and sloshing her bracelets. There was no expression on her face. Kyle lifted her off the ground, digging his fingers into her flesh to keep hold, and the two of them nearly fell.

"Now throw me in a heap," she said. "Toward the carpet, not the steps."

Kyle put a hand on her ribs and a hand in her armpit and slung her with all his might. She was upright in the air a moment, as if she'd leapt off a cliff, then she tumbled and splayed on her back, her skirt bunched around her hips. She took a couple breaths, then sat up. She put a hand through her hair and it regained its form. Now her face was stirred. Kyle imagined she'd wanted to ask someone to do that for a long time. She bounced up and collected her things, gave her skirt a tug, slipped back into her shoes, and swished toward the door. Kyle stopped her on the porch to get an art quote. He wanted her to stay a little longer, wanted to hear her speak more. He half-expected she wouldn't have a quote ready, but she turned pertly and began.

"'I am a believer and a conformist. Anyone can revolt; it is more difficult silently to obey our own interior promptings, and to spend our lives finding sincere and fitting means of expression for our temperaments and our gifts—if we have any. I do not say 'Neither God, nor Master,' only in the end to substitute myself for the God I have excommunicated.'"

Kyle had no way to keep her any longer. She hopped in her car and was gone.

Kyle's interior prompts were not loud or clear, he reflected; they were muttered by his gut. The type of expression that fit his temperament was no expression at all. His gift, realism. Kyle had never had occasion to cast God out because God had never been interested in him. Like the bums of Little Rock, who had never asked him for change, God knew better than to bother with Kyle.

He took a towel to the attic and kneeled before it, imagining a continuation of the episode he and Wendy had shared. He saw her pick herself up from the rug and begin giving him orders. She was on top of him, pinning him, slithering in ways that made her clothes fall off. She said not to worry now. She said Kyle would keep them all safe.

It had been three weeks since Bright had been killed. Swin figured he didn't have long before the cable bill went unpaid and he was left with two fuzzy networks to choose between. He'd had his keys in his hand for two hours and could not set down the remote or pry himself from Bright's easy chair. *Murphy Brown*. Robots fighting. South American stock reports. How hats were made, once.

Swin fired up the minivan and aimed it toward Feston, the town where he and Johnna had seen the kids from Nova Scotia sing. Johnna's pregnancy had given him his first sense of the rushing-by of life. Swin could count the steps to his death: have kids, raise kids, get old, die. He felt tricked—not by Johnna but by luck. You weren't supposed to get a girl pregnant the first time you slept with her. He'd gotten Johnna pregnant because he'd been distracted by Bright's death; the pregnancy was a punishment for not paying attention to one of life's sweet moments. Well, not a punishment; luck didn't care what you thought of it. If your mind was fit enough, you could think of *all* luck as good luck. Swin's mind did not feel fit. His mind felt like a man in a backward country who'd ingested tainted drugs and hadn't slept in days and had an important meeting to attend. Each attempt to get a grip on himself only thickened this man's disorientation. This was no way to think, Swin thought. Why was he rushing his mind into this news instead of trusting it to get its bearings? His mind always got its bearings. And his mind would figure out why Kyle had chosen to tell Johnna everything. There must've been a reason. Kyle, unlike Swin, did not have an unruly mind.

The baby store was three stories, with low-hanging mobiles and lots of cradles in the way. Swin went down an aisle of scrapbooking gear and high-stepped over a stuffed elephant. He saw a narrow door marked BOOKS and when he pushed it open, it revealed a dark staircase. He made his way down and found a light. He was in the basement. He arranged some crates into a chaise longue and opened a window that looked out at ground level onto a drugstore and a flagpole. He made a casual sweep of the stacks. Many of the books could be eliminated by their physical condition—falling apart or warped or emitting a urine smell when moved. Swin felt the reverent calm he always fell into in dim rooms of ignored books. He wished he'd brought a sack lunch, so he could hide down here for the night, approving of himself, validating the toil of these authors.

He began with the books meant for children to read. He planned for his son or daughter to have three or four toys, minimal sports equipment, and a thousand books. He didn't care for the rhymed nonsense of Dr. Seuss, but preferred anything that instilled basic knowledge sets. He could abide a talking animal, but not an inanimate object that spoke. Swin would be careful not to spoil the kid for serious reading; he didn't want books that were mostly pictures or had pop-up images or offered some visual reward for reaching the final page. He found a complete set of biographies about famous thinkers and a set about how different inventions had come to be. None of the books were priced. Swin figured they'd been purchased in one lot, for next to nothing, and the owner of this baby store didn't consider them hot enough items to pick through and price and shelve upstairs. Swin could likely get them for a quarter apiece. Twenty cents. Whatever he offered. And he had a van. He went on to check the entire back wall, discovering books about musical instruments, forms of government, dinosaurs, Roman deities, bullies. He piled the books on the staircase, leaving a passage in the middle.

Time for something *he* could read. He snatched a dozen volumes at random and reclined on the crates he'd set up. He learned about infant sleep, infant coordination. He read about behavioral disorders that struck at random and had no cure, little sociopaths who had the same feelings for humans as they had for plastic grapes. Swin was happy to learn that parents with diverse genetic material made better babies, like the opposite of inbreeding. He wondered what Johnna's IQ was, and whether he would consider her well adjusted. He was going to be a fucking dad. There would be a brand-new family in existence and Swin would be its leader.

He loaded hundreds of titles into the minivan, filling the entire back cargo area, and handed the old woman a wad of bills. Once back on the county road, he checked his phone and saw a message waiting. He knew the area code: Kentucky. It was the private investigator. Swin had built up the courage to ask for a report on his mother and sisters. The PI started with Swin's mother, who, as Swin knew, did not work. She did go somewhere each afternoon from say one to three-thirty, returning just before the girls got home from school. Wherever it was she went, she went simply dressed, carrying a small, black case, and always waited until Swin's stepdad, who came home for lunch each day, had gone back to work. Both parents were home in the evenings—content, almost sedate. His mother had come out on the porch last night with something to drink and stared at nothing for an hour until one of Swin's sisters disturbed her. But, the investigator reassured him, all middle-aged women were wistful—every single one. He said he could contact the oldest sister, drop a note somewhere only she would get it. The note could advise her to skip school on a certain day and meet Swin at a remote spot. Drop a note? No way, Swin thought. Swin didn't like the idea of the investigator doing more than observing. He didn't want the guy contacting his sister. Rosa took walks at night, the investigator's message continued, around the block, when the neighborhood was quiet. As for the other sisters, the youngest was a small version of the mother. The tenth-grader was in the clouds—distracted and skinny, a long-distance runner who did no primping and was still the beauty of the bunch. The one that was thirteen was involved in everything. She always came home right at dinnertime, laden with boxes and outfits and posters. None of them seemed to have any major problems. The PI signed off, saying he needed to take a monthlong nap.

Beauty of the bunch? Swin didn't want this scumbag getting attached to one of his sisters—a professional stalker. It was time to give him specific questions and forty-eight hours to answer them. Swin wanted to know where his mother went in the afternoons and whether his two oldest sisters had boyfriends. He simply wanted to make sure his sisters were how he'd left them, which for the most part they seemed to be, except that Swin's stepdad must have relaxed the rules. Before, each child was forced to participate in two extracurricular activities—no more, no less—and no one was allowed to take walks at night. The girls weren't permitted to leave the house unless every hair was in place, and there were constant chores.

The dark thought Swin couldn't resist, blowing through a short tunnel and past a gang of weary sheep, was of the private investigator jerking off to fantasies of four island sisters dressed in tight outfits, play-fighting one another for the right to sponge his wrinkled old pecker.

Kyle had been calling Her for days with no answer. It had been a long time since the last packet. Kyle was worried that he and Swin had been cut off, or that something had happened to Her.

Saturday morning he drove the minivan to her trailer park, parked a couple blocks away, and strolled past the pampered parcels of lawn. Kyle knocked several times and heard no stirring. The stand by the door was bare. He circled the place, the grass resilient under his feet, looking for nothing in particular. And finding nothing—blankets on the windows, resounding silence. Maybe she got her wish, Kyle thought. He remembered her speech about wanting to be struck dead, about being afraid to commit suicide and wanting the Lord to strike her dead. Maybe it had happened. Kyle stood under Her's carport, wondering whether he should break into her house, and there he saw the packet, almost touching his knee, sitting atop a case of organic soap. Her wasn't dead. She was sitting in there being difficult. Why the hell hadn't she called? Or maybe she had and Kyle and Swin had missed the call. Kyle, frustrated, spat forcefully onto Her's doorstep.

Emerging onto the gravel driveway, he was stared down by that old man, the neighbor with the sunglasses pushed up on his head. When the man began to speak, Kyle said, "Tell the woman who lives here that a no-good thug was snooping around and you scared him off." Kyle walked past him and paced down the middle of the street.

In the van, he checked out the next trip. Hardy, Arkansas. Chevy Malibu. First they had to go to a town called Cobin—it sounded familiar. Saturday the twenty-first? That was today. They had to be in Hardy in... ten hours. What the hell was Her's problem? Kyle raced home, realizing in stages that he didn't have to panic. Ten hours was enough time.

He and Swin ate and packed. Swin figured Cobin was forty-five minutes away, in the flat, soybean country. The Malibu would be waiting for them behind an old children's museum. Since they didn't know a thing about Cobin other than what Swin got from his *Lost Arkansas* travel book, Kyle didn't want to leave the minivan sitting there overnight. He didn't care about the van itself, and especially not the hundreds of books in the back of it, but he didn't want anyone wondering why the van was there. Johnna could've dropped them off, but Swin said that was out of the question. Even though she was basically living with them now, she didn't have to be involved in their work. So the only way to get to Cobin was to take a cab and get dropped in the town square. The cab company was a half hour from the park and had a fleet of two cars.

The driver had a bowl cut and high-top sneakers, and he drove a Camry station wagon. He claimed to be a master of many professions. He asked if anyone had ever heard the term "Renaissance man," and Swin said no, he hadn't. The driver told Swin he was looking at one—a graphic computer artist with a passion for working wood. He recounted an argument he'd had at a flea market involving a guy who carved famous logos with a chain saw. This fool with his Husqvarna thought he was hot, but he couldn't create his own designs, was limited when it came to detail, and stank the place up with exhaust. The driver slowed in front of a fragmented tree stump. He hopped out, heaved the largest piece into his trunk, then resumed the journey. Kyle asked for his card and was handed a wafer of bark with a name and number etched into it.

"Tinsel plant?" the driver asked.

"How's that?" said Kyle.

"You boys got spots at the Christmas factory?"

"No," Swin said. "We tried to work there last year, but it's all politics at that place."

"They opened a new building for tree-toppers," the driver said. "Everybody's sick of angels. Know I am."

Swin stared out his window. "We're Ivy League students on a new kind of fall break. We go to places nobody would want to, and get to them in ways nobody would want to."

"Learn about the real folks, huh?"

"Being poor and handy doesn't necessarily make you real," Swin said.

"No?"

"Being threatened," Kyle broke in. "Having your life threatened makes you real."

The driver mulled this over, then fell into a tour-guide mode, pointing out where things had burned or where tornadoes had blown through. He coasted into downtown Cobin and rocked to a stop in front of a barber school. Kyle handed him a fifty and the man thanked him and asked if maybe he needed an ornament, not one that was knocked into shape by a machine in a factory, but a sample of old-fashioned craftsmanship. He held up a display box of holly sprigs and sleighs, five dollars each. Swin put his face close to the display for a long time, then said sure, he'd take five for twenty.

The pink spiral on top of the children's museum looked very close, but in fact Kyle and Swin walked seven blocks before reaching it. The back lot was hidden by some kind of quarry, also abandoned, and there was the Chevy.

In Hardy, they exchanged the Malibu for a Caprice Classic, an old cop car that, as they cruised the main strip of town looking for a place to eat, they couldn't help fidgeting in. The bolts and flat hooks that had once held the caging were still there, as were the switches for the lights and sirens, now attached to nothing. They felt conspicuous in the cruiser, disliked; cars around them drove straight and stiff. Kyle wondered how many guys had taken the ride in this very car, guys in shock, wondering about a lawyer, wanting to cry or bash the window out with their foreheads, while the cop sat where Kyle sat, fiddling with his radio, sat up here chewing on mints and wondering where everybody was meeting for darts.

Kyle and Swin made it back to Cobin and again waited for the cab driver in the Camry, who drove them back and dropped them off at the market where Swin had met Johnna. Swin called Johnna for a ride and he and Kyle sat under the awning to wait, getting nodded at by everyone who entered. One guy stopped short in front of them, snapped his fingers, and said, "Bright's boys."

They kept quiet.

"I left a note, little ways back."

Kyle thought. Something about the guy smelled like a cop, smelled like the car he'd driven around earlier that day. "Cooper," he said.

"Lawfully yours."

Kyle didn't want Cooper to ask why they were sitting in front of the market, why they needed a ride. A helpful cop was the worst kind.

"Yeah, Bright got transferred," Kyle said. "Supposed to be a little training trip, then they kept him there permanent."

"Where at?"

"Oklahoma."

"I'm Suarez," Swin said. "This is Mollar. You off duty today?"

"Off as I get. We need a couple barrels for the PAL field."

"Well," said Kyle. "We'll let Bright know you were looking for him."

Kyle stood and Swin followed, the two of them hedging toward the front lot.

"Come on out to Stumbler's Tuesday," Cooper said. "Green building on 411. You can't miss it."

"We just might do that," said Swin.

"It's trivia. Everybody likes trivia."

"Thanks."

"We'll make you have a good time, the hard way or the easy way." Cooper made a clicking sound with his cheek, then swung around and went inside.

Kyle and Swin shuffled up the road in the direction Johnna would come from, veering into the weeds when cars passed, watching the farthest hill for a clay-colored hooptie.

"I know who doesn't like trivia," Swin said. "Kyle Ribb."

The next day, Swin rented a video called *Savannah Smiles* and watched it out in the minivan. This was his sisters' favorite movie. They used to watch it hundreds of times and whenever they did Swin would act put out but would plop onto the couch and stare at it beginning to end, keeping his tears in with great effort. It was dusk now. A fervent wind blew, finding nothing to whistle against but the van. Swin rolled up a blanket to lean on and hit the play button. The movie was about two convicts—one tall, one short. The short one was in charge of scaring up meals, meals that the tall one always found fault with. The tall convict made gruff, astute remarks about the fact that half the world was rich and half the world was poor. Savannah, adorable and ignored, was from the rich half. Her father was an ambitious politician who held dinner parties at which he put on airs. Events conspired to force the convicts to kidnap Savannah. The short convict took to her right away, while the tall one viewed her as a dangerous nuisance. Savannah taught the convicts games and songs. Over the course of the movie, the tall convict accepted that his life was ruined and worthless, and also, despite himself, grew to love Savannah.

On her lunch break, Johnna got Max, her favorite patient, out of his room and wheeled him to the hump of a small hill. They had a view of the clinic. Max was senile and for this reason Johnna wasn't afraid to give him the snuff he was always asking for. He spit in his plastic cup and told the only two stories he had left, the one about riding the freight train and the one about seeing the dancing girls. Max gave Johnna a jar of barbecue sauce each day and each morning she sneaked it back into his room.

"Suspension bridges are amazing," he said. Then a minute later, "How's your love life, dear?"

Johnna pulled a sugar packet from her chest pocket and emptied it down her throat. It gave her a shiver.

"Love life's swell, Max. The guy that knocked me up is sticking to me like white on rice."

"Those shoes are damned unattractive."

Johnna turned her feet in and admired them. "This outfit is the reason Swin fell for me."

"What's a Swin?"

Johnna huffed, conceding that it was a valid question. "A Swin is a rambunctious, handsome boy whose own intelligence is a burden to him."

"You an Arkansas girl?" Max asked.

"Am now. I'm a convert."

"You're almost a mama. Means your mama's almost a grandmama."

"Mama's dead," Johnna told him.

He snorted.

Johnna's mother had raised her in Texas. Johnna was an only child and had had no contact with her cousins because her mother had been ostracized from the family. Her mother had fallen in love with her nephew, who was only six years her junior, because he always did unpleasant chores for her and ate her food and understood her moods. She turned down an offer of marriage from the fire chief, and from that day forward was thought of as nuts.

Johnna's mother wore a lot of turquoise jewelry. Her favorite thing to call Johnna, when Johnna acted up, was "numbskull." When the nephew stopped coming over, she complained incessantly about her monkey grass and took to having rum for dinner and just a slice of white bread before bed. Her only passion in life was her nephew. She never committed to a career or a hobby. Johnna had been in high school when her mother had her heart attack. Afterward, Johnna lived for two years in a well-appointed shelter where she ate jam on everything and read newspapers.

"Shit, Max." Johnna scrambled over and righted his spit cup. He'd dozed off and spilled on his pant leg. She dumped out what was left and gave the cup back to him. She'd have to wash his pants herself, so no one would know he'd had snuff.

"When my old lady died." Max made a face, swallowing some tobacco juice. "My old lady died, she didn't know who anybody was, but she knew a thousand movie-star birthdays. Every morning she'd rattle off three or four."

It wasn't hard to relish each day when you saw as many old people as Johnna saw, as many people who'd managed to accumulate money and retain dignity and raise families only to have it all go down the drain in their last years. Johnna had no desire to live a long life. Everyone was always claiming that life went fast, but that wasn't her experience. Days were as limitless for her now as when she was a teenager. Each hour still had its own personality, and if it didn't she could fill it up with her memories. She could walk herself through her younger days.

In high school, Johnna could never bring herself to preen. She couldn't bring herself to tell the gossips what boy she liked and then wait for that boy to find out. She liked boys who had unique hair and a bashful, snide way about them. Because she was pretty, she had to press herself on these boys. They often thought a joke was being played, but if she held her head close to theirs long enough, they'd kiss her. They'd kiss her like they were in hell and she was iced tea. A week later, when she moved on, they would accept her departure with docility, happy with what little they'd gotten. She'd been a confusing case—a girl with nerdy glasses who was eager to talk to anyone during school hours but couldn't be found at night or on weekends, who kissed dozens of boys but didn't do more than kiss, who either aced classes or failed them.

Sophomore year she went out for soccer. She thought the girls looked cute in their cleats and shin guards and a lot of the games took place during school hours. She didn't understand soccer; she would run down the field dozens of times without touching the ball and the coach would praise her. At halftime the girls would put on lipstick and straighten their socks. These girls had money. They were pleasant to Johnna out of a courtesy that had been trained into them. One game, while everyone was in a bunch awaiting a corner kick, Johnna picked out a girl on the other team and, when the ball came floating into the box, rammed the girl from behind, sending her sprawling into the goal post. Three of the girl's teeth were knocked out. Johnna received a red card. The principal called her down to his office and said she was off the soccer team. He asked her to sign a disciplinary report, and to see what would happen, she refused. The principal watched the wall behind Johnna for a time, then sighed and dismissed her.

"I'm free to go?" she said.

The principal put on a snooty face. "We can't *make* you sign it."

Junior year, she had a crush on her history teacher. He wore pants that were too big for him and showed the video of his trip to Australia every chance he got. Johnna started holding his gaze longer than normal, until he'd smirk and

148

look away. Brushing past him after class, she would touch his hip. She would tell him he looked nice and he would scoff. Her grades in his class improved. He stopped calling on her. When he stood outside during the passing period to count down the seconds, singing to everyone that they were going to be late, Johnna stood behind him and mimicked him. She used her French book to construct amorous declarations, which he pretended not to understand. Johnna felt the power she had. During quiet reading time, when this teacher would try to foster a dreamy tone in the room—telling the class to focus on the gong of the flagpole, the shouts from the distant ball field, the buzzing of a fly—Johnna would sit there with her book shut, feeling sharp, pressing her breasts against her T-shirt, knowing he wouldn't return her glare. After school one day she went into his classroom and propped herself on his desk, right on a stack of quizzes about some embargo. She slipped her glasses off and dropped them on the desk. She mussed his hair and he turned purple. His voice splintered when he told her to get down. She tossed her head back and tied her T-shirt up in a knot, slid toward him until her brown tummy was inches from his nose. His face was bright with pain. She wanted to giggle at him, in his rolling chair. When he shoved off from the desk, Johnna nearly pitched forward. He backed himself into a corner and slipped out of the chair, his body crumpling.

"Stop it, Johnna," he said. "I'm begging, okay? You win."

"What do I win?"

"Just stop."

"God," said Johnna. "Don't cry."

But he did. Johnna felt adult and mean. Her mouth went sticky. She untied her T-shirt and smoothed the creases, found her glasses. She kneeled, not wanting to look down on him, and he pressed his eyes shut.

Senior year, Johnna started watching Del Dial. Del didn't take normal classes. He was allowed to haunt the library all day, writing articles that were published in magazines, his only friends the librarians. Sometimes, when everyone else was in class, he roamed the halls with his hands clasped behind his back. He had a lock of colorless hair that flopped from one side of his forehead to the other.

The last week of school, Johnna walked out of an awards ceremony and went to the library. No Del. She wandered the halls, checked the bus loop, checked by the trailers—nothing. She sat on a brick planter near her locker, feeling cheated, letting her eyes zone out. Half of the lockers were wagging open. Johnna felt no attachment to the school, yet didn't feel ready to leave it.

She heard the tread of soft shoes and caught Del out of the corner of her eye. It was like a movie; right when she'd given up, here he was. He'd have to walk right in front of her. His lock of hair was undecided, hung forward. Johnna stuck her leg out, planting her foot against a locker, and Del slowed gradually before coming to a stop.

"What are you contemplating?" Johnna asked.

He looked at her leg, starting where her skin sprang tanly from her shorts, stopping a moment at the knee, squinting toward the ankle.

"What were you contemplating before you started contemplating my leg?"

"Is this a toll situation?"

"I can't *make* you sit down. That's how the principal would say it."

Del shrugged with his cheeks and sat. Johnna set her foot down slowly and edged toward him, not wanting to frighten him.

"I like your jeep," she said.

"My dad gave it to me. It's military issue."

"It's one high car."

"It's a hunk of shit. None of the gauges work."

Del was sweating with nerves but had no problem studying Johnna's cleavage. Her skin was shiny with the heat.

"I go with the traffic," he said. "And I get gas once a week. I always drive to the same places."

"Never been on a date, have you?"

"I thought those were out of style."

"Never drank. Never did drugs."

"I've done heroin. It was research for a piece."

"You should write a piece on girls."

Del flattened his hands onto his thighs, drying his palms. His fingers were reddish and he had huge writing calluses on his right hand. Johnna leaned against him and crossed her legs. She took his hand, guided it under her shirt, and pressed it to her. Del sat bolt upright and gazed raptly into an open locker. He pressed his fingertips against her bra, tugged it insistently, fumbling.

"Shove it out of the way," Johnna said.

He got to the skin. She felt his callus against her nipple. She let him get his fill of both breasts, waited until he was heartened enough to squeeze them, then she pulled his hand back out and he stared at it like he'd never seen it before.

After high school, Johnna signed on with a temp agency and found that she excelled at any traditionally female job, anything organizational or bookkeepy, anything at a hospital, anything involving phones. She excelled at most anything. She was hired full-time at a lingerie-distribution warehouse—aisles and aisles and shelves and shelves and crates and crates of underwear. She started out filling orders and was soon overseeing the filling of orders, soon running the shipping and receiving department. She was signing for truckloads and people were coming to her to request days off. After six months, she was sort of comanaging the place, still earning her starting wage of eleven dollars an hour.

One day she sought out the actual manager, a fairly young guy named Toby who spent his days in a cluster of small, carpeted rooms that served as the warehouse offices. These rooms were dim and empty. Toby had desks back there, some plastic file trays, copy and fax machines. Several times a day, Johnna would get a creepy feeling on the back of her neck and turn to see Toby spying on her from the shadows of the office area, and he would scurry back in.

When Johnna sought him out, in the deepest, best-hidden of the office rooms, he seemed as though he'd been expecting her. He sat squarely behind his desk, feet flat on the floor. The office was tidy, a bunch of brand-new pens in a cup. Toby's diploma, from the University of Central Florida, was prominently displayed.

"I know why you're here," he said.

"You do?" There wasn't a chair on Johnna's side of the desk, so she came to the center of the room and stood there. Toby looked at her warily, like he'd just woken up and had been pushed in front of a searchlight. Johnna knew all too well what was wrong with him. He was bewitched, smitten, whatever you wanted to call it. Instead of simply asking her on a date the first day she'd showed up at the warehouse, he'd let himself become ruined with obsession. He was a fairly successful guy, fairly good-looking.

"Toby," Johnna said.

Toby coughed, a fake cough to help him recover himself. "You're too good for this place, probably too good to even *manage* this place. Corporate will only allow one boss here. For everybody else, fifteen an hour's the roof."

"I don't want a raise," Johnna said. "I want a responsibility reduction."

Toby straightened even more, stretching his neck. He wanted to see Johnna's feet, to see every bit of her at once. "That's not really a bell you can unring. You can try to hold yourself down, but you'll keep popping up to the top, like a..."

"Like a football in a pool?"

"Sure. Any air-filled object in any body of water."

"It sounds like you're firing me," Johnna said.

"I couldn't bring myself to do such a thing. I'm suggesting, for your own good, that you resign."

"When you make eleven dollars an hour, it's called quitting."

Toby nodded. There was a little panic in him now. He knew Johnna was about to leave and that he might never see her again.

Soon Johnna figured out that she needed to go to nursing school. In nursing, there wasn't much in the way of a chain of command, your coworkers were mostly women, and the pay was excellent. Johnna financed her education by doing the books at a car lot. She had no set hours at the lot, which allowed her to take extra classes and finish in just under two years. A couple clinics near the school offered to hire her, but Johnna, not sure why, turned them down. She took a couple weeks off and drove around on country roads, lost, which led to yet another discouraging encounter with a guy, a kid Johnna's age who was a guide at an underground lake. He took Johnna out on the calm water in a canoe and started crying, blubbering about his ex-girlfriends and the various musicians they'd run off with. He had one of his most recent girlfriend's fuzzy pink socks in his jacket pocket, and he threw them into the water, an act meant to prove that he was over this girl. The guide then lunged at Johnna, trying to grope her, and the canoe nearly capsized.

Johnna sat at home and went through stacks of papers she'd accumulated during her time at the nursing school—flyers for seminars, classroom handouts, magazine order forms. She came across a sheet that explained reciprocity. With her Texas nursing license, Johnna could work in a number of states, one of which was Arkansas, a state that was only forty miles away and that had always exerted a faint pull on her. To Johnna, Arkansas had a cozy, tucked-away quality. Also an underdoggish quality. It seemed a place for common sense and minding one's own business. The next day, Johnna's last free issue of *Advanced Nursing* arrived in the mail, and in it was a want ad for an energetic, team-oriented nurse. "Come to the Natural State," the ad read. "Laidback living in the Ozark foothills. Sign-on bonus." Johnna imagined nurses from all over the country racing toward southern Arkansas. They were coming by train, jet, automobile, however they could, packing the local hotels, clogging the dusty roads. Johnna called the phone number and was relieved to find that the position had not been filled. She showered, packed enough for a night or two, and got on the road. In an hour and a half she was approaching the clinic. The dirt roads were not clogged with eager nurses. The hotel—well, she didn't see a hotel. At the clinic she was sent straight to the director of nursing, who shot the shit with her for ten minutes and then hired her. No pressure-packed interview. No selection process. The director sent her to a small apartment complex where she signed a lease. She brought her bag into her new apartment and sat in the middle of the carpet. She'd made a new life for herself in one day. Her head was in a slow spin. Arkansas. She would stay here as long as she wanted to, and then she would leave. Johnna thought about the fact that she had never felt like Texas understood her. She had often felt at odds with the windy, hot weather, with the widened Southern accent, with the vastness, that famous size that Texans took as some kind of accomplishment. Johnna had always thought of Texas as a bully.

Swin had been working for hours in one of Bright's yellow rooms, turning it into a nursery. He'd painted the ceiling like a dusky sky and adorned the walls with geometric shapes. Swin was more unsure than ever about his and Kyle's predicament, about the scope and urgency of their problems, about how their lives were coming together. Swin, lately, felt oppressed by a diffuse tension born of the fact that with each day that passed he felt more placid and more like he belonged in this Arkansas life, but at the same time he felt less certain about anything having to do with Frog or the Parks Department. Anything was possible. Swin found himself trying to convince Kyle that Frog didn't exist, that "Frog" was a company name, or that if there *had* been a real Frog at one time, by now he'd fled the country or something. Swin found himself asking the same questions over and over. Why had no one come for the money? Where did Her's packets come from? He found himself believing Her could be the boss of the whole thing. And what about the boss in pink? They had no proof that she worked for the Parks Department. Maybe she'd had something on Bright. Or perhaps they all worked for an enormous foreign cartel. It took operations like that a long time to notice they were being stolen from. Swin could think himself silly with these kinds of thoughts, but he knew the important thing wasn't figuring it all out. What mattered was remaining vigilant, keeping the guard up. Things had gone okay to this point and they would continue to go okay.

Swin had hung a mobile of the solar system, stood some of the baby books on an antique postman's desk, and found a wooden trunk that would hold a couple toys. Swin didn't know how long he would live in this house, didn't know if one day soon he'd have to grab Johnna and flee, but it appeared likely that they'd at least be around for Johnna to have the baby, and Swin wanted each day his child had to spend in this backward place to be the least bad day it could be. If his child got to enjoy Swin's nursery for one hour, the work would be justified.

Swin took a break and joined Johnna in the living room. She was straightening up, her attention on a talk-show host who was explaining the psychological need for curse words. Johnna had placed a doily on the television and hung lace around the windows. In the kitchen she was bringing along a citrus theme, anchored by a huge bowl of browning lemons.

"Know what Jews do?" Swin said. "Not American Jews but the real ones. They give babies a book with honey soaked into it, to suck on."

"Books are dirty."

"That's the attitude the Jews are trying to avoid."

"Ought to avoid germs." Johnna plucked a cereal bowl off the end table.

"So I need to borrow your car, whenever your next weekend is."

"Why *my* car?"

"It's not a trip," Swin said. "It's not work. It's just… something."

Swin wasn't about to take the van and have Kyle bitching and asking a thousand questions. As for Johnna, though she was about as trustworthy as they came, she was still of the genus Woman, and could still fall prey to feminine desires for family connection. Swin didn't want her to know that he was going to check on his sisters, didn't want her to know where they lived, because he didn't want her trying to contact them behind his back, trying to fix things for him.

"Old girlfriend?" Johnna asked.

"Not quite."

Johnna stepped into the kitchen and ran the water.

"I wouldn't mind you knowing every single thing I do," Swin said. "It's just better for you if you don't."

"You sound stupid when you say stuff like that."

"Don't you think it's sexy?"

"I never thought anything was sexy in my life. You can take the car, but I need to change the oil if you're headed out of state."

"I am."

"Want to learn how to change oil? I could show you."

They heard footsteps on the porch and Swin told Johnna not to mention his trip to Kyle, who bumbled in with his hands full and handed Johnna a clock. Instead of numbers, it had different fruits. Johnna thanked Kyle warmly but said she couldn't use it. She was going strictly citrus, not apples and grapes and any old thing.

"Why'd you get a soda?" she asked. "We got that here."

"Value meal."

Kyle's yellow bowl and numerous small cups were from the Japanese fast-food place. It took him several minutes to parcel out his sauces and seasonings and ginger strips.

"California rolls, fried rice, and chicken satay." Swin grunted. "They're threatening Japan—not exactly hitting it."

"These lemons are about done for," Johnna said. "Y'all got any mint?"

"Think so," said Kyle, mouth full. "The cabinet right there."

Kyle heard a car and stopped chewing. He swallowed the whole lump in his mouth and peered out the window.

"The elderly frat boy came back."

"The who?" Johnna brought her attention out of the cabinet and sneezed at the dried mint in her hand.

"Determined," said Kyle. He walked down the hall and into the bathroom.

Swin hurried to the door and opened it before the guy could knock, then sat at the kitchen table and waited for a head to pop in, which it soon did, in a ski cap, followed by the rest of the guy. Cap'n Crunch T-shirt. Sweatpants.

"Oh," Johnna said. "You never called."

"I was far away. I didn't want to torture you."

"I believe I remember this," said Swin. "Your daddy the rich tree remover was buddies with Bright, and since Papa croaked, you want to annoy all his friends."

"Why don't you fetch him for me. I'll keep the lady company."

"Sour timing. He got transferred to Oklahoma."

"What for?"

"They needed him."

"Where in Oklahoma?"

"A new park near Stillwater."

"Come on, where is he?"

"Why don't you leave your number again?"

"When I find out he's not in Stillwater, I'll just come back here."

"Why would I care if you spoke to Bright or not?"

"Who's thirsty?" Johnna had water and ice and mint in a pitcher and was pressing a lemon against the table, rolling it around under her palm. She reached back and grabbed a knife out of the dish drainer.

"You must have her drugged," the guy said. "Lady like that settling for a junior ranger."

"You dress like you're on the JV snowboarding team."

The guy stepped farther into the room and shut the door behind him. "Found out where Copernicus is from. Also found out that the rest of the Latin world hates Ricans because they butcher the language."

"I'm thinking it might be best if you take your lemonade and go."

"Believe I will. Why bother myself when I can have someone else figure all this out? A professional. The best private investigator in Baton Rouge owes me a favor and I've already talked to him about you all."

"Good," Swin said. "It's been a long time since we've had a professional *anything* around here."

"I'm a professional," Johnna said.

"*You* must know where Bright is," the guy said to her. "Huh, darling? Every time I come over, you guys are hanging out in here, nothing to do, acting suspicious."

Kyle emerged from the hallway with a crowbar. As the guy began to turn, Kyle clubbed him in the back of the head. He raised the crowbar again, but there was no need. The guy slumped, then gently toppled onto the ceramic tile. Johnna dropped the thermos and lemonade glugged over the floor. Kyle knelt and removed the guy's ski cap. He wasn't bleeding but he was dead. The crowbar had struck him at the base of his skull and broken his neck. Swin picked up the thermos and sat Johnna down. She was shaking, staring at the guy's face, which looked like a distorted modern sculpture, pinkish liquid escaping the mouth and nose.

"What the fuck?" said Swin.

"I got to do CPR," Johnna said.

"Not this time." Kyle spoke to her softly. "We have too many chores to do."

"What the fuck?" Swin repeated.

Kyle ignored him. He stayed composed. He explained that he and Swin would get rid of the body and the 4Runner, and Johnna had to disinfect the whole area by the door and clean the carpet. Then she had to retrace their steps where they'd carried the wrapped body to the car, to get any hair or fluid that might've fallen.

"Fluid?" she repeated.

"We have to do these things without thinking about them."

Kyle thumbed through the guy's wallet, looking for the number of the PI the frat boy had threatened them with. Lots of plastic. Beachy photos with too many people in them. AAA. Hyatt rewards. Insurance. Video store. Between a couple ten-dollar bills was an unlabeled number on a slip of white paper. Kyle didn't recognize the area code.

He dialed. He dreaded hearing a raspy voice, trained to sound jaded. This voice would ask for a short description of the case, giving the impression that no matter what it was, it happened a hundred times a week in every neighborhood. Go ahead and put me to sleep; that would be the voice's meaning. Or else the voice would be flat, not unkind, the voice of an ex-cop who'd found religion, who said his name and then said, "What can I do you for?" After a few rings, Kyle was clicked over to an automated system which listed many regional headquarters in the voice of a classy woman who'd gone wild. Kyle chose Tampa for no reason, becoming sure that the number he'd dialed wasn't a PI. They wanted Kyle's age and he gave it. They wanted to know if he was male or female, if he was gay or straight. They wanted him to rate how active he was. The woman's voice said a computer would choose the best vacation for Kyle and he'd be transferred to customer service. He hung up.

To Swin, the rest of the day went in fast-forward. It was strange that he and

Kyle knew what to do, strange to be digging another grave. Swin felt sorry for the aged frat boy. One was supposed to be allowed some verbal jousting, some threatening and bluffing, without having to die over it. Swin had drawn him in, had goaded the frat boy. And Swin had had the situation under control. Kyle had overreacted. Kyle couldn't read people like Swin could. In Kyle's world, consequences were too prescribed. He was paranoid; that was the only way to put it. Of course, Swin couldn't tell Kyle he was paranoid without making himself seem the opposite of paranoid, which was... well, feeling a false sense of security. Swin certainly didn't feel *that*. He didn't feel secure.

They didn't bury the frat boy near Bright. They took him to a muddy hollow on the other side of the pond. This time they did not go the full six feet deep. They flipped the dirt back in at an almost frantic pace, then rolled a couple rotting tree trunks onto the spot. Then they drove up and sank the 4Runner in the swamp near Little Rock. The whole business was over by two in the morning and Swin and Kyle were in the van, barreling back into the hills.

"Who needs a gun?" Swin said. "*Shit.*"

"That guy would've sunk us."

"Maybe not."

"Maybe's enough."

"It's our ship now? We have the title?"

"It's keeping us afloat. If it sinks, we drown."

"Okay," said Swin. "I still don't think you had to do that."

"If you haven't noticed, we're in pretty deep. Getting in a little deeper doesn't make much difference. Going to jail would, though. That would make a difference."

"Well, you shouldn't scare Johnna like that. Not while she's pregnant."

"I hope not to have to do it again."

"Let's not kid ourselves and say you *had* to do that."

"How was I supposed to know if he was bluffing about the PI? My gut told me I had to do it, so I had to do it."

"Your gut again," exclaimed Swin.

"If you get a feeling like it's him or you, you better trust that feeling. You better not say, '*Him?* Really?' That's probably how we'll die. Someone will feel that way about us." Kyle leaned forward and squashed a bug against the windshield. "This wasn't a bad thing that happened."

Swin dug his tongue into his cheek.

"It was good for us and it was good for Johnna," Kyle said. "It was only bad for old... Barry?"

"Good for Johnna?"

"Now she's one of us."

———————

Stumbler's was tidy and high-roofed. The only people in the place were cops—seven of them. Cooper wasn't there; he was pulling an all-night watch at a rest home that had been vandalized, but he'd told the other cops to expect Mollar and Suarez and they'd been greeted affably and offered stools. Everyone crowded the bar, eyes on a TV above the liquor bottles which displayed question after question. Each man gripped a remote answer pad, answering questions about movie stars and rock bands.

The cops sported similar hair and clothing, had names like Jeremy and Jake and Jack. After a few beers, Kyle couldn't tell them apart. He could not follow their running inside jokes. These cops were treating Kyle and Swin like old buddies, buying Kyle's beer and allowing Swin to make fun of their boundless knowledge of celebrity feuds. They were trying to show the outsiders that cops were regular, good dudes. Or Kyle and Swin *weren't* outsiders. They were fellow low-ranking authority figures. Anyway, it made Kyle nervous, which made him drink faster, one draft Michelob after another. This was another chore, coming down here and pacifying these cops with his presence—always another chore. Kyle would've traded a week in the booth to get out of it. Cops made his skin crawl. Luckily, this was Swin's sort of chore.

Swin was working on a bottle of pink wine he'd brought from home. He'd introduced the owner of the bar, a man with mutton chops who tried to keep his nose in a book about submarines, to the practice of corkage fees. The cops chided Swin for drinking wine and he steered into the skid, swirling and sniffing and holding out his pinkie. Swin guessed at their inside jokes—two remarks in particular they kept repeating: "Somewhere on the seventh floor" and "I'll be your campaign manager." The first one, Swin said, referred to a mild hazing ritual in which a rookie cop was told to go check for evidence on the seventh floor of a six-story building. The campaign manager thing had to do with the overblown desire of some cops to be named lead investigator for even the pettiest crime—indecent exposure, truancy. "Lead investigator?" the cops scoffed. They were friendly, dumb guys. Kyle knew he didn't need to worry about them. The only advantage cops had was time; they waited and waited, not even knowing what for, and then eventually you screwed yourself.

Not Kyle, though. Kyle had no greed and no ego. He took what came to him. A park came, he took it. He would stay alert, go on his trips, cook Bright's muck, keep the park clean, smile at old ladies, and once in a while bring Swin down here to charm these cops.

1991

Thomas and Tim, now forging through their early twenties, have never killed anyone or beaten anyone or even threatened anyone, and this begins to worry you. Little Rock's crime rate keeps nudging higher, the bad neighborhoods claiming another street and another. You can feel that you and the boys have competition of the worst kind—unorganized, desperate. To this point, Thomas and Tim have worked around this swell of grubby hoodlums, but it only takes one confrontation, one clash in which neither party has a side alley to sneak down, a face-saving route of escape. The need for animal toughness has not found Thomas and Tim on its own, so you will bring it to them. One far-off day they'll remember all the pains you took to make them the best, how they rose from farm boys who'd never been on a farm to expert criminals.

You choose Steve, pretty much a drunk, a guy you pay to paint high awnings, clean the basement, do yard work. Steve has a ponytail and symbolic tattoos. He fancies himself to have strong Indian blood, which you doubt. With the thousand dollars you're paying him, he plans to buy a canoe made of reeds and pitch and also a deep freeze. He will be able to catch fish and freeze them. He accepts the offer without thinking about it, perhaps scared to think about it. You tell him to come back that night, sober.

You call Thomas and Tim and tell them to meet you on a mud road that runs through a swamp east of town, a spot where the city is planning to grow rice. You caught a junkie trying to break into the bakery, you tell them. He's got to be working for someone. You tell them to bring whatever they'll need. It's their show.

They arrive with a canvas beach bag that contains gloves, Clorox, rope, elastic cords, tape, and a few yards of steel wire. You tell them they have until midnight, that a proper Q & A takes no longer than twenty minutes. Steve is relieved at this. You step back and lean on the hood of your car. Steve's wrists and ankles are already tied, but the boys decide to bind him to a pine tree. They undo and retie the knots three or four times. You point to your watch and say, "Tick, tick."

Here is where the difference between the boys fully shows up. Thomas looks Steve in the eye and his movements are certain and rigid, while Tim seems to have shrunk, capable only of grunts that answer his brother's questions. Steve sees it, keeps his attention on Thomas. Steve's eyes blink crazily and he sweats, wanting to be asked something, wanting to get on with it already.

When all the knots are secure, Thomas reaches in the bag for the steel wire. Tim starts to speak but doesn't. Steve says, "What's that—" and Thomas slugs him in the stomach. Steve wants to double over but the ropes hold him tall. It wasn't Thomas's best punch; he drifted on it. He tries again, stepping into it, and Steve spits up and looks over at you through his hair.

"That's *our* boss," Thomas tells him. "Now who's yours?"

Steve gets his breath lined up, presses down his foot to stop it from tapping. "I've never had a boss for more than a month."

"How about *this* month?" Tim asks, feeling his way.

"I was hungry is all," says Steve.

Thomas holds the wire up, giving Steve a chance to say something that will save him.

"I hate twins. One's always mean."

"We're not twins," Thomas tells him. He frees Steve's arms and winds wire around one wrist. Steve wants to lash out in this untied moment, break Thomas's nose, but all he can do is shake and look at his hands. Thomas puts on a pair of gloves like ranch hands wear and gives a pair to Tim. They each hold an end of the steel wire. Thomas begins to pull and Steve gasps. Tim yanks back and the wire sinks into Steve's wrist, replaced by a neat line of blood. Tim puts his head down and clenches his teeth. You have to stop this before the guy's hand is on the ground. You wish you hadn't said that about the twenty minutes. You hop off the hood and slap Thomas on the back, tell him to slow down; it's a delicate act, a session like this. If you go too fast, you tell the boys, the tortured man has no time to doubt his toughness.

"Hit him in the face a few times. Nothing like intimacy to get them yapping."

Tim steps up and Steve spits to the side. Tim swings sidearm and glances his fist off Steve's forehead, drawing no flinch.

"He thinks you're a pussy," you say. "Thinks you're pink as bubble gum inside."

Tim wraps Steve's hair in his fist and pulls it to the side, holding the guy's head in place, then pushes a straight right into his eye. Tears fall down Steve's cheeks. Tim hits him again, busting Steve's lip, catches him a good one in the jaw, a good one in the temple. Steve goes limp in his ropes. You produce a pocketknife and order Tim to nip off the end of Steve's tongue. Tim tells Steve to open up, but Steve's eyes are closed and he pretends not to hear.

Tim is calm but impatient. "Piece of the tongue or the whole ear."

He presses the flat of the blade onto Steve's earlobe, perking him up. Steve works his mouth and manages to say he doesn't know nothing, doesn't work for nobody. Tim clutches him by the chin and you see Steve wondering if he should give up the secret, say it's all staged. He knows you'll kill him. As miserable as his life is, he still wants to live. You nudge Tim out of the way and kick Steve in the balls. You steady the knife against his Adam's apple. Steve loses his legs and his eyes roll. He whispers something you can't make out.

You hold him there a long moment, then shrug and close up the knife. "Telling the truth. It happens."

You tell Thomas and Tim to scat, that you'll take it from here. They round up their wire and gloves, disappointed, and lower themselves into their car at the same time, making it crouch. When their taillights vanish, you untie Steve and sit him down, a shivering heap, blood running from his wrist and face.

"Now you have to make sure they never see you," you say. "Avoid them around town."

Steve nods.

You get a six-pack of beer from your trunk, peel one off, and set the rest in the mud before him. You're happy for Steve; these will be the best beers of his life. And you're proud of yourself. You still have the old nastiness in you.

By 1992, Thomas and Tim have people at Memphis State. They avoid Frayser and Orange Mound, instead making the campus their western border and creeping toward the chipper, white, suburban high schools. They have a guy in north Mississippi who makes speed and a guy who runs back and forth from Paducah. Thomas and Tim send a boy they met in Little Rock, a chubby finance major named Colin, to clean the Memphis money. Colin founds a company that promotes underground parties, then he expands to the motivational-speaking market. He rents out ballrooms in downtown hotels, then cancels the events. Sometimes he caters these events and lets the hotel staff chow down.

It is a panel truck half-full of cocaine, heading from Texas toward Little Rock, that gets lost and pulls into a park and causes you to meet Bright. The driver is a new guy named Gregor, who you plant in a shop in the bad part of Little Rock and forbid to ever drive again. Gregor's blunder is for the best, though. Bright is steady and able. He lives away from everything, doesn't haggle. He wants everyone to get their fair share and stay out of trouble.

In 1994, the biggest supplier in New Orleans is chased off when one of his warehouses floods and tons of drugs go floating down the streets of a blue-collar neighborhood. The ports now crawl with DEA and NOPD and Coast Guard, strolling with coffee and flashlights, tossing sandwich crusts to their dogs. Without the water or I-10, which shoots across from Jacksonville on one side and Texas on the other, a road that now teems with highway patrol, the only way left is from Memphis. The boys spend a month in New Orleans, a place they despise, securing three good-sized customers.

Thomas and Tim have taken over the business. Little Rock keeps embarrassing itself by trying to attract tourists, claiming to be a technological hub and cultural capital. Capital of what? The Northwestern Mid-South? Certain areas, to compensate for other areas that have gone to shit, have been made cute, and now no one wants to go to any area. Filthy or antiseptic—those are the choices.

You take your time about moving, enjoying it. You sell the townhouse to the boys and go to the boonies, out near Bright's park, a quiet place where people aren't nosy. Bright doesn't know you're his neighbor and you see no reason to tell him. He wouldn't know you if he saw you. You make your new place into a sort of curiosity shop. For the second time in your life, you are a shop-owner. In Memphis you struggled upstream against the currents of commerce, making ends meet, saving. Now you live in your shop, your inventory existing only for your amusement. You put the shop in the yellow pages, post hours, and make no effort to sell anything—in fact, refuse to sell anything. You're like the mob bosses in movies who sit around in pizza joints. The word semiretired sounds privileged, luxurious. The boys have made this possible—Thomas and Tim. You can snooze all afternoon, cozy in the knowledge that they won't do anything stupid. Your snores are full of confidence in them. You let them grow the business the way they wish to grow it. You don't demand or forbid. Unless there are people stupid enough to provoke you, to create a threat to your business, to the boys, or to yourself, to, through ignorance or youth or cockiness or whatever brand of idiocy it would require, rankle you and draw you out, you'll gladly stay warm in your shell.

PART THREE
ONE-WAY TRIPS

November began peacefully, with Kyle, Swin, and Johnna falling into a domestic routine shaped around Johnna's work schedule. Whether they wanted it to or not, the park had become Kyle and Swin's stomping ground. They weren't watching over this place for someone else, weren't placeholding. When they did chores, they did them for themselves. The leaves were floating down in drifts, and with each stroke of the rake, Kyle and Swin staked more claim. Swin was able to relax while he exercised or read, and Kyle took long drives and listened to *Also sprach Zarathustra*, hearing all the instruments distinctly, beginning to get the strategy of the thing. He understood that there was no way to know what was going on with Strauss. The music was a cover; it was how Strauss wished to be.

Kyle cooked each day, and it didn't take long for Bright's presence in the kitchen to fade away. Kyle made pork dishes for himself and Johnna and steamed things for Swin. Swin had put Johnna on even more supplements, which Kyle mixed up for her in fruity desserts. Using chicken, olive oil, wine rather than beer, and carrots instead of potatoes, Kyle made a version of Bright's muck that was agreeable to Swin.

Swin took one book at a time out of the minivan, read it, and stacked it in a corner of the living room. Sometimes he only scanned the words, thinking of the book *he* would one day write. He'd decided that having a child in the narrative would make it more human. His and Johnna's child would be the moral touchstone. Swin would be honest about the child's faults, and honest about his and Johnna's faults as parents—honest about everything. Swin didn't feel he'd have to make anything up to improve the book. He would simply record all that had happened in a diary format. When Swin's kid was in high school, he or she would be assigned Swin's book, *The Mule to Emeritus Diaries*, and all the other students would marvel at his or her crazy Arkansas upbringing.

Swin said he wanted to choose the baby's name by process of elimination. He told Kyle to call out names that he had even the slightest negative association with. As a child, Kyle shared, a boy named Clay had ratted him out for knocking down mailboxes.

"That's a bit Keifer Sutherland, isn't it?" said Swin. "*Stand by Me.*"

"I don't know that one," Kyle said.

"Skip it. Give me more names."

"At my high school there was a male cheerleader named Ivan."

"Those guys are smart," Swin said.

"In seventh grade I kissed this girl named Dana, then some kid asked me if I'd kissed her and I said, 'Yeah.' The next day she made a whole opera out of it, like I'd dishonored her. Me betraying her was the hot gossip for a whole week."

Swin jotted the name down.

"I truly hated that girl," Kyle mused.

"For making you seem like a scumbag?"

"For making me the subject of gossip."

"I guess you knew enough not to apologize or deny it."

"I never said another word to her."

"At my high school, girls were deemed either two-faced, conceited, sweet, or shy. Those were the choices."

"You were probably popular," Kyle said.

"Very," said Swin. "Weren't you?"

"What do you think?"

"I honestly couldn't say."

"Nobody bothered me. Put it that way." Kyle drew himself into an erect posture and belched. "Your turn."

Swin said a girl named Tess had ruined a scam he had where he checked books out of the public library with a fake ID and kept them. He'd gone to school with a kid named Dean who had webbed toes and was a notorious kiss-ass.

Kyle began regarding his and Swin's situation less darkly. He and Swin had a house *and* some money. If the Parks Department got wise and Kyle and Swin had to leave the house, they'd still have the money. Frog's people, though they might come for the money, had no claim on the house. Someone might come to kill them, of course, but to Kyle that seemed like a condition of life, like the price of doing business. You could get killed anytime. There were a lot of other ways to die than by the order of a drug boss. Florists and teenagers and princesses got killed. Hikers and firemen. Mothers. One thing was obvious: neither Kyle nor Swin would be able to get a setup like this by his own devices. If they left Felsenthal, they'd be poor. They'd have the same chance of ending up in jail or dead, and they'd also be poor.

The fact was, Kyle could feel his fear of Frog dwindling. His fear was now a mighty oak tree so rotten under its bark that a child could push it over. One of these mornings, Kyle would awaken to find his fear of Frog toppled over onto some power lines. Kyle wanted to know about Frog, wanted his questions about the man answered, wanted to know what Frog thought of him, but it was as much for curiosity's sake as for self-preservation. Kyle couldn't see himself dying. He found it hard to believe anyone could extinguish him.

One morning Kyle brewed coffee, filled a thermos that read TEXAS: NOT JUST STEERS AND QUEERS ANYMORE, and walked up to Bright's grave. When he got there, he was annoyed with himself. He had no idea what to do or how to feel. He could've brought some whiskey to pour out, but that was stupid. Kyle's mild sorrow for Bright had settled, had joined the other disheveled shadows of Kyle's brain.

Swin spoke to the private investigator for the last time. It turned out there was nothing untoward about his mother's afternoon jaunts. She was bored in the house and liked to spend time at the wine shop and the quilt museum and at a new shark aquarium that had been constructed at a defunct racetrack. She carried a disposable camera and took pictures without aiming. Swin's second oldest sister, Rita, who was in tenth grade, "sort of" had a boyfriend. It was one of those best friend/boyfriend deals where the two, although not fully dating, scare potential dates away from each other. Swin could not have wished for better; the best friend/boyfriend rarely scored, and if he did, it was a shaky grope session the girl wasn't hot to repeat. Rosa, the oldest, had a jock and a nerd after her. The

PI said nerds weren't like they used to be. Today's nerds had knowledge about obscure music, marketable computer skills, and a fashionably unfashionable way of dressing. These days, the PI asserted, a varsity jacket was as much a hindrance as a help.

Swin drove Johnna's hooptie to Kentucky. It had been weeks since he'd asked if he could use her car, and finally she didn't have to work and Kyle didn't have chores planned and there was no trip to go on and no dead body to deal with and even the weather was pleasant. Swin had told Kyle he was making a trek to a liquidation sale at a huge book and music store somewhere in Alabama, and he'd asked Johnna, if Kyle inquired, to go along with this fib. When Swin returned, he'd say he'd been too late, that the place was already cleaned out. Or he could just buy some books somewhere. You couldn't have too many.

Swin, steering absently, felt anxious in a hopeful way, a man with a full and cryptic heart. Taking a trip for personal reasons was freeing. Kyle wasn't there deciding when they would stop and what, if anything, they'd listen to. Swin found a blues station out of Jonesboro and heard a song that went, "Crying is my business, and business is good."

It took forever to get past Little Rock, but then Memphis and Jackson whipped by and Swin was bearing down on Nashville. He decided to stop for lunch at an upscale Asian place just off the Vanderbilt campus. He saw the medical building and the stadium and a shady spot where he used to sit with a book and watch girls in shorts walk by. It was like he'd only been gone a week. The same banners hung over the same walkways. The same signs were tacked to the same telephone poles. Kids dressed like vampires scuttled from corner to corner. Kids. Kids in ties and hunting hats. Eastern Europeans reading Tennessee Williams. Krishnas. There was twenty-four-hour sushi delivery in little foam coolers embossed with dragons. Laptops. Marxists. Espresso. Swin felt at home and alive in this jumble of ambition, this mess of intent.

He ate grilled duck, enjoying the under-thump of foreign hip-hop, trying to convince himself that the grass was always greener, that if he ever got back to a university, he would get sick of it. Of what, though? He loved it all, and now he was an intruder here. Swin heard a familiar voice. One of his old professors, the guy that had confronted Swin about his gold chains, walked by with a spiffy, middle-aged woman. Swin put his hands in front of his face. He was so jealous, it felt like his ribs were straightening. He couldn't get up from his table. He ordered tea and prepared it and sniffed it. It tasted bad but Swin was going to drink the whole miniature pot.

He would never be a professor. This knowledge was an old wind that had just grown cold. Now that he'd been out in the world earning money, setting his own schedule, committing felonies, how would he ever fit into a place where you got pissy at copy machines and devised attendance policies? Swin had to get the idea of cushy professorship out of his head. No one would want him. They'd want a token Rican who strove for gold stars, a Rican they could set up next to their token black guy and token Eskimo woman.

Swin felt betrayed by his mind. He put both hands on the table and lowered his face to the steaming tea. If he ever lived in a college town, it would be as a hanger-on, one of those too-old young guys that the students looked at sidelong. Or as a drug dealer. Universities didn't hire people with diverse backgrounds; they hired people with similar backgrounds who *appeared* different. They wanted you to have been reading Jung and Plato and Henry James in Trinidad, rather than in Maryland. They wanted accents. It had never occurred to Swin that his life was tragic, but it was. His sadness was a stiff jacket that his mind was racing to shed. His mind was fumbling with the zippers and buttons. He gulped his tea.

He would still write his book. It would be a groundbreaking book. It would include every murder and every drug deal, down to the day and the hour and what the breeze felt like. It would include Bright's phantom wood-shavings and the boss in pink's art quotations and Her's rare disease. Kyle's moods. Johnna's tits. There was always a chance Swin could become an authentic genius, one with cult status, one that never goes within a hundred miles of a college, one that hates professors and, mostly for that reason, gets taught in their classes.

Swin watched his oldest sister, Rosa, from a park down the street. She was trimming bushes over at the neighbor's, a skinny widow who wore running shoes with pantyhose and spent the winters with her niece in Florida. Rosa was a patient trimmer—stepping back often to survey her work and pluck off individual leaves with her fingers. Her hair was pulled under a ball cap and a rag hung from her jeans pocket. Swin slipped up the street, avoiding the eye-line of passing drivers, and cut behind the widow's house. He stepped right up to Rosa, who froze mid-clip but kept her eyes down. She dropped the shears. Next she was smiling and saying she was doing great and hugging Swin. She smelled like nuts and candy. She was taller. Her skin glowed. Swin struggled to get his bearings. He was in his neighbor's yard, in his sister's arms.

"I knew you'd come back," Rosa said.

"You're the only one that can know I'm here."

Rosa reached up and skimmed her palm over Swin's hair.

"Seriously," Swin told her.

Rosa's smile waned. She picked up a thermos and chugged. Swin knew it was grapefruit juice. He hated the stuff, and she didn't bother offering him any.

"I want to say I'm sorry I made up all those theories," Swin said. "So you guys would hate the Blond Baron. He's a good guy, in case you were wondering. Better than our real father."

"It didn't work," said Rosa. "We don't hate him."

"I had him checked out."

"Checked out how?"

"You know, his background."

"Like on the Internet?"

"Something like that."

Rosa looked at him. "And?"

"He's got a couple black marks, but they're honorable black marks."

"Was he ever married?"

"Nope. And no other kids."

"You got all this off the computer?"

"Not all of it."

"He said he felt like somebody was following him."

"I guess the guy I hired wasn't too good."

Rosa blinked. "Did you have this guy spy on *us*?"

"Of course not," Swin said. "No."

Rosa picked up her shears and led Swin around to the front porch, which had a cloistered garden area that would keep them from sight. She began snipping a shapeless shrub.

"Those are clip-on earrings," Swin said.

"Can't get our ears pierced until we move out."

"You're seventeen, just get them pierced."

"Rebellion?" She scrunched her nose. "No thanks."

"How's Mom?"

"Down lately."

"Why?"

Rosa shrugged. "She's like the stock market. She surges back."

"I can't think of her as my mother, but I can't think of her as a regular person, either."

"She's both."

"She's like somebody I only know from dreams, somebody it would be creepy to see when I was awake. I don't feel like we owe each other anything."

The top of the shrub was taking shape under Rosa's shears. Swin sat on a wicker lawn chair and voiced his wishes—that Rosa would get all her sisters together and go for ice cream, so he could watch them from a distance.

"Ice cream might work on Lizzie," Rosa said.

"Well, shopping or… I don't know."

"We'll all be at the track meet tomorrow at Shorn Hills. Rita's running at four-thirty."

Rosa was now boring holes in the bush. She worked in silence a few minutes, clipping and extracting stems one by one, then she stood tall and regarded Swin.

"Stealing, right?"

Swin winked.

"Do whatever you want," she said. "Just don't start hating everything. The only things Dad liked were salt water and Cuban sandwiches. The only things in the world."

"I hate an awful lot of stuff."

"It doesn't matter if you never get a master's degree or have a corner office. You can do whatever you want with your own brain."

Swin leaned on the house, the bricks snagging his shirt. "I trust you've avoided moral compromise with the opposite sex."

"They're persistent."

"You can outlast them."

"If they're in love with me, I can."

"They are."

Rosa had fashioned the bush she'd been trimming into a B. Swin recalled that the widow's last name was Bunson. The B leaned to one side but was well proportioned. Rosa sat down and told Swin she'd been working on becoming sane. Sanity was a thankless achievement. It was rising above indulgences like stress. One had to avoid meetings, leave phases behind. She was working, in particular, on fickleness. She didn't want to change her opinion of people because of one isolated act of meanness or ingenuity or haste. She classified Swin as a bursting, elite human, she told him, and wherever his bursting, elite humanity led him, that was where he needed to be.

Shorn Hills was an old high school, a three-story brick building with brown yards. Swin was early for the meet. He strolled the soundless corridors, looking at graduation pictures from the fifties and trophies from a time when white guys in tight shorts ruled the basketball court. Swin was settling into the idea that his sisters didn't need him, that no matter where he was, there were bad things that could happen to them that he couldn't stop. It was a privilege, being depended on by a woman. You got more out of it than they did. Johnna was the woman depending on Swin. Johnna was the chance he couldn't squander, not his sisters. His sisters were out of his hands. He had to view his sisters the way Rosa viewed *him*. His sisters were bulbs of cheer that would forever glow in the universe, however dark it got, bulbs that would sometimes pass into Swin's sight and warm him. He was rationalizing, trying not to miss them, but that was okay. His mind was trying to win back his trust, to prove itself an ally.

He made his way upstairs and went into an empty classroom. On the board were vocabulary words that started with the letter A. Stacks of *A Separate Peace* crowded a low table. Out the window, a view of the athletic fields. This would be Swin's perch. He paced, watching birds peck around outside, and then he was struck with the relief of a new plan. He needed a manly skill that would allow his mind to idle. He needed a way to make money that would leave his intellect at leisure, that would remove the shadow of looming trouble a life of crime casts. A person never questioned themselves after a day of physical labor. Johnna would respect him if he could provide for her with steadiness, if he came home smudged and bedraggled and complained about taxes. She'd await him with a healthy dinner and an arched back. And Swin's brain, knowing what was expected of it and having rested all day, would explode into dexterous profundity each night

176

when Swin sat down at his desk. His book would fly along. Before he knew it, he'd be writing about this very day, this day of spying on his sisters at Shorn Hills. Before he knew it, the literary world would beckon, plying him with readings, interviews, panels, awards, and Swin would look at them with pity and decline. Very kind, he'd say, but I believe I'll stick with welding. Exceedingly flattering, but I'll not turn my back on shortwave radio. Swin would learn every trade there was to learn. He had to find out how long all this would take and how much it would cost. He had to figure out whether to use his real identity or be Suarez from the park or be an entirely new person. Would he be in unions? Would he be an independent contractor? He didn't even know which questions to ask.

He watched the first runners arrive and stretch, then perused a map of Kentucky. He pulled the teacher's chair over to the window and sank himself into it, falling into an agreeable, shallow reverie and passing a good twenty minutes, until the field below was littered with high-schoolers in tank tops. Rita was lining up with two dozen other girls, staring down the track, making a task out of being calm. The girls put one foot forward and the gun sounded. By the pace, Swin could tell it was a distance race. Rita edged to the inside and stuck with the pack, while a tiny girl with buzzed hair took out a lead. Lizzie, Swin's youngest sister, was helping with refreshments, peeling oranges and filling water cups. Rosa was off by herself, sitting under a tree, speaking into a handheld tape recorder. There was Luz, cheering, and Cory, Rita's best friend/boyfriend. The runners went out of sight at the far end of the track, then reemerged in the same order. Rita looked like she knew something, like she was waiting for an inevitable sign.

Johnna slid into her Oldsmobile and aimed it at the tanning parlor. Swin had outlawed tanning, but Johnna wasn't about to get pale right before winter. Winter was the most important time to be tan. Swin didn't let her get her nails done anymore, either, so now she bit them and they were gross. There were two kinds of nurses—those with nice nails and those with gross nails. Patients noticed. Doctors noticed. It had been refreshing having Swin gone for a couple days. Johnna still had her place, but she only stayed there when Swin and Kyle went on trips. She pulled some peanut brittle out of her purse and sniffed it. Being pregnant had keened her sense of smell. Her lips were plump. Her balance had improved. She gobbled the brittle and popped a handful of chocolate raisins. No matter what Swin thought, she wasn't going to deprive this baby of sugar. Or a tan mother.

Johnna had quit her church. She knew that when she started to show more, the fat ladies would regard each other solemnly and press her hand with big, frozen smiles on their faces, smiles that meant Johnna needed pity. The skinny sons would pull chairs out, hold doors, make her plate, want to *sing* for her. The pastor would have a private session with her where he would skip from one idea to the next, describing the importance of family and fellowship and whatnot, and the preacher's son, that idiot, would probably ask her how it happened. They would all say they wanted to meet Swin, would expect Johnna to recruit him into the church. Furthermore, she had missed the last minute of Razorback football that she ever intended to miss. This church was easy-come and easy-go for her; she'd picked it out of the phone book. After she was through nursing and the baby could understand things, she would find a new church. Maybe she'd find a Catholic church, where the services lasted a set amount of time and involved pretty candles and statues. Catholic folks, she knew, liked to drink. They liked holidays.

At the tanning parlor, Johnna got her card punched and locked herself in a room. She stretched out in the dark chamber. A Taylor Dayne song was tinking away in the speakers. Johnna drifted. A couple times she felt that the buzzer had gone off but it hadn't. She dreamed she was sitting in a big crowd, at a stadium. It was a Razorback game. The roar in the stands was so constant, it was like silence. The Razorback coaches had gotten the wrong weather report, so their players were wearing galoshes. They weren't, by rule, allowed to change into cleats. The opposing team wore blue and grinned behind their face masks. They were good sports. They kept giving their condolences about the galoshes and helping the Razorbacks up when they slipped, and this enraged Arkansas's head coach. He stalked the sidelines, screaming, "This ain't buddy-ball. That's the enemy over there." His assistant coaches chewed things—leather straps or pieces of shingle. It was a sunny, sunny day. The players of the blue-clad team, while on the bench, donned sunglasses.

Johnna knew a secret. The Razorback quarterback, the day before, had gone to lunch with some old friend he had from the other team. Johnna couldn't decide whether to share this information with the coach at the weekly meeting she had with him to discuss the game plan. The coach would go apeshit; he'd choke the quarterback dead. But didn't the quarterback deserve death? Wasn't he a traitor?

———————

Wendy, the pink boss, called Kyle and told him she'd be in Little Rock in two days and she needed to see him, that he should expect an envelope the next morning containing instructions of a nonbusiness sort, that she would leave her hotel room door cracked so he could barge in.

Kyle bought a shirt, a green button-down with a pointy collar, and drove to Little Rock. He parked in a pay lot across from Wendy's hotel, stepped into an elevator, located 631, heard a bath running and a television doctor being blackmailed. Was he going on a date? It was a bizarre idea, Kyle going on a date. Wendy didn't have the usual ideas of romance, and that had to be good for Kyle; maybe these meetings could be a recurring thing. He took a couple sharp breaths through his nose, then shoved the door open. Wendy called, "Who is it?" from the bathroom and Kyle said, "You know goddamn well who it is." He jerked Wendy from her tub of bubbles, leaving the water running, then slid open the closet and threw clothes at her. He told her to quit being a tramp. As she struggled into some underwear and a large sweater, he yelled, "Where is it?" and rifled through her suitcase. Wendy yanked Kyle's elbow and he slung her into a chair. He threw shoes this way and that, flung a curling iron, dumped a pouch of jewelry. Wendy's makeup case had many compartments and clasps, like a tackle box. Kyle patiently opened each one, forcing her to watch. He asked if she thought any amount of makeup could help her, then turned the case upside down over the trash can, clattering half the compacts and pencils and bottles onto the floor. Finally, Wendy unplugged the alarm clock and chucked it at Kyle, and he caught it and rested it on the bed. She darted for the door but he got her by the arm and gathered her in and swung her into the bathroom, the tub now overflowing. Her lapses into limpness made this fake-drowning harder than Kyle had imagined it would be. The two of them were slipping and splashing and he began to think of the noise, the other guests, the staff, the police. He loosened his grip. Wendy asked what was wrong. Just like that, they were out of character. She patted his face and told him he'd done fantastic, a lot better than she'd expected. She'd known the drowning would be problematic.

She asked Kyle to go downstairs and have a drink while she cleaned up. She'd meet him in the restaurant.

The restaurant was silent, and all who worked there seemed stoned. Busboys wandered in the distance, nothing to do, grouping and disbanding. Wendy sat across from Kyle. Her dress was the lightest pink, a shade of white.

"Here you go," she said. "'A man cannot attain excellence if he satisfies the ignorant and not those of his own craft, and if he be not singular. As for those other meek spirits, they may be found without the need of a candle in all the highways of the world.'"

"That one's a load of shit."

"What's the matter with you? You're mad because we didn't sleep together?"

Kyle scoffed. "It's the quote. First off, attaining excellence is for douchebags. Second, saying one human is ignorant and one isn't is splitting hairs. Third, the highway is the *best* place to find singular dudes."

The hostess came around the corner in a huff and apologized that Kyle and Wendy had had to seat themselves.

"Can we have a sober waiter?" Kyle asked.

"You want Eric. By the fountain." The hostess handed Kyle two menus and pointed at a stone horseman surrounded by spitting bronze children.

Kyle and Wendy switched tables. They read the short menus over and over until Eric stopped by. He was deliberate and depressed. He told them the special was New York strip with blue cheese on it, and that the steak enchiladas were bland. Kyle and Wendy ordered the special. Eric nodded and turned on his heel.

"It's obvious to me that Bright is no longer affiliated with the Parks Department," Wendy said. "*Why* is none of my business, but I have to report it. I have to."

"Report what?" Kyle said.

"That's he's missing."

"Jesus, I'll need some time."

"Once I process the paperwork, it's maybe thirty days before you got a new ranger out there."

"How will that work?"

"You can't let him know your certification is false—him or her. I don't know it's false, either. I'm a victim of fraud. And I'm only taking a few more payments."

"I'll believe that when I see it."

"I can buy my houseboat soon."

"Then you'll quit the Parks Department?" said Kyle. "Hang out in the harbor and paint?"

Wendy shook her head with self-pity. "I saw a color on the plane the other day, out the window—this seething orange. I knew I would never paint it. I knew I'd…"

Before she could finish her thought, Eric came with bread, glasses, and a metal pitcher of ice water. He informed them that the butter tabs had been heated, bowed crookedly, and left.

"Crime is a sinking ship," Wendy said. "As is art. I'll have a nice pension from the park people. Insurance. It's an easy job."

"I'm no expert, but I think you lack the balls to be a painter."

"Painting is childish, Kyle. I'm a single woman and I have to be smart."

"What does being single or being a woman have to do with it?"

Wendy gave Kyle a withering look.

"I'm a single man," he said.

Wendy looked away, toward the busboys at the far end of the restaurant, and Kyle let her. Neither spoke again until the steaks came. Kyle ate his and most of Wendy's, then slouched in the booth. Wendy said he could pick any story he wanted about Bright, and Kyle said how about the truth, that one morning he was just gone, his clothes still in his closet, whiskey still in the cabinet, an atlas on the kitchen table open to the state of Alaska.

"Alaska sounds like a lie." Wendy handed Kyle a packet of forms. She would be in D.C. for five days, she said, for pamphlet meetings. When she returned home she wanted to find those forms in her mailbox.

"How come you don't have sex?" Kyle asked her.

"For days afterward I can't do anything. Regular life doesn't interest me after I sleep with a man."

Her answer sounded practiced. Kyle wondered if she did these charades with a bunch of other guys, if she had stacks of scripts lying around amongst her piles of pamphlets.

"You can pay for dinner," he said. "I'll be in touch."

Driving home, Kyle knew he'd never see Wendy again. He'd have Swin fill out the paperwork, but they wouldn't pay her another cent. Bright had made her believe she was blackmailing him, but *he* had boxed *her* in. She had a lot more to lose from trouble than Kyle did.

———

Kyle took Swin with him. This time they parked right in front of Her's trailer, two wheels on her lawn. It had been too long since the last packet, and though it didn't make sense that Her would withhold packets, Kyle couldn't put it past her. Her's job was to give Kyle and Swin the packets, and, like everyone else, she didn't want to lose her job. On the other hand, she was nuts.

The second part of Kyle's mission, aside from recovering a packet if there was one to recover, was as simple as letting Her know that he and his partner were not to be fucked with. Frog was the CEO, but Kyle and Swin were now regional managers and they needed to start doing a little managing on Frog's behalf. Kyle was sick of Her's act. He was sick of having to beg for the packets and having to tiptoe around her schedule and walk circles around her trailer and check her little carport area and sick of having her annoying neighbor stare at him. He was sick of her condescending attitude, that she would only deign to allow Kyle and Swin into her trailer if it suited her mood.

Kyle and Swin knocked a long time before Her unlatched the door and stuck her head out. She said the envelopes were on hold until she talked to Bright, so Kyle forced his way in, sending Her wobbling backward, the indignation in her face drowning out the shock. She was slick with sweat, flushed, beautiful. A squishy, waist-high ball rested in the corner.

"I was exercising," she said.

"Feminine perfection," said Swin. "Aside from the unprecedented disease."

"Why would you be exercising?" Kyle asked. "If you want to die as soon as possible, you shouldn't exercise."

Her ignored Kyle. She looked at Swin. "I wonder what your rude friend wants to do if I don't have a packet."

"I intend to kill you by strangulation. And it *will* be suicide, because I'm giving you a warning. You won't be able to say you didn't know you were about to get strangled."

Her brushed her neck with her fingers. "Why not shoot me?"

"All I brought are my hands."

Swin pointed at the big ball. "So, what, you push it around in a circle five hundred times?"

"Shut up," said Her.

"So, is this an order from Frog?" Kyle asked. "Frog said no packets until he finds out what's happening over here?"

"That's right. He wants to know what happened to the ranger."

"Right," Kyle said. "And we're probably supposed to tell you so you can tell him."

Life sprang into Her's eyes. "That's right," she said.

Kyle sighed. "Bull-fucking-shit."

Her's mouth hung open.

Swin winked. "Are you the boss of this whole thing?"

"Don't be an idiot."

"Are you the Frogman?"

"If you want to call him Frog then he's Frog. Could be Bob Hope's cousin-in-law, for all I know." Her dabbed her cheeks with a napkin. "You can lie, but you have no intuition."

"Intuition is for women," Kyle said. "You don't need to worry about intuition right now. You need to worry about the fact that you're an unnecessary middleman and we've been thinking about streamlining. Frog will be impressed if we can make his operation more efficient."

Her looked to Swin and he shrugged. "You *are* superfluous," he admitted.

"You can't do that," Her said. "You can't streamline."

"We do a whole bunch of shit we're not supposed to do," Kyle said. "Frog doesn't seem to mind."

"I'm a buffer," Her insisted. "I'm a vital layer of insulation."

Kyle cracked his knuckles. "I'm convinced you have a packet sitting in here, and I refuse to tear the place up. You're going to hobble right over and get it for me."

Kyle peered into Her's eyes, tried to make her understand that he was indeed a killer and she was helpless. It was working. She was frightened.

Swin cleared his throat and asked if there were ways to practice intuition.

"Do you pray?" Her asked him, prying her attention from Kyle. "Most prayers sound hollow inside your head, but every so often a prayer is full and it echoes. That's the same feeling as intuition."

"I'll pray for you if you pray for me," Swin said.

Kyle wrung his hands. "Packet," he said.

"It's stuffed in the ball, you asshole."

Kyle and Swin looked at each other.

"Why would you hide a packet from us?" Swin asked.

Her considered this. "I'm scared, same as you. I want to know what happened to Ranger Bright. He was my friend, you know?"

"Your *friend*?" Swin asked. "You think distributing a manila envelope to someone every two weeks constitutes a friendship?"

"To me it does," Her said. "To me and the ranger it did."

"You're never going to know what happened to Bright." Kyle pointed to the ball, wanting Swin to get the packet, then went to Her's kitchen sink and splashed water on his face. He used his shirt to dry off.

"We're not scared," he told Her. "You just said we were scared, same as you, but that's wrong. We're not."

The packet from Her's exercise ball sent them to Huntsville, Alabama. To find the Celica, Kyle and Swin walked five miles, half down a dirt road that skirted the park, the other half through fields of rotten berries that stained their shoes and the bottoms of their pants. It was hard to know if they were walking the right course; there were no landmarks on the map, only distances and compass directions. The berry fields contained no streams, misshapen trees, barns—nothing of note except a hole someone had dug and thrown hundreds of real estate signs into.

The Celica had no hubcaps. Kyle barely fit in the driver's seat. There were napkins all over the dash. The console contained a mess of punch cards for getting free coffee and videos and ice cream and such. Kyle dropped these out the window, along with an air freshener shaped like a T-bone steak. Swin popped in a tape that taught basic Russian. To him, there was quite a distinction between being bilingual and knowing three languages. He had chosen Russian because it was the only language tape he could find in the shops near Felsenthal, but Russian *was* a great language, the language of many strange poets. Swin shut his eyes and mouthed the words. Though the woman on the tape didn't have a Russian accent, Swin told Kyle, she had a Russian attitude; she held the student in contempt for not being born Russian, for living a portion of his or her life in ignorance of the greatest cultural heritage of the last several hundred years.

The Celica drove with a whine that got under Kyle's skin. The window didn't shut flush. This car, he thought, should belong to an anorexic waitress. It was going to be a long way to Huntsville, and when they got back, Kyle and Swin had nothing to look forward to but the new ranger. They'd have to take orders, would have to act dumb and outdoorsy. Kyle could no longer picture himself with a day-to-day boss. What if the guy wanted to kick them out of the house, wanted them to return to their trailers? What about the nursery Swin had fixed up? What about the baby and Johnna? What if the new ranger blabbed to Cooper about what really happened to Bright, that he'd disappeared without a trace?

"The best way to throw off a hound dog is hot pepper," Swin said.

"Throw off a hound dog?"

"Like if they bring one out to the park ever."

"No one's bringing a hound dog."

"Someday they might."

"That works? Hot pepper?"

"I'm as convinced of it as I am that man walked on the moon."

"Meaning you saw it on TV?"

Swin nodded. "We could test it on Bedford."

"Wouldn't that be mean?"

"Not very."

The drive seemed endless. Kyle's knees ached from being jammed under the Celica's dashboard. Swin took restless naps. He awoke at one point and informed Kyle that Johnna didn't want to get married until after the baby came, to prove some kind of point. Kyle told Swin that Johnna probably knew this was no time to be filing paperwork with the government, that maybe she wanted to wait until they could have an old-fashioned, expensive wedding that would include Swin's family, that maybe she thought all this stuff with Frog would blow over.

"It will," Swin said.

"I guess," said Kyle. "Getting a new ranger is going to be a monumental pain in the ass."

"Monumental, huh?"

"Monumental."

"You think there's a chance the new ranger will be a Frog guy? Could his reach be that great?"

Kyle had not thought of this. The possibility had not occurred to him. He kneaded the steering wheel. "Doesn't seem likely," he told Swin.

"It would be too good to be true," Swin said.

"It really doesn't seem likely."

"No, it doesn't. But nothing about my life seems likely to me."

They pulled into the parking lot of the NASA museum and escaped the Celica. Immediately a man with watches on both wrists walked over. He rummaged under the driver's seat, pulled out a small clipboard full of forms, flipped through them, then tossed Kyle a bundle of cash wrapped in deli paper, marked TURK/PROV. They got back in the car and counted it—twenty-two thousand dollars. They took out a grand for expenses and put the bundle in the glove box. Kyle wasn't ready to be cooped back up in the car, and said he was going for a walk. Swin said he was going in the museum to see if he could figure out once and for all whether we really went to the moon.

You flip through a book about Negro League baseball, wondering, if it was so ignored, where all these wonderful pictures came from. Lately you've prepared and cleaned up after three elaborate meals a day, learned about the first half of the twentieth century, listened to politicians on the radio. Your retired life is oiled and humming—operational, at least—but as always, here is another problem, a problem like an iceberg too large to be sailed around, an iceberg that has to be smashed to cinders.

Gregor was killed. The cops busted into his shop and shot him. This is not good. Gregor was dependable, well suited for his sunless, solitary duty. The cops have been slithering around Little Rock for weeks, questioning every hoodlum they can grub up, emboldened by the fact that they have a specific, large object to ask about, a car they dragged out of a swamp, and a specific, smaller object, a body, a toothless boy from Louisiana. Most of this was on the news, but Thomas and Tim can find out anything they want to find out in Little Rock. The boy was identified even without his teeth—probably had a juvenile record with fingerprints—and tracked back to his uncle, who was found dead, and the uncle, the cops figured out, was connected in some way to the Little Rock drug trade. None of this is good.

Ranger Bright's body has not turned up, but you feel he too has been killed. You know he would never up and leave. He would never abandon his park. You don't know how, but these new boys, Kyle and Swin, had something to do with it. Possibly everything to do with it. Bright lives almost fifty years, not a scratch on him, then the boys show up and boom: dead. Then they come sniffing around for guns and Swin asks you if you want to purchase a set of human bones. The boys don't know who you are. They couldn't. Swin couldn't have been taunting you, offering you Bright's remains. Could he have?

Kyle and Swin had something to do with Bright and the sunk car and the uncle and the nephew and, indirectly, with Gregor. Her called the other night and said she couldn't sleep because she was scared of Kyle. These two are supposed to be working for you, but they're about the worst enemies you've ever had. You've never had anyone kill your associates and steal your money. Whether they are accomplishing these things according to a plan, or whether they're lost in a maze of their own fuckups, you cannot say. And it doesn't matter. What could you think but the worst when they kept trying to contact Colin? They don't contact higher-ups. Everyone knows that. They can't genuinely believe they're going to be able to speak to you directly. More likely, their idea is to turn your organization against you, to feel Colin out, see if he's turnable, get him and the other runners to break off on their own. Those idiots think the park is theirs now. They think they've found a weak branch of your company and they're going to lop it off and replant it for themselves. Maybe this is true and maybe it isn't, but what can you assume but the worst?

And then there's the book bonfire. You watched from the woods one night, more amused than shocked, as Swin and Johnna went into your shop, into your home, and took half your poetry books outside and burned them. You know it's not possible that those jackasses know you're Frog and are pretending not to know. You know it was Johnna who wanted to burn your books and Swin was along for the ride, too weak to say no to a pretty woman. But that's just it. These guys are stupid and that's what makes them dangerous.

If Kyle and Swin are stupid enough to let all this happen, there's no telling what else they're up to. They will be caught, soon, and brought up on serious charges, and it will somehow lead back to you. Every minute that passes, you are closer to jail. Every minute you sit idle, you deserve jail more. There are troubling questions everywhere you look, and they all have the same simple answer.

You will keep this job close. You will instruct Her to give Kyle and Swin one last trip, to keep them comfortable—something not far away, maybe Fort Smith. You will run into them, casually, and tell them where they can get as many orphan guns as their little hearts desire. They will feel lucky, like something has gone right for them, but nothing will ever go right for them again. They will not get orphan guns. They will get Thomas and Tim. You've wrestled in circles about sending Thomas and Tim, knowing all the while, hard as you may wish to wrestle, that you would lose. You can guide your boys, but you can't shield them. This is what they're for and they know it. They know that the practice of dealing drugs is always, at its core, a reward for violence. That's how you see it; that's how you taught them. If you allow them to dodge this live-bullet assignment, their entire ascent will ring hollow. You know all this, so why is it so tough to send them? You're more attached to them than they are to you; that's something you have to face. This assignment is a standard aspect of the business they're in, and you're treating it like sending your sons off to war. You're making an opera out of it. It's not that big a deal. You'll make sure it's done right. You'll have the boys scout the place out, have them lying in wait, prepared and resolved. Thomas will lead. He will look after Tim. They'll corner Kyle and Swin and separate them. Thomas will carry a shotgun. Tim will be better off with his size as his weapon, a weapon that can't be taken and used against him. They'll have to practice frisking. Thomas will have to be ready to shoot, in case they charge him. One shot for Swin, right there where they are, then drag Kyle off for a few questions… drop *him*—whole thing over within a half hour. The boys will be back in Little Rock by dinnertime, where you'll meet them for ribs and begin the fun work of keeping your heads down.

A fearsome pitcher who was thirty-nine years old in his rookie season stares at you. His teeth gleam. He is amused at playing a child's game for a living. In your mind, you flip through a catalog of venues for your setup. You wonder if Thomas and Tim should try to recover what's left of the money. You wonder if Felsenthal has a different ranger now. You wonder about the girl, Johnna. Your heart skips a beat and you toss the book off your lap. You were supposed to take your prune tarts out of the oven twenty minutes ago.

Swin had arranged to phone his sister Rosa each Wednesday at nine, when dinner would be over and pre-bedtime scurrying would be in full swing. Rosa toured the house, pretending to speak to one of her suitors. Swin pressed the phone into his ear. A sitcom with a sarcastic toddler could be heard, and then a radio playing a racy version of the hokey-pokey. Swin heard Luz raising her voice over and over in light, wordless song, Rita reciting the Gettysburg Address. He heard Lizzie begging for help with her homework, mispronouncing the word "diorama."

"Use spaghetti," Rosa told her. "You need spaghetti and you need food coloring."

Rosa calmed Lizzie down, then went outside to give Swin updates on each sister. Rosa herself was close to a decision about her dating life. She was leaning toward the jock because the nerd was too cocky and because the jock said "Yes, sir" and "No, sir." Her project of becoming sane had hit a roadblock: she couldn't keep herself from watching politics on TV. The desire for sanity was not a phase, she believed, but it was something that could only be accomplished by going *through* phases. Rita had quit organized running, and now ran on her own. She'd had a falling-out with her best friend/boyfriend, who, she'd discovered, had another best friend/girlfriend at another school. She had saved up and bought herself a microscope. Luz had gotten busier, and somehow calmer. She'd been granted her own cell phone by their stepdad. The only news about Lizzie was that she'd recently been sent home from school for laughing too much.

Swin headed to the market for picnic supplies. He'd never been on a picnic, but he knew that fresh fruit and wine were standard. In Confederate areas, people brought fried chicken for the main course and a nut pie. The market didn't carry a woven wood basket or a checkered sheet, so Swin put his bounty in a soft, blue cooler. This once, he would not urge vitamins upon Johnna, offering her instead an assortment of chocolate-dipped gummy things. Chocolate made her predictable, less likely to demand picnics or throw out all her shoes, both things she'd done the day before.

Swin chose a shaded spot halfway to the berry fields he and Kyle had tromped through. The hike gave Johnna an appetite. She devoured the chicken and pears with little help from Swin, but wouldn't touch the pecan pie because it looked, to her, gelatinous. Swin accepted a smooch for the candy and uncorked the wine, a nonalcoholic type that tasted like carbonated fruit punch. He had prepared a picnic game, like in a Victorian movie he'd seen. The two of them had to alternate saying facts the other did not know.

"I'll tell you one. Our star receiver's a turncoat." Johnna slipped her legs underneath her. "He's transferring out to California. That's what happens when you recruit guys from out of state."

"That's not what I had in mind. That's more a news update than an obscure fact."

"The guy's a pretty boy," Johnna said. "That's another fact."

Swin drank a little wine from the bottle and the sweetness made him pucker. "I put forth that the finest pinot noirs the world over are produced in the state of Oregon. I've heard that."

"I got one: My mother's uncle-in-law invented the dude ranch."

"Is that true?"

"In Arizona. He got the idea from all the Western movies they shot out there."

"Well, in Japan…" Swin racked his brain. "If a kid misbehaves, the other students beat him up. They have that much respect for authority."

Johnna stared at him.

"They don't cross the street without the walk signal," he said. "No matter how clear."

"It's a boy," said Johnna.

"Is that for sure?"

"It is."

"You said you didn't want to know."

"One day I did."

"It's *sure* sure?"

"A no-doubter."

"A boy?"

Johnna nodded. "You never put a PI on *me*, did you?" she asked.

Swin stared. "Never even thought about it," he told her. He kept looking at Johnna. He'd never considered the notion that she wasn't trustworthy.

"I wouldn't care that much," she said. "Just curious."

"I trust you," Swin said.

"Why?"

Swin ate a chocolate, sucking on it hard and then gulping it. "You're too strong a person to need to do anything scummy."

Johnna sighed. "That's a pretty good answer."

"You don't have any sneakiness in your heart."

"Don't overdo it," Johnna said. She waved the topic away with the back of her hand. "I don't want to exchange Christmas presents," she said. "I want to get the baby some savings bonds so he can go to college."

"Or clown school," said Swin.

"Or open a gun range."

Johnna showed Swin her new sneakers, holding a foot up in the air and flexing it around, and this, oddly, gave Swin a boner.

"Why don't you want to get married?" he asked.

"I don't *not* want to get married." She dropped her leg with a thud. "But we're still in the infatuation stage. Even though we're having a kid, there's no denying we're infatuated."

"That's not an easy thing to deny."

"We should wait till we're not attracted to each other to make a decision about marriage."

"What if that never happens?"

"Give it time."

When they returned home there were two phone messages, both inquiring about an annual chili cook-off that Swin knew nothing about. He and Kyle had also received the following letter:

Greetings Suarez and Mollar,

You two will have to hold down the fort a bit longer. (I'm sure you're capable of it.) My arrival at Felsenthal has been set for January 8th. I don't know what you've been told about me, if anything, but I'm coming from Wyoming. I was at a Federal Game Preserve that's been rezoned for a Military Woodland. What does that mean, right? I'd tell you if I could. It must've took some hard looking to find a state park in Arkansas for me, but I assure you I'm glad they did. I need to commend you for what it's worth on running the park without missing a beat after the disappearance of your superior. I've been told that a full investigation will take place in March, so until he comes up deceased, we can always hold out hope. Have safe holidays. Me and the birdbrains will meet you soon.

Ranger Marcus

Kyle and Swin packed up the money from the dryer, over sixty grand, and took it to an out-of-business hardware store behind the Japanese fast-food joint. They picked their way into a garden section overrun with vines, shrubs that had busted their pots, rotten hoses, infested irrigation fittings. They pulled limp bags of fertilizer off a pile and buried the money underneath them. Neither felt the need to mark the spot; if anything, that would attract the attention of a marauding teenager.

They brought out their litter-grabbers and wandered the park at random angles, eyes trained for wrappers and cups and bags. Mostly they spotted discarded pamphlets. The entire haul, compressed, fit in one garbage sack. They spread new mulch in the flower beds and medians, pruned the branches that overhung the road. They had to replace a strip of rubber that ran around a section of mud near the pond. They didn't know why this area was special, but the guy from Wyoming might. Swin righted crooked signs while Kyle weed-whacked around the porch and trailers and around the booth. The damn booth—sunup to sundown, each man a six-hour shift. They collected fees and answered questions, but thankfully the cold kept most people away.

Swin found he could think in the booth. His mind was finally catching up with itself, showing signs of settling. He understood that he hadn't escaped anything, in this life of crime he'd forged. It was the same life lived by sales associates. One tried to avoid pissing off one's bosses, tried not to get caught in one's illegal dealings, wondered what to do with one's excess income, all the while finding time to exercise and keep the yard spiffy. There was no more rebellion for the thinking man, Swin knew. Rebellion was stored in a distant warehouse under a fake name. When you completed your quest, whether it was spiritual or intellectual or physical, and turned the last stone to claim your hard-won wisdom, you found that your wisdom, your reward, had been marked down for the Labor Day weekend, that your reward was cheaper if you possessed a club card, that if you bought ten spiritual and intellectual rewards the eleventh was free. Swin was a fool. Other people knew all this. That's why smart people went into the kind of crime that ended them up in country-club jails in Connecticut for six months. The kind of crime Swin was involved in would put him in an state prison for the rest of his life.

The booth contained a heater that crammed itchy air into Kyle's nose. He got nosebleeds and ended up sitting his shifts in a coat and a Razorback ski cap. This much quiet was too much even for him. He told Swin to leave his ghetto-blaster in the booth and sat through *Also sprach Zarathustra* day after day until he felt he'd never heard it. The notes wanted to show each other up; they were pageant contestants who behaved with courtesy but secretly hated each other. The composition dragged on forever, then other times it seemed comically brief, a mere treatment. Kyle stacked boxes in the booth to rest his feet on, brought blankets and a deep Tupperware of batteries—in the mornings, a place mat to block the sun. When a visitor interrupted Kyle, he would rewind the tape and start from the beginning. He was okay with the fact that this piece of music would never change, not a note, that it was perfect no matter what anyone thought.

Swin was using the ghetto-blaster to learn more Russian. He incessantly told Kyle what various household objects were called in Moscow. When he had to speak English, Swin used a Russian accent and a humorless facial expression. He fielded dozens of earnest calls about the chili cook-off, all from the same couple people. Apparently the cook-off was a long-standing event, an event that, at least for a few folks, had prestige attached to it. These people would not be evaded, Swin could tell. There was no getting out of it; he and Kyle had to pick a date, and that date had to be soon.

They remembered about the chili peppers and minced some up, mostly for the hell of it, because it was something to do, scattered them over Bright's grave, dropped Bedford in the middle of them. He tottered in a circle, snorting, then looked at Kyle and Swin with wonder. It worked, they guessed. But wouldn't police dogs know that trick? It would be obvious something was being hidden. Anyway, when the cops got to the bottom of Bright's real identity and saw his history, they might decide he just slipped off to some better scam. Kyle asked Swin how long the pepper would work for and Swin had no idea. It had been a mistake to bury Bright in the park, but it was way too late to do anything about it now.

They decided to go ahead and get rid of Bright's Bronco. When they moved it from its spot behind the house, it was apparent a car had been there. They raked the area and covered it with picnic tables. They found a hilly forest in Texas and dumped a gallon of gas on the Bronco, removed the license plate, tossed in a match, and watched the seats and carpet and console burn to nothing while the frame only grew sooty. They stood there and finished their cans of soda, wondering why the gas tank hadn't blown. Oh well. Outside of a chop shop, there was no way to truly get rid of all traces of an automobile. The important thing was that when the authorities found the Bronco, it would be nowhere near the park.

They were as ready as they'd ever be for the man from Wyoming. Kyle had a sense of accomplishment but he sensed the accomplishment was meaningless. His and Swin's loose ends were tangled all over each other like a wad of shoestrings.

Kyle deemed himself judge of the cook-off and declared that, to avoid being influenced, he had to stay up at the house until the tasting. Swin, as competition oversight chairman, set up tables and place-markers for his eight contestants: five solo women, an outfit from the Methodist church, two guys opening a diner out on the highway, and the pawnshop owner whose books Johnna had burned. The pawnshop owner suggested that the judging be blind, but the women found this idea sleazy. The pair opening the diner had failed in an attempt to bring North African cuisine to Fort Smith, and had now given up broadening Arkansas's culinary horizons; if people wanted chili and burgers and chocolate ice cream every day of their lives, they would have yet another place to get it. One of the women was an unknown with a slippery accent and designs inked onto her hands. She'd come to America because it was a country where one could choose not to be religious.

"Should've moved to LA or something," Swin said.

"I want churches *around* me, and pious people." For the moment, she sounded Indian. "I like the clothing and the holidays."

"You can keep holidays," said the pawnshop owner.

"My aunt raised me," the woman offered. "I am my aunt's niece."

Swin asked where the woman was from and she said she was born in the Ukraine, but her aunt was not. Her aunt's sisters, one of whom was the woman's mother, had all died on a boat.

"And your father?"

"He was an agent of tile. He spoke many dialects. He once bought a barge of hats for the village."

"No dialects in America," Swin said. "Black children invent slang and in time it makes its way to the dictionary."

One of the church men cleared his throat. "You probably think since we're Methodist, we want to recruit a new arrival like you, but let me clear up a misbelief. We southern central Arkansas Methodists keep our God clear of school and City Hall and chili cook-offs. We *are* glad you didn't go to California. They recruit in their own way with TV and movie screens. Nobody even—"

"We get it," said the tall woman. "Please, nobody mention California around him. This is what happens."

"Who mentioned California?" asked Swin.

"You did."

"When?"

"I don't know, a minute ago. Let's just start this shindig."

"Here, here," said the pawnshop owner.

The cook-off ran itself. Everyone sampled each chili, then they all broke into a song that glorified the loneliness of ranch hands and the power of good chili to, if only for a moment, alleviate that loneliness. There was a sack race, after which the African bistro chefs were forced to swallow hot peppers. The Methodists insisted on a prayer. It included veiled thanks for the earthquakes, fires, venereal diseases, and budget problems that plagued a certain West Coast state.

Kyle strode down from the house with the trophy, which was covered by a towel. Silence fell and spoons were unsheathed. Kyle solemnly shook hands before each taste, employed a rolling, thoughtful chew. He made noises, squinted. After each chili he had a single cracker and a swig of Coke. He took his time, paced about, then whispered to Swin that he couldn't tell one from another. Swin nodded, then gravely pointed at the foreign woman, whose chili contained a lot of cumin and lamb.

When everyone else cleared out, the pawnshop owner came back to the house, claiming to know something Kyle and Swin might be interested in. It put Kyle on edge having the guy in the house, having him peering down the long hallway, surveying the kitchen, smirking at Swin's dumbbells and jump ropes tumbled up in the corner. Kyle was glad when the pawnshop owner turned down coffee, refused to sit. He had no profitable link, the pawnshop owner stressed, but was passing information along out of courtesy. Two fat twins with an arsenal of orphans were taking appointments. Hot Springs. Weekend after next.

"Nobody does anything without a profitable link," Kyle said.

"Old people do," responded the pawnshop owner. "I'm old at heart."

The pawnshop owner recited a phone number with a Memphis area code and told Kyle and Swin he hated to leave in such a rush.

The parking lot of the Adult Vocational Learning Center was governed by a system of colored passes that Swin couldn't figure out. He had a purple pass but there was only one purple lot and it was full of reserved spaces. The bare trees were somber and secretive, like boys who were trying to behave. Swin turned on his flashers and pulled over a curb onto a patch of brown grass. He reasoned that vans with their flashers on never got towed or ticketed. He remembered the couple hundred baby books and left a note on the windshield: BOOK DROP-OFF/ CHECK BACK OF VAN.

He crossed a footbridge and strolled past a couple recruitment booths—the Army, the Coast Guard, something where you worked from home—and into a windblown gymnasium. The men inside hoped to be mechanics and plumbers and masons. They acted warmly toward each other, clapping shoulders with the comfort of common ground. They had sweat in common, and usefulness, and probably beer. Swin had given up on bourbon but surely he could learn to like beer. You had to have a beer after you got off work, and if you stayed and had five or six then the little woman would get mad. She wouldn't really be mad, though; she'd smile as she scolded you, like you were a naughty dog she loved. The men included Swin in their greetings, no idea he wasn't one of them. Maybe you faked being one of these rugged men for a while and then one day you weren't faking anymore. Maybe these guys knew as little about engines and drywall as Swin did.

He had decided to use his Suarez identity. He couldn't use his social security number, so he would be his own boss, a freelancer. He'd gotten hold of a catalog of courses and intended to take four of them, plus CPR, and four more in the spring. He would be a hyper-skilled handyman. He would be the greatest handyman there ever was *and* one of the most notable thinkers of his generation.

An old man with a shiny tie and a tattered, understanding way about him took the podium. He held his head at angles, trying to clear his throat, then started talking about television production, about the crucial jobs that had to be done behind the scenes in order to get a show off the ground. He rattled off names and asked if anyone was familiar with them. When no one was, he said, "See?" These people were highly successful, wealthy. The old man chided his audience for believing that TV shows came from some magic mill in the clouds, rather than from people just like them. A man with a firm belly and a goatee raised his arm. The old man glared at him but did not interrupt himself.

"One thing, Pops," the man with the goatee said. "One little thing, Pops."

The old man had to look at him.

"One thing you're forgetting. TV shows suck."

The old man's face clouded. "TV is immensely popular and its popularity grows with each passing year."

"Nature shows, maybe. And football. But those ain't shows. That's setting up a camera and hitting the button."

The crowd was getting behind the man with the goatee. The disagreement obviously stemmed from something personal, yet the crowd glared at the old man. A couple insults were hurled. Swin found the scene discouraging. He didn't want these sturdy men who built things with their hands to be so defensive, so quick to take sides. They no longer seemed united by wholesome camaraderie. They were a clique of cool kids in high school, ridiculing a nerd who was running for a student-government office. Swin found humans vastly unimpressive. There was no limit to their ability to disappoint. Who cared if some old man wanted to talk about TV for a minute? The men in the crowd didn't. They just wanted to be involved in the confrontation. Everyone was defensive. Everyone was ready to bristle up like a wolf guarding its hunting ground. But people weren't wolves. It was high school, Swin concluded. Life was a big high school. Maybe crime *was* the right life for Swin. Maybe his most dominating characteristic was hatred for run-of-the-mill human beings. In crime, you saw very few people, and not many of them were run-of-the-mill.

Swin yanked his collar. He was getting worked up. It was about a hundred degrees in the gym. How come as soon as the temperature dipped below fifty, everyone thought they had to crank their heater to the hilt? Swin had to stay. He had to get the information he'd come for.

"I believe you know shockingly little about television production." The old man coughed, finally clearing out whatever was in his throat. "It can take a crew of twenty-five to film a fishing show. Two dozen friends, down in the tropics—"

"*I* believe you don't belong here," said the man with the goatee. "I believe your department's failing and you're trying to recruit these men away from honest work and into your faggy TV business."

The old man's expression was serene and resigned. He looked more understanding than ever.

Kyle's Christmas miracle was that Her called, sweet as a plum, and said the bad news was she was still alive and the good news was the next envelope was ready, that she'd leave it on the porch. Kyle fetched it and saw the trip wasn't for another week—Fort Smith. He busied himself. He roasted a goose and prepared a cherry topping for it. He fired up the chain saw, cut down a rotting pecan tree, and sliced the trunk into small lengths that, when he and Swin attempted to stack them, collapsed into shards. On an unseasonably warm day, Kyle rented a pressure washer. He ran it up and down the vinyl siding in uniform strokes. He splattered the bricks. He made the porch wood gleam.

Johnna took time off work, the first time she'd ever done so, and her good mood infected the house. She hung stockings and filled Kyle's and Swin's with coal. She hid shoes. She got Bedford drunk. She painted Swin's nails. She put blue lights on the porch banister and reindeer heads on the doorknobs. Kyle sawed down a small pine tree. Making a stand proved too difficult without welding equipment, so he leaned the tree in a corner. Swin slathered it with tinsel and hung the five ornaments he'd bought from the cab driver.

"I'll make a stand next year," Swin said. "When I'm a certified welder, I'll fashion a tree stand the likes of which will make you shudder to behold it."

Johnna framed the baby's savings bonds, along with the dollar Swin had won from his lottery ticket. Kyle's gift to Swin was a juicer endorsed by a spry man with unruly eyebrows, and Swin gave Kyle a tape of Arnold Schwarzenegger crooning in German. Swin believed this present was hysterical and forced everyone to listen to the tape in its entirety. Johnna presented Kyle with a chess set. Swin agreed to teach him the game, but said before Kyle learned the rules, he needed to clarify his general philosophy of war, whether he was a compromiser, a savage, or a statesman, whether he would use subordinates cruelly, whether he was loyal to kings or sympathetic to coups. Kyle replied that he would stick with checkers. To Johnna, Kyle gave a draw-stringed cashmere hat that Swin said could be worn by a gay fighter pilot, and a novel about a nurse who solved crimes.

For the short trip to Fort Smith, they drove a black Saab which they picked up in broad daylight at a Circle K. They made Fort Smith without seeing one cop and met a surfer-type with white hair and a long-sleeved T-shirt that read ROCK N' ROLL: NOW IN LOW VOLUME in the parking lot of a run-down petting zoo. The surfer retrieved a coffee canister from a compartment in the Saab's trunk and handed Kyle a carton of cigarettes containing ten thousand dollars. Llamas with wadded fur hung their heads over the fence and stared dryly at the transaction.

"If they get aggravated they'll spit," Swin said.

"Irritated's the word you want," the surfer said. "Spit like how?"

"Yeah," Kyle added. "Just saliva?"

"I think so."

"That's the lamest defense I ever heard," said the surfer.

Swin tilted his head, weighing it all. "I'd imagine they spit far and hard and precisely, or why would nature have them spit at all?"

The surfer's eyes lit up. "Nature doesn't always make sense. It can be every bit as stupid as God."

Kyle threw a handful of acorns at the llamas. The acorns, rotten, veered off target and mostly hit the fence. The surfer struck a karate pose and crab-walked toward the llamas. He made airy shrieks. He waved his body like a cobra, calling the animals "llama motherfuckers."

"They're domesticated," Swin explained. "Or they could be depressed."

"You're domesticated," the surfer told Swin.

"Not really," rebutted Swin. "Not that I've noticed."

"You know, when I got here the sun was shining." The surfer didn't look skyward. He looked right at Swin. "You guys show up, now the sky's like a slab of cement."

"It didn't turn gray for us until we saw you," Swin said, amused to be getting drawn into the surfer's argument.

"You and I both know who brought those clouds." The surfer made a face that appealed to Swin's sense of fairness. "Let's be honest," he said.

"I'll be honest," Kyle said. "You're a fuckface."

The surfer froze, peeking upward. He raised his finger expectantly. The rumble of thunder could be heard, loudly after a moment, and the surfer took this as proof that he was right. He chuckled and went to his car, as the first shy drops of rain tapped Kyle's and Swin's shoulders.

Johnna thought Bedford deserved some pampering, so she took him to a dog spa down near the Texas border. His fur was shampooed, his eyes and ears cleaned, and then he was sent to the "pawdicure" room, where a girl with a loose bun spoke softly to him, telling him she expected him to behave like a gentleman. The girl set Bedford's front paws in a soak and lined up a bunch of filing and clipping implements. She was the type of person who didn't have to look at what she was doing with her hands. She told Johnna about the history of dog spas and remarked on the weather and on a diet she was attempting. She said Bedford seemed wise.

"Don't feel like you have to talk to me," Johnna said.

"Really?" said the girl.

"If I want to know something, I'll ask."

"That sounds fair."

The girl had worn-out sandals and stately posture. She was stern with Bedford. She dried his paws then rubbed lotion into the pads. When she clipped a nail, she looked right in his eyes. The clippings shot this way and that, popping against the walls. The girl wasn't wearing any rings, but that could've been because she put her hands in solutions all day. Johnna asked if she was single and she said she was.

"I got a friend that might like you." Johnna tried to look at the girl in a conspiratorial way.

"I'm sure he would," said the girl. "Would I like *him?*"

"He's taller than average. Kind of a loner. He's got this solitude that, I don't know, needs to be broken."

"What are you, his ex?"

"No, I go with his buddy."

The girl jockeyed Bedford around and started on his back paws. She positioned her own feet for better balance. Her sandals were so old they were curling up.

"Smart?"

"It's hard to say," Johnna said. "He's good at his job."

"What's that?"

"He works for the Parks Department."

"I don't like outdoorsy guys."

"He doesn't prefer being outside to being inside."

The girl set her clippers down and adjusted her bun. "He seems good but not *too* good," she said. "I think you're describing him fairly."

"Fair as I can."

"My name's Jasmine."

Bedford made a noise, wanting to know if he was finished or what. Jasmine touched his side.

"Write that name down," Johnna said. "With some numbers next to it."

Jasmine searched for a pen. Johnna observed her, wondering if she and Kyle would hit it off, wondering if Kyle ever hit it off with anyone, if being set up with someone would annoy him. The only information Johnna had given out was that he worked at a park. Jasmine hadn't even asked his name. If Kyle thought dating this girl was a bad idea, he could rip up her number and forget about it.

Jasmine clapped a scented powder onto Bedford and set him down next to Johnna.

"As a rule, I don't get hopeful," Jasmine said. "Still, I can't help feeling that you and your friends are compelling people."

On her way home, Johnna tore up Jasmine's number and let the pieces flutter out the window. This was no time to bring anyone new around. Johnna and Swin had a baby to concentrate on and Kyle had his hands full keeping them safe. It seemed unwise to Johnna to rock the boat she was in. The boat contained two guys to look after her, a nicer house than she had ever expected to live in, a baby that appeared healthy, and an even-tempered dog.

The only kept-up houses in Hot Springs were the ones that had been turned into massage parlors. The town was hilly and rustic and, though clouds filled the sky, bright. It was the BOYHOOD HOME OF BILL CLINTON. Kyle and Swin walked down the main drag toward the baths. They were to go in the third one, with the empty flower beds and green shutters, at eleven-fifteen. Here they would finally procure guns, guns that were not defective, guns that would offer them a measure of security; that would, by Swin's thinking, put them on even ground with anyone who might want to harm them; that would, by Kyle's thinking, allow them to stop talking about and looking for guns.

A courtyard with many fact-bearing placards separated the bathhouses from the rest of town. The naturally steaming water was once thought to cure syphilis and, when combined with walking on inclines, obesity. Wealthy families once flocked to Hot Springs for vacations, but now the place was eerie, like a set for a play or something. Kyle and Swin had walked a quarter mile and seen two parked cars.

"They *all* have barren flower beds," Swin said.

He and Kyle approached the third house and noticed there were no windows; the shutters were tacked to the masonry for show. Inside was a cavernous lobby with stands meant to display statues. The light in the bathhouse came from above, through panes of tinted glass in the ceiling.

"Men lounging naked together has fully passed from fashion," Swin said.

"Don't see much syphilis, either."

"Rich guys in clubs still hang out naked. And the poor fucks in jail, when they shower."

"With these guns, we'll never have to go to jail if we don't want to. Gives you the option of ruining their party."

"Whose party?"

"When they bring in fourteen cruisers and SWAT and the chopper—all of them with hard-ons to call you a fuckbag and break your teeth on the floor. You make them stand out there all night, till they're lathered to their ears, then you just shoot yourself and they all have to go home and beat up their dog."

They made their way down a wide hall that led to the main bath. Swin called hello and his voice echoed. Kyle peered around the next corner and saw rows of individual baths and racks of towels. He waved Swin over and the two of them stared at the towels ponderously.

Swin nodded. "Perhaps we'll leave now."

Halfway down the hall a pair of beefy twins stepped in from the lobby, blocking it off, one cradling a black rifle. They seemed to cast a shadow down the hallway and onto Kyle and Swin. They were a dark cloud over all of Arkansas.

"Gray Cypress," Swin whispered. "Tell Johnna—Gray Cypress, Kentucky."

"Your sisters?" Kyle asked.

Swin nodded.

"What'd you say?" said the twin with the gun. "Don't be talking in code."

"Can you guys communicate with each other?" Swin inquired. "Telepathically."

"We're not twins."

"Where are the guns?" Kyle asked.

"Forgot them."

"I'm guessing you still want the money."

"Sure, why not?" The gunless twin hocked up some phlegm and swallowed it, trying to seem tough. "Set it on the floor with your pistols, then back up three steps."

Kyle dropped the wad of cash on the tile and he and Swin backed off. Kyle didn't have anything to tell Swin, in case Swin made it out alive and Kyle didn't. Kyle didn't have any secrets. He had nothing to confess, nothing to reveal that would help anyone.

"And the guns."

"We don't, uh…"

"The *guns*."

"We don't have any," Kyle said.

The twin with the rifle told his brother to frisk Kyle and Swin. He lumbered over and stripped off their jackets, pawing them like a bear. He paused, checked their ankles, then turned with a quizzical look.

"Told you," said Swin.

"You came to a firearm deal with no firearm?"

"If we had them, we wouldn't need them," Kyle said.

The twins again aligned themselves, walling off the lobby. They forced Kyle and Swin toward the personal baths and stashed Kyle in a stall. The unarmed twin stayed to guard him, towering over Kyle. Kyle heard the other twin direct Swin out of the room, their footsteps fading.

"Get in the tub," the unarmed twin told Kyle.

Kyle did so. He felt cold. The porcelain or ceramic or whatever it was felt like ice. It was as if the twin had his own weather system, his own chilling gales. Kyle strained to hear something from the rooms beyond but it was no use. When Kyle's guard shifted his weight, his sneakers on the tile were like a horn blow. Kyle's breathing was coming under control. He noted that the stall walls didn't reach to the floor. There were no locks on the doors. The ceiling and its windows were fifty feet away. Anger at Swin was welling up in Kyle, because Swin had kept harping about getting guns, but Kyle knew it was his own fault. People were built to harp, but that didn't mean you had to listen. Kyle had let himself wear down. He'd been weak, agreeing to come to this remote spot in this unfamiliar town, and he deserved to be in this tub.

"We work for you, don't we?" Kyle asked.

The twin nodded.

"What were we supposed to do? What would you have done if you were us?"

"You know damn well you don't have to *do* anything to get in this spot," the twin said. "Anyway, I ain't you. Not by a long shot."

"No," Kyle said. "You're fat and you're also lucky."

The twin was not going to laugh at this, or glower. He'd swallowed any good humor he possessed, any rage, and wasn't going to let any of it gurgle up until this was over with.

Kyle made every effort to appear resigned to his tub, hanging his arms over the rim and resting his head. "What about the pawnshop guy that doesn't sell anything? Why'd he set us up?"

The twin sniffed heartily. "Paid him."

"He's got money."

"Told him what he was going to do and told him we would pay him for it."

"I was starting to think that was Frog."

The twin laughed in a forced way. Kyle was right. The pawnshop guy *was* Frog. He was there the whole time, six or seven miles away. It was Frog they'd tried to buy guns from, Frog's books Johnna had burned, Frog that had entered the chili cook-off so he could send Kyle and Swin to their deaths.

"So this outfit's based in Memphis?" Kyle asked.

"It's not based anywhere."

"Why so secretive? You're planning to kill me, right?"

"It's past the planning stage. First we'll need the money, location of the bodies, the girl."

Kyle raised his weight off the bottom of the tub, testing. "Should question Swin. I'm not bothered by torture."

"If I was going to question Swin, I'd have to hurry. He'll be dead in a minute." The twin cracked his knuckles. "And if it's a pain to get *you* to talk, we'll go ahead and shoot you in the head. We don't care that much about the cash and we can find the girl on our own. Or not."

"Girl doesn't know shit."

"Apparently not, hanging out with you two."

"If I was you, I'd speed the plan up. I'd go ahead and shoot me in the head. Keeping me alive will only end badly for you. You'll embarrass yourself trying to scare me." Kyle waited for the twin to answer. "Of course, your brother's the only one allowed to have a gun, so we'll have to wait."

"Why don't you go ahead and shut the fuck up?"

Kyle flexed his toes in his shoes. He tensed his torso. "I'm the real deal, bud. You and I both know it's true." He thumped his chest with his thumb. "Nothing in there."

The twin looked Kyle in the eyes, afraid, Kyle knew, to look away. Kyle knew he had the upper hand with this guy. The problem was, the other twin would return, the tough twin, the one with the gun. Kyle had to do something. And he felt he could. He felt light and indestructible. Frog was no longer his boss. Kyle was unemployed and homeless. He had nothing to explain. Kyle felt like himself. He felt that this was how he was meant to die, and therefore he had nothing to lose.

The sound of the shot was a blinding, ear-boxing charge that caused Kyle's guard to loose a shriek and duck his head. Kyle flopped onto the floor, squirmed under to the next stall, and raised his foot to the door. He was on his back, one leg in the air, the sole of his sneaker an inch from the wooden door, his strength surging. He heard the twin coming around, saw the twin's big boots, then thrust his leg, slamming the twin, dazing him. Kyle stood, toe-to-toe with a stack of doughy muscle that would any second regain its bearing. The guy staggered toward Kyle and Kyle jabbed the only weak spot, the eye, working his thumb into the firm jelly. It seemed to take a long time for Kyle to get in up to his highest knuckle, into brain. He didn't feel the twin crushing him against the wall, making his knees wobbly, but he was aware it was happening, that he was being pinned up by the leaning heft of this dude. He plunged into the twin's skull, knowing he was stirring something important. The two of them buckled against the tub in a heap and it was all Kyle could do to keep them out of it. They were face-to-face. The twin's unmolested eye floated and rocked, no target. He shook Kyle and groaned, but he didn't know where the hell he was. He snapped his mouth open, but couldn't speak. Kyle thought the guy might kiss him. He slid out his thumb and wiped it on the twin's shirt.

"It's all right, big guy," he whispered. "It's okay now."

The twin made a noise that meant he knew he was being lied to. Kyle extricated himself and sneaked down a side hall, no clue where he was going, sticking to an outside wall. He didn't know where the other twin was. All he knew was Swin was dead and this place had no windows. Swin was dead. Kyle kept creeping along on his toes until he ran into a set of steps. He peeked over them and recognized the front hall, then sprinted for the door, exhilarated by the thought of being felled from behind by a rifle blast. He was in the crisp air, huffing past the courtyard. He passed a car on the street and wished he had a pocketknife to puncture the tires. There wasn't a soul around except a guy with long blond hair in a flannel shirt, riding a bicycle with one hand. Kyle got into the minivan, pulled a U-turn in an intersection, and searched out the highway. He got the van up to ninety. The twin with the rifle had to clean up whatever mess he'd made with Swin, do something with Swin's body, then guide his lobotomized kin to their car, the poor sap drooling and pissing himself.

Swin. Kyle had not been able to protect him. Swin never belonged in that bathhouse. Kyle didn't know where Swin belonged, but it wasn't in this life. Unlike Kyle and the twins and Gregor and Frog and all the rest of them, Swin had a lot to regret. Swin wasn't single-minded enough for crime. He had too much intelligence, not enough instinct. He took crime too seriously, and not seriously enough. Kyle felt he had no business knowing Swin, but maybe no one did. Maybe Swin was his own race. Kyle had often worried about Swin, had thought about the fact that Swin might get killed, but now that it had happened it seemed impossible, sudden, hard to grip. Swin was gone. It felt like a terrible, embarrassing joke.

Kyle wished he could drive straight to the pawnshop and beat the guy to death. He wanted to throw Frog against a wall over and over until he was dead. Kyle was embarrassed that he'd glamorized the guy in his mind. Kyle wished he had time to search him out, probably hiding in Little Rock until his little plan was carried through, but the twin with the rifle had already sent the alert. People would be looking for Kyle. For Johnna's good, and his own, he needed to forget about fucking Frog. He needed to see if this van could do a hundred.

At the park, Kyle saw no strange tire tracks. The porch Christmas lights glowed in the daylight, but the inside of the house was dark, the door locked, Johnna back at her apartment because Kyle and Swin had been away on the run to Fort Smith. Kyle slipped inside and hit the switch, illuminating a glinting birdcage on the kitchen table. A blue and yellow parrot stared at him distastefully. There were other birdcages in the room, the birds in them still and serious. A man shot up from Bright's big chair, causing Kyle to bump the cabinet of whiskey.

"So sorry," the man said. "Dozed off there."

"Lazy bones," said the bird on the kitchen table. "Lazy bones."

"Oh, put a sock in it, you."

The man introduced the bird as Rodney, a macaw, then directed Kyle's attention to a kookaburra named Shemp and a pair of fluffy cockatiels. He approached Kyle with his hand out, a small man with an uneven mustache and a bulging vein in his forehead. "Ranger Marcus from Wyoming. My guess is you're Ed."

Ranger Marcus was early. Kyle did not have it in him—did not feel he had the time or energy or will—to kill this man who had already made this house his own little zoo, this man who evidently was not Frog's man and who probably had only his feathered pets for friends. Kyle reared back from Marcus's handshake and peered about, horrified, as if seeing menacing spirits. He dodged, pursued, pitching into the cabinet, hard enough this time to send plastic bottles of FILED TALON thunking down on top of one other. He asked the ranger who the fuck Ed was, man. It seemed to him that crazy people said "man" after their questions.

"Where the fuck am I, man? Why are those birds looking at me?"

Marcus had frozen, his hands open but not raised, his face almost mirthful. Kyle didn't know how else to act crazy so he walked in a tight circle on the balls of his feet and grasped at the front of his pants.

"I'm just a ranger," Marcus offered.

Kyle crouched and tackled him by the legs. The little man seemed to throw his weight *with* the impact, causing the two of them to tumble across the living room as if ejected from a moving car.

"Good move, Grace," the parrot said.

"That bird knows my sister," gasped Kyle. He held Marcus down with ease and quaked from the inside out, yawping.

"We just got here," Marcus said. "We're your friends."

"How do I know you're in charge, man?"

Marcus looked at Kyle as though he'd asked a valid question. "They do whatever I say," he whispered.

Kyle dragged Marcus into the kitchen and bound his wrists and ankles. The ranger kept assuring Kyle it was okay to feel suspicious of birds, that he'd often felt the same. He was on Kyle's side.

"Rodney loves you," the parrot squawked.

Kyle took Marcus to a bedroom. He asked where Marcus's car was, if he'd flown here like a bird.

"I haven't had an automobile for ten years. I took a cab from Little Rock."

Kyle stormed out of the room, shut the door, and breathed deeply. He unzipped Marcus's red suitcase and dumped out bags of birdseed, packages of fig cookies, bundles of newspaper. In their place, he packed armloads of juice drinks and energy bars, then fetched T-shirts, socks, another jacket, and anything that seemed important from the bathroom. He hoisted the suitcase onto his shoulder and, as he left, stomped at the parrot, causing the bird to flutter and crow in its own language.

Kyle went to Swin's trailer and threw the rubber container of jewelry in the minivan, then ducked into his own trailer for Bright's old bones and his Strauss tape. He sped to the hardware store where the cash was hidden, loped into the garden section, threw bags of fertilizer this way and that. A litter of kittens was cozied up on the money. They were sweaty and relaxed. They were not in a nest that could've been lifted intact, so Kyle gently unzipped one end of the bag and slipped out the wads, replacing them with handfuls of mulch. He plumped the pockets of his pants and jacket with bills. His socks. Some of the money he carried out in his hands and dropped in the glove box.

Johnna knew something was wrong. She stood in the doorway of her apartment in a sweater and faded camouflage pants and said, "Jesus, go ahead and tell me." Kyle told her Swin was never scared, never begged or tried to sell Kyle out, that Swin had been exactly Swin to the last. Kyle hoped this was true. He hoped Swin had turned off the salesman in himself and said, "Pull the trigger, you piece of shit."

Kyle told Johnna she had ten minutes to pack up her Oldsmobile and leave Arkansas for good. She would take half the cash and, of course, Bedford, and she would find the Kentucky town where Swin's family lived: Gray Cypress.

"Kentucky?"

"Kentucky."

"I thought he came from Florida."

"Originally. When you get close, get a good map. I think Gray Cypress is in the center somewhere."

Johnna pushed a laundry basket out of the way with her knee, then slid two book bags from under the end table. "One for the hospital, one for skipping town."

She zipped open a satchel and stuffed it with bottled water and candy. There were three dozen postcards tacked on the wall, each bearing a Razorback football legend, and there was no way, Johnna said, she could face a new life without them. Kyle took them down one by one, dropping the pins in an orange coffee mug. He handed the stack of cards to Johnna, who was heatedly gnawing on a wad of taffy, realizing she would never see her possessions again, her coworkers, the leafy brown hills that marked the petering out of the Ozarks. She dropped her name tag from the clinic in the trash.

Something ran through Johnna—rage, it seemed. She glared down at a small table standing nearby, and Kyle thought she might kick it. She didn't. The rage passed, slackening her shoulders.

"The baby knows something's happening," she said.

"Swin's got like forty sisters," said Kyle. "The little guy'll have more attention than he knows what to do with."

She gazed at her belly. "Kentucky," she said.

Kyle said, "His real name is Ruiz."

"I know. But I'm looking for the Dutch stepfather's name."

Bedford had plodded out from the bedroom. Kyle scooped him up and put him in Johnna's car, then took her bags out. The bags contained mostly clothes, but Kyle could barely keep them off the ground. The world itself was getting heavy. The air, the light, the scent of Arkansas—it was all weighing Kyle down. Maybe this was sorrow, he thought. Whatever had brought himself and Swin and Johnna together—fear, mostly—the thought that he'd never see her again was wearying him physically. He had to get her on her way before he collapsed.

When Kyle came back in, Johnna was slipping packages of SweeTarts into the pockets of her army pants. He approached the television and unplugged it, cutting off an English guy who was complaining that American teenagers had killed punk rock.

"Dog food," Kyle said. He was trying to think of practical things.

"My son will hear all about you," said Johnna.

"I'd like that."

"You and Swin'll be his heroes. Come visit him sometime, when he's old enough to know who you are."

Kyle couldn't manage even to nod his head. Johnna yanked him by the hair and hugged him. She forced herself out the door, jangling her key chain and shushing Bedford. It was early afternoon, the sun roaring, drowning out the chilly breeze. Johnna shaded her eyes. She turned back toward Kyle, squinting, her mouth in a hard smile. He wondered if it was crossing her mind that she and Kyle could flee together. It was a terrible idea, terrible for Johnna, and Kyle wouldn't have allowed it, but he hoped it crossed her mind.

"I'm sorry," Kyle told her. "So is Swin."

Johnna's face went stony. "Don't be sorry."

"I'm sorry for myself. I liked it here. I liked living with you and Swin." This seemed, to Kyle, an important thing to say, but as soon as the words were out he knew there was nothing he could say that would mean anything.

Johnna stared at Kyle, ignoring Bedford, who was making timid noises at her knee. She dragged herself the last couple steps, steadied herself on the open car door. "Where will you go?" she asked.

"North, I suspect. Or maybe west or east. I'll see what feels right when I get behind the wheel."

Johnna nodded. "I'm not crying," she said. "I need to cry."

Bright's house. No car outside. The blue Christmas lights on the porch make everything seem even more still. In the living room, you find some sort of birdie zoo. The things don't bat an eye at you. You search the refrigerator, looking for some juice, and don't find any. There are all those nature books you saw when you spoke to Kyle and Swin after the chili cook-off. There are the half-empty whiskey bottles, some cheap brand you've never heard of.

"Stupid bird," you chime. "Shithead bird."

Kyle and Swin have their crap everywhere. Swin seems to have gotten the master bedroom, so he either won a coin toss or, more likely, Johnna had been living here. Yes, you see the womanly touches now, not exactly subtle—the fruit motif, the frilly curtains. There are baby books. You push back a door: a dead man, splayed face down, stinking. You tug your gloves on and kneel for the man's wallet, and when you touch his leg he flops over like a fish. The man has crazed eyes that remind you of a gym teacher you once had. He has a stiff mustache and there is no distinction between the hair on his head and on his back, which combine at the scruff of his neck. You know his type; he's a ranger. You straighten his shirt and fasten the top button, but do not untie him. The room you're in is some kind of nursery, with circles and triangles on the walls and a model of outer space hanging from the ceiling. Jesus, a baby?

"So, you're not dead," you say.

The man is pained, dramatic. "Don't kill me, sir. Do not kill me."

"Did you shit yourself?"

The man swallows.

"You couldn't have been tied up more than what, five hours?"

"I'm still tied up. You can get bad burns this way, you know."

"I'll untie you in a minute."

"I wanted to stay in Wyoming. Just me and my birds."

"Let me guess. Young white guy, pretty tall, nondescript haircut."

"That's the guy."

"You're initiated. They won't bother you again."

"Into what?"

"There's a whole band of them, like to shake up newcomers. It's all in fun. One visit per customer."

The man looks you over, discouraged by what he sees.

"We think of it as a prank," you assure him.

"What are *you* doing here?"

"I sell things—go around and see what people need. Like you, you need a pocketknife and an extra hand, which I'll provide free of charge."

You rest your hand on the man's head and he doesn't mind. You tell him he reminds you of Coach Zoll, a guy that failed you because you didn't have the right shoes, because you only had work boots.

"PE sucked," the man agrees.

"A lot of folks would think less of you, a lawman, if they knew you were brought to this sorry state by one of our random punks. We can keep this between you and me, be the best thing."

"I'm not a lawman."

"You got an outfit, don't you? Around here that's enough."

You take Thomas and Tim to your shop, to your home, to stay in the boonies awhile. You hire an Asian nurse with hammer thumbs to look after Tim. You and the nurse train him to stay in his wheelchair, though his legs work perfectly, because he's too large to be stalking about. You teach him to call for help when he wants something. You train laziness into him and he takes to it. He laughs without making a sound when the nurse tries to squeeze her shoes onto his giant feet. He will only eat cold, bite-size cubes. The nurse bakes pan after pan of chicken and stores it in the fridge. He loses weight, no longer appears to be Thomas's twin. Thomas cannot stand to look at his brother but asks the nurse endless questions and reads hour upon hour, evening upon evening, about brain injury. Thomas often stands behind his oblivious brother, a few feet distant, and stares at him, trying to accept the fact that there's no hope. Tim is healthy, in good spirits, yet there's no hope—no surgery for this, no therapy, nothing but... what, prayer? The pain in Thomas's face sometimes looks like a smirk, like he's up to mischief, like he's getting ready to snap the strap of Tim's eye patch. You're almost sure you've convinced him not to go after Kyle, to stay in Arkansas and attend to his legitimate business, to stay here and build up the courage to face his brother.

As the weeks pass, you grow accustomed to Tim's condition. He's a demanding pet. You let the nurse fully take over his care, which allows you to concentrate on Thomas, who moves from room to room with no purpose, who sits and listens to audio tapes from the library about who-knows-what. Thomas is the one who needs you, who needs purpose, who needs marching orders. The lying low is over. The sooner you get yourself together, the sooner Thomas can get himself together. You begin waking each morning feeling like things could be a lot worse, feeling relieved to be through with retirement. You feel more alive than you've felt since first moving to Little Rock, when you had to dig up mismatched pieces all over the state and assemble them with your bare hands. Soon you will go back to the city. A new plan is needed, a plan to make Thomas a legitimate businessman, strictly aboveboard, to have Thomas sitting across from Southern Ivy League types, having his meetings in broad daylight, at brunch and at golf courses. He will be safe. One day, he will tell your story. He'll knock all his designer-suited cronies out with the tale of his old boss.

You go into the screened back room, which Thomas has claimed and strewn with half-eaten bowls of cereal, and tell him you care for him very much, and he seems to take this as an unavoidable development, as something to be weathered.

The morning before you and Thomas and Tim and the nurse are set to move to Little Rock, the U-Haul almost full in the mud driveway, the Goodwill bags huddling in the hall, the kitchen bare except for the coffeemaker, the sun still hidden but casting the rugged horizon in soft pink, you stick your head into the den, where Tim spends his nights, and for a moment he appears cured. His expression is closed up, as if after weeks on end of chasing, he'd lassoed his mind, corralled his intellect. His mouth is shut. His good eye is staid. He looks grumpy, a mood you haven't seen in him since he went to Hot Springs. He doesn't look over at you. You bid him good morning and he remains still. It's like he's refusing to be interrupted, ignoring you. The thrill that had leapt into you leaks out. It finds the floorboards and finds the cracks between the floorboards and is gone. Tim is dead. You see the pillow. It rests primly on the seat of a rocking chair, but it's rumpled in a permanent way. Thomas's huge fingers have disfigured it. You go through the house, front to back, no need to hurry. Of course, Thomas is gone.

You sit at the kitchen table and wait for the Asian nurse to present herself. You listen to her shuffling around in her room. You want coffee, but it seems a complicated procedure, getting the pot going. It's very quiet, but you only hear one bird outside, and not an enthusiastic one.

When the nurse comes into the kitchen, she is startled by the way you look at her. She thinks she's done something wrong. She touches her American clothing here and there, wondering if she's missed a snap or a zipper. She is American in her dress, but walks and sighs and kneels down like an Asian woman. You tell her to sit. You tell her she is being relieved of her duties, by no fault of hers. Tim has passed away, you say. "We've lost Tim." You don't know if it's because she's Asian, or if it's because she's a nurse, or because she spends a lot of time in the homes of strangers, but she seems like a particularly discreet person. She won't ask questions. You can give her a bunch of details or none at all. Whatever words you say to her, she'll act like those are the most appropriate, tasteful words that could've been said. You tell her only that Tim was from a faraway town and that his body will be returned to his family, that he is locked in his room, that you don't wish to call the proper authorities until she has packed her things and cleared out. You tell her you'll give her a ride to the bus station or the train station or anywhere she needs to go.

"To the market will be fine," she says. "I get a ride from there."

You nod, but she does not stand up.

"All right I make tea?" she asks. "Every morning I make tea."

"Make enough for me," you say.

You can count on one hand the number of times you've had hot tea. You know when one of them was: the day you met the boys. At the hotel that morning, there were tea packets and little cookies on the counter. The hotel had an English theme. The tea was called Earl Grey. Until you put the powdered creamer in it, it tasted like nothing.

You drop the nurse in town, then hop on the interstate to Little Rock, wanting, as much as anything, a drive, but knowing you can find out a thing or two. The right lane is full of sluggish semis, but the left lane is wide open. You rocket out of the hills, reel in the soybean country, speed the city skyline into view.

You hit the boys' condo first, knowing Thomas won't be there. You climb up the stairs and try the knob. Locked. You dig out your keys and study them one by one. You have eighteen keys on your key chain and can identify maybe nine. You recognize the key; it's got a bulldog on it. It slides into the knob, but the lock won't turn. The locks have been changed. You put your nose to one of the slim windows that flank the door. Thomas didn't stop here. He didn't take anything with him. You see piles of the boys' clothes inside, bags of chips, movies from the video store. Even some cash. In a recliner, you spot a neat stack of brightly colored boxes. Board games—some brand new, some lightly used, some the tattered games the boys had brought with them from Magnet Cove.

Next you visit the boys' investment guy. You know him from when the boys' got their first rental house; you'd come down here with them to oversee the deal. He's your age, this investment guy, but wears shoulder-length hair and a beret. You remember thinking he must be pretty good at his job, to get away with looking like a B-list beatnik. When you walk past his secretary, she protests half-heartedly, not looking up from her computer screen. You poke your head in and there he is, same beret, same beat-up boots under the desk. He gives you a rapid series of nods, letting you know with this gesture that he was sort of expecting you. He gets off the phone. He offers you a chair, but you decline it.

"I apologize," he says. "I can't recall your name."

"Quite all right," you say. You don't offer your hand. "I'm worried about the boys," you tell him. "I need to know if they've done anything strange lately, as far as money's concerned."

The guy pulls a loud breath in through his nose and blinks protractedly, a way of answering your question affirmatively. You take a glance around his office. He likes a band called Phish. He went to Northwestern University.

"I'll be honest," the guy says. "They've gone against my advice. It's Thomas who's been calling, and he's defied my advice quite a bit."

"Buying or selling?"

"Selling. Selling everything."

"Everything *what?*"

"The rentals, the stocks, the silver. That lake out near Benton. I suppose they've got a whopper of a scheme cooked up. They won't tell me. I think I did something to piss them off."

"What could you have done to piss them off?"

"I've pissed plenty of people off in my day," he says. "Only on occasion have I known why."

You take a step backward and allow your weight to rest on the office door.

"I saw a movie where John Candy wears a hat all the time." The guy points at his beret. "He says, 'A lot of people hate this hat. The sight of it enrages them.' Of course, his wasn't a beret."

"Did they sell the condo? I put it in their names."

The guy nods. "That was the last thing to go."

"The sale is finalized?"

"As of two days ago, yeah."

"And where's all the money now?"

"In some account I don't have access to. I've been relieved of duties."

You look at him and he looks at you. It feels like you've got the exact same expression on your faces.

"When did this sell-off begin?"

"Almost two months ago. Thomas kept saying time was of the essence, so I didn't get the best price on a lot of it."

"Thomas said 'Time is of the essence?'"

"He said 'Hurry the hell up.'"

So, Thomas had begun selling right after Hot Springs. You wonder if his original plan was to take Tim with him. Once he became convinced his brother was hopeless, the plan changed. They were both gone for good. You think of darting over to Magnet Cove, but Thomas won't be there. The aunt might be, but what's the use of harassing her?

There's nothing else to say to the investment guy. You're still gazing at one another with a look of forced amusement, a false boys-will-be-boys look. You bring your weight off the door and pull it open.

"I seriously doubt you've pissed many people off," you say. "Irritated them? Yes. Pissed them off? Not likely."

You leave the building and wheel out of the parking lot toward the interstate. A couple blocks up, you pass the Barnett Building, the building you took the boys to the top of when you handed them the reins. You feel yourself hardening toward Thomas, and softening toward Tim. You wish you could have Tim's body cremated and go to the top of the Barnett Building and let his ashes blow all over Little Rock. You wish you didn't have to drag him through your house and down your steps and across your yard and bury him in the woods.

———————

You are taken under. You don't know what is taking you under, but you are aware of the sinking as it happens. It pulls you part of the day, then most of the day, then around the clock. You are unable to scold yourself with the correct phrases, unable to find a tone that you will respond to. When you attempt to talk yourself up, it comes out in an urgent whisper, a whisper from the next room, something you wish you could ignore, something you pretend to ignore out of spite. You lose your old talent for registering emotions only in your brain, for not letting badness invade your guts. It invades and invades. You don't struggle against the pull, afraid of sinking faster. You don't surrender, either. You stiffen up inside. You are untrained for this sort of fight. You've never had children to disappoint you, never had a woman break your heart, never had a ton of money and lost it all. You wonder if it's a midlife crisis, *want* it to be a midlife crisis. It isn't. You have no desire for a faster, newer sports car, no desire for a trophy wife or a woman of any kind, no desire to play the music of your adolescence at high volume, no desire to improve your appearance. And no desire, you realize, for heirs, no desire to secure the future of all the grubby green paper you squeeze out of the world.

You lay your mattress down flat in the U-Haul, where it had been packed along with most of the rest of your stuff, awaiting a ride to Little Rock, and get whatever sleep you can. Your dreams are of a city, a city like Little Rock but not Little Rock. The streets are canals, like in Venice. There are no bridges. The only way to get around is by small, oval-shaped boats, which are rowed by children. The children keep tiny books in their pockets and burn the hours reading, their legs draped over the edges of their boats. These children have no use for money. They give you a ride only if they like the look of you, if they are touched by your begging. They never take you where you want to go. Sometimes they just paddle you to the other side of the canal. You spend your fitful nights in the U-Haul struggling to get to the other side of town and never getting there. You sleep less and less. When the sun goes down, it seems it will not return.

You carry the television back inside, set it on the floor, and, from time to time, sit and stare at it. What you see on the screen is comforting, but you can't follow it. You can't construe the morals of the sitcoms, can't tell cops from criminals, can't tell anyone's age. Even commercials become obtuse. You don't know what anyone's laughing about, what anyone's being sly about. You can't find your radio anywhere. It's packed under an avalanche of lamps and curtains and toasters and tools. The Cardinals' first-baseman is hitting tons of home runs, half a dozen a game. He's breaking every record. He's muscle-bound, barely limber enough to swing the bat, but every time he connects, it's out of the park. Is this baseball or a show about baseball? You think about smashing the TV, but can't bring yourself to do it. You nudge it roughly with your leg as you walk by, knocking it sideways.

Whenever you walk past the coffeemaker, it regards you accusingly. It doesn't understand what's wrong with you. It thinks you're lazy. If it knew you at all, it would know laziness wasn't the problem. The longer you go without running the pot, the less chance there is that you will ever do so. You don't like to look in the cupboards. Tim had about a week's worth of food left when he died, and this is what you subsist on—rubbery slabs of baked chicken, dried fruit, miniature chocolate bars. At the rate you're going, you can make this food last a month.

One day you're walking past the phone and it begins to ring. You stop and stare at it. It's a timid ring. You answer the phone and it's a guy from U-Haul calling. He wants to know what happened to the truck, if you ever made it to Little Rock. You tell him everything's peachy, that his truck's in good hands. He informs you of the late fees you're compiling, informs you of some of the processes that will grind into motion as a result of your delinquent account. Contract. Grace period.

"You can send somebody out to get the thing," you tell him. "Of course, he'll have to unpack it. You can always charge me for the retail price of the truck— that's another option. But do not, under any circumstances, call this phone again.

Call this phone again, you'll be sorry."

You take your mattress and box spring out of the U-Haul and stack them in your patchy, muddy yard. You begin keeping a fire. At first you gather fallen branches and kindle them with unread newspapers, but the branches and papers run dry. You lug boxes from the U-Haul to burn, pieces of furniture, bundles of towels, boxes of cereal, wooden hangers. You keep one chair, a dining room chair, and set it over near your bed. You bring the bags of Goodwill stuff from the house and burn those.

You come across the rest of the poetry books, the ones that weren't burned. You read each book unhurriedly, and upon turning the final page, toss it in the fire. The books burn hot and fast, almost making sparks. The wisdom you fail to pry from them is released into the breeze. There is a guy named Vallejo who believes he'll die in Paris, alone, and doesn't seem upset about it. There's a guy named Donald Justice who says he'll die in Miami. He says the ground in Miami is black marl. You can picture it swampy or sandy, but not black marl. Is he lying? Are poets allowed to lie?

When Tim's food runs out, you eat whatever turns up in the truck, whatever food you'd packed. You eat hard, tart pears from a tree at the back of your property. They taste awful. You can eat two or three bites of one before you throw it in the fire.

The moon is the same night after night, then suddenly it's a sliver.

You begin to stink so badly that the smoke from the fire doesn't mask your odor, that running a hose on a rag and wiping your armpits has no effect. It's an ancient stink. It's not unpleasant.

Most of your mail goes to the fire, but a letter from U-Haul catches your eye. It says NOTICE on it. You open and read it. It's vaguely threatening, but still businesslike. The next day, you get another letter from them, almost identical to the first. The print is bolder and it says NOTICE in red this time.

You find that you cannot imagine the future, not even the near future. Your days are more or less the same, but you can't see tomorrow. The present has been beyond your control for some time, and now the future is gone, too. You have only the past—snapshots, growing clearer by the day. These are your memories. They don't move. They don't try to make you feel any certain way. They haunt you. They replace your dreams. You wake each morning with dew in your hair, missing the wizened, rowing children. There are so many snapshots that if you stacked them and flipped the edge with your thumb they'd appear as coherent episodes, like cartoons.

The daytime hours lose meaning. You notice that every day a bee appears, lands on whatever's handy, then buzzes on. The bee completes an enormous lap each day and you're part of that lap. You wish you could leave flowers out for him, like milk for a stray cat. When the bee visits, you know the day is more than half over.

When you discover your baseball in the U-Haul, you spend the sunlit hours of an entire day throwing it as far as you can and walking and finding it and throwing it again. You follow it into the woods, near the spot where you buried Tim. You imagine that if you dug down to find Tim, his body would be gone, taken somewhere better. You imagine that if you dug him up, he'd stand and walk back into the house, no hard feelings. Anything is possible except that Tim's body is right where you left it, dead as ever, pale and crushed and newly found by insects. Tim is a side of white meat. There is no Tim. At the end of the day, you kneel down by the fire and roll the baseball into it.

You get another letter from U-Haul, this one with even bigger red letters that say FINAL NOTICE and LEGAL DOCUMENTS ENCLOSED. You slip the envelope into a plastic file case, then deposit the file case in the fire.

You notice your driveway has hardened. The mud on the tires of the U-Haul is like cement. It hasn't rained. You realize it then. Since you began living out of doors, not one drop has fallen. Of course, that very evening the clouds roll in. They waste no time. As soon as the sun goes down, they open. You pull a big comforter and part of a tarp over you and manage to sleep.

You come across your radio. It's a worthless plastic box. You burn it.

Your bed and your body begin to smell like mildew.

There are no more holes in your snapshot memories. You can see everything you've done.

Whatever's wrong with you, you can sense it's burning off. You're running out of body fat and out of possessions. It's burning off slowly, and there's nothing you can do to rush it.

A guy shows up, looking for antiques and oddities. Someone at the market told him there was a shop down here.

"Was," you tell him. "Closed now." Your voice is grainy.

The guy wears a T-shirt advertising a band called Shirt of Apes. The T-shirt has a pocket and in the pocket is a bottle of aspirin. The guy doesn't seem at all disappointed to find the shop closed. He's young, a teenager.

He makes to get back in his car and you tell him to hold on. You rummage on the porch, looking for something to give him. The best you can find is a platter with a picture of Elvis on it. You find it facedown in some leaves, pick it up, and give it a hearty dusting-off with your hands.

"Take this," you say.

He accepts it with two hands, feeling how heavy it is.

"This used to belong to a crime boss," you say.

He wants to believe you, wants to believe this piece of tacky kitchenware he's been handed was once the property of an important criminal.

"What was his name?" he asks.

You nod toward the platter. "People call him Frog."

"How long ago did this belong to him?"

"Till right now."

His mouth opens. He really wants to believe you. He wants to believe, but he can smell you and see what's going on in your yard. Most likely you're delusional and never broke the law in your life.

You're coming out of it. You begin reading the newspaper each morning. There's an article about Felsenthal. The article doesn't draw conclusions, just details all the oddness that's transpired at the park. It starts with Ranger Bright, a fixture at the park, who disappeared mysteriously and never turned up, moves on to Bright's underlings, two youngsters who also disappeared and never turned up, then moves to the new ranger, Bright's replacement, who claims to have been accosted and tied up by one of the disappeared youngsters, then untied, later in the day, by some stranger he's never seen again. The article mentions a woman named Wendy Vasgar, a person you know nothing about, who is in charge of all South Arkansas parks and recently purchased an extravagant houseboat. The article presents all these occurrences as coincidence, but is sure to imply that a smart reader would know better. The readership of this paper, you think, all the bored bumpkins of Union County, are like the guy with the aspirin in his shirt pocket—hoping, for once, to have a claim on something out of the ordinary.

You need to get moving. They may not be there tomorrow or next week, but cops *will* descend upon Felsenthal. You don't know what they'll find, but whatever it is, it'll bring them a step closer to you. You never know what scrap they'll connect to what other scrap. The ranger would remember you. Kyle, if they ever turned him up, would remember you.

You go inside and take a look at the coffeemaker. The cream is bad. The sugar is all gone; you ate every packet. You look everywhere for your keys and finally track them down in the freezer. You remember stashing them in there, one of the first days you were feeling bad. You go start your car, the old Nissan, and the engine rumbles. You head for the market. You need cream and sugar, but also something else. You'll have to stop at the electronics store. You need a tape recorder. You have to rid yourself of the snapshots in your brain. You have to translate them to audio and reclaim the space in your mind. There is no deal in place, you know; you won't trade the tapes for a full mental recovery. They're separate events, both inevitable. Your mind will recover. The tapes will be made. You'll shower. You'll eat at a restaurant. You'll give voice to the countless pictures of your life. You'll make a plan.

And all of it does happen, except the plan. You buy new clothes and get a car wash. You buy an inflatable mattress and move back into the house. You hold one last fire, and in goes your old mattress, your box spring, your trusty chair. You eat seafood and vegetables. You keep the coffee flowing. You have a mug that you keep filling and taking into the bathroom with you. The bathroom is your recording studio. You look into the mirror and think of yourself as a stranger. You don't sit down while you speak. Each time you enter the bathroom, you fall into a trance, a good trance, a bright one, the kind of trance artists must fall into. You are excited, but patient. There is Memphis— the barbecue and the blacks and the Baptists. Buttons. There is Pine Bluff—the foggy hills, Almond, the casserole dish. There is the empty fountain in Magnet Cove, the waitress who calls you a drifter. There are the trips to the flea market to buy art for the walls of your bakery. There is the insomniac elf-carver. And Steve. Your move to the boonies. There is the smell of Johnna's apartment, the smell of the caged birds in Bright's living room. There is the dainty precision of the Asian nurse. There is your time in the yard, which, though it just ended, seems distant. There is this morning, when you clipped your nails and ate a mess of sautéed scallops with sourdough toast, and this afternoon, when you paid a tow truck to take the U-Haul to Little Rock. There is the last session in the bathroom, at the end of which you enjoy the sigh of all sighs and soberly press the stop button.

I go to the bank and get a cashier's check for $150,000. The banker thinks I'm a real-estate speculator from the city, and I let him think that. He talks up the loan department and I nod and smile. I mail the check to Delta Corporate Entertainment, an outfit Colin uses from time to time to scrub Thomas's and Tim's money. It's just a PO box. I enclose instructions for Colin to keep forty-five grand and give ten grand each to the Tennessee runners, ten to the Alabama runners, ten to the Mississippi runners, ten to the Little Rock guys, five to the guy who replaced Gregor, and twenty to Her. On the envelope I write SEVERANCE. Colin will give the runners the money. He's that kind of person. There are some other folks who will feel it when I pull out, but they're freelance types, people with options, people who've never directly put their necks on the line for me.

I pack. I want to bring only what will fit in my car, and this is no big trick now that I've burned all my things. I go to the drugstore and buy one of everything they have in a travel size. I buy a miniature TV. I buy a couple maps, the smallest ones they have. I almost buy a heated pillow to put behind my back while I drive. I don't, though; I'm not planning on more than a day on the road. I go to the electric company, the gas company, the phone company, and tell them what day to cut the service. I leave them each a hundred bucks and tell them to keep, as a tip, whatever's left over after the last bill. I tell the post office to hold my mail for a month. I check the fluids in my car—oil, brake, power steering, antifreeze, washer—and none of them are a drop low. My car is getting better with age.

I want to make a clean break from the people I work with, the people Thomas and Tim and Colin work with. I don't want to be found. I don't want to be hounded by people who expect something from me, who have hard feelings toward me. Any thoughts I had of going legitimate were clouds over my mind, gloomy fluff. One day my story will come to light, and it will have a grand final act. I am a drug dealer. No one knows they're a drug dealer until they become one, and once you do, there's no resigning the post.

I have only one good connection left, a guy I haven't talked to in years but who I know is still active. I dial his number. One ring and here he is. He's got a voice you don't forget—deep, but squawky and struggling. It makes me think of a crippled hawk.

I can find no other way to identify myself than as Frog, Froggy, Froggy from Memphis. It feels undignified, referring to myself as Frog. It's something other people should call me. He's not sure. Colin's boss, I say, and that brings him around.

"I thought Colin's bosses were two big twins," he says.

"That's right," I say. "I'm *their* boss."

"Okay, I know who you are. I figured you'd be retired by now."

"I was, but it didn't suit me. I make a lousy lazy man." I know what he's thinking, that I blew all my money. I blew some of it, sure, but not all. Not hardly. If I lived a certain way, I could stretch my savings out fifteen, twenty years—if I ate generic bran flakes and went to matinee movies and kept a penny jar. I'd rather die than put myself on a budget, and it's not because I like spending money; it's because going on a budget now would make my whole life to this point meaningless. I might as well have been working in a supermarket all this time.

I tell the guy I'm getting my hand back in, attending some meetings personally, doing some runs. What I need, I tell him, are weekly shipments to Oklahoma City.

"Oklahoma City?" he asks. He leaves it at that, dead air on the line.

He doesn't trust me. I called him out of the blue, for one. It's *me* calling, for two. A regular, volume customer seems too good to be true. I don't blame him; it's fishy. If I try to convince him it's not fishy, it will stink all the more.

"Look," I say. "I'm trying to stay in shape. I don't want to get fat and get ripped off. I want to be able to do what my people do."

"Makes sense," he says. "I'm not taking new clients right now, though. I can hardly please the ones I already got."

"Is there some kind of shortage I don't know about?"

"It's not like the old days," he tells me. "Supply dips and rises from month to month."

"What old days?"

"The eighties."

"Don't worry about your other customers," I tell him. "Whoever used to be your biggest customer, now they're your second biggest."

"Can't," he says. He gives me another number to call, and I act like I'm writing it down. He says in Oklahoma it's all meth, and meth is all local. He says Oklahoma's a bad choice. He says these days there are nothing but scumbags in the business.

"There's always been scumbags," I tell him. "I'm a scumbag."

He doesn't chuckle at this. He apologizes again and hangs up.

I hold the phone up and turn it this way and that in the light.

"Oklahoma's whatever I say it is," I tell the phone. "If Arkansas is what I say it is, Oklahoma's what I say it is."

I'll go to Oklahoma with nothing arranged. I wouldn't have it any other way. I'll tell them what they like and when they like it. I'm not frustrated or scared or excited or determined; I'm simply ready to do what I do. Maybe I'll get new boys, maybe I won't. Maybe I'll work for somebody; that'd be a fucking hoot. Maybe I'll leave right now. I'll put some coffee in a travel mug and throw the tapes of my life, these tapes of an unfinished tale, in the trash can. Tapes aren't a proper home for my story. My story should never be recorded. It should be pieced together and passed down, exaggerated, doubted, insisted upon.

After Johnna left Union County, it took her six hours to get a hold of herself, to grasp the situation, and only then could she take a break from driving, at a dusky truckstop exit a ways past Jackson, Tennessee. She put her Oldsmobile in park and pushed warm breath after warm breath against the windshield. She brushed her fingertips through Bedford's fur. She ate a couple handfuls of smoked almonds that tasted like meat, drank a bottle of something called vitamin water. A team of semis were lined up dutifully across the way, all parked at the same slight angle, their lights glowing. They were watching over Johnna, daring anyone to mess with her.

When Johnna reached Gray Cypress, she was going to tell Swin's family exactly what had happened, leaving nothing out, answering any and all questions, and they were going to respect her for this. She would hand the cash over to Swin's stepdad, however much it was, and let him do with it whatever he thought was right.

Before that, she would get a hotel room a couple miles from Gray Cypress and relax for a day or two, get her nails done and go for a tan. She would get her car washed and waxed, get a new dress. When she rang the doorbell at Swin's stepdad's house she would be stunning. She would be as beautiful as any of Swin's sisters, but she would be a grown woman with a small, insistent, radiant belly. They would know in a glance that she hadn't come to take, but to give. They would know she was a gift.

Johnna had never been more alone than now, pregnant and unemployed, pulled off the road in a foreign state, night falling, but she'd never felt more secure. She had surpluses of toughness built up, and it was an embarrassment of riches. She'd never need as much toughness as she had in her right now. Things had gone bad and she was handling it. She had Kyle's grit in her guts and Swin's cleverness in her brain. The next time things went bad for Johnna, and the time after that, the badness would be no match for her. Bedford nuzzled his nose into her thigh. His tail was twitching. He was a wuss, this dog; thank God he had Johnna to look out for him. Johnna rolled down her window. The air had sharp notes to it—the exhaust from the semis, the cold night on its way, a nearby cow pasture. She tilted her head out the window and there were the stars, faint but numerous, pushing everything that ever happened before tonight further into the past.

ACKNOWLEDGMENTS

The author thanks Paul Winner, Anna Keesey,
and Heather Brandon. Their help was invaluable.